"Niklas," I said, not knowing what I would say next, but a strange thin sound from the distance stopped me from saying more. We both turned in the direction of the mill. Over the treetops we could see its thatched roof. And then the sound again, climbing into the sky darkly like smoke. It was a howl of pain.

Then we were running along the riverbank, seeing ahead of us the waterwheel. It sat in the water as big as a scaly brown beast, next to our old millhouse. Coming around the far corner of the mill were one, two, three men—armor glinting in the sunlight—and this glimpse sent me hurtling into a clump of bushes, with Niklas following.

We breathed against the ground while hearing them yell into the air. They were calling to one another and laughing, but from inside the mill there were screams and clanging, as though great lengths of metal were hitting together. Holding Niklas's hand, I scrambled up and led us across the verge of bushes until we came around the mill to face its entrance. We crouched behind a large bush and stared across the snowy yard at the big door flung back. Through its empty darkness a man staggered into the sunlight and blinked.

He was a soldier in red tattered hose and tall boots with the tops turned down. He wore a long-sleeved doublet and a padded woolen jacket with a dirty breastplate strapped to it.

I would remember it all.

MALCOLM BOSSE is a distinguished author of numerous highly acclaimed novels. His books for children include *The 79 Squares*, an ALA Notable Book, *Cave Beyond Time*, and *Ganesh*. His many novels for adults include *The Warlord* and *Fire in Heaven*. Mr. Bosse lives in New York City.

QUANTITY SALES

Captives of Time

Malcolm Bosse

LAUREL-LEAF BOOKS bring together under a single imprint outstanding works of fiction and nonfiction particularly suitable for young adult readers, both in and out of the classroom. Charles F. Reasoner, Professor Emeritus of Children's Literature and Reading, New York University, is consultant to this series.

Published by
Dell Publishing
a division of
The Bantam Doubleday Dell Publishing Group, Inc.
666 Fifth Avenue
New York, New York 10103

ISBN: 0-440-20311-2

RL: 6.6

Reprinted by arrangement with Delacorte Press

Printed in the United States of America

April 1989

10 9 8 7 6 5 4 3 2 1

KRI

For Mary Heathcote

"Something is added to the everlasting earth;
From my mind a space is taken away."

And for Marie-Claude and Malcolm-Scott
With love

Come what may,
Time and the hour runs through the roughest day.

Part I

1

THAT morning, when sunlight came over the edge of the world, I said to my brother, "Niklas, you can feel the spring." I took his cold little hand in mine and leaning out of our bed held both our hands in the light coming through slits in the window boards. His fingers began to wiggle like worms. "That's what spring does," I told him. "It warms you after the winter." I was sixteen; he was four years younger. At the start of recent springs I had held his hands in the warming sunlight, in just this way, but I couldn't be sure if he understood what a season is.

After I said our prayers and we dressed and aired the blanket to rid it of lice and each ate a wheat cake and drank a bowl of milk in the kitchen with our mother, we gathered firewood in the forest. Finished, we sat by the river, watching the ice break off along the bank to whirl through the sluggish water. The sunlight and warmth made the ice look heavy, just like the snow looked heavy in woods across the river. Out of this melting snow the sun was making mirrors to see itself in. "Look at the green patches of grass, Niklas. The spring brings them back."

We sat awhile, listening to the birds singing and the lumbering creak of the waterwheel upstream. "That's the sound of the wheel turning. It's free of ice now. With the river unfrozen, the mill can work. Father will soon be making paper again. Above the wheel, where the big shaft turns—do you remember that? The hammers will be rising and falling all day long to beat the wet rags into paper. Then the monks will buy it from us to write their prayers on. Remember last year, before winter came? How we'd lie in bed each morning waiting for Mother to call us and we'd lie there and we'd hear the hammers above the

13

wheel? And I told you it was the sound of God walking through heaven? Can you remember so long ago?"

As if he could answer such questions. But I thought he liked to hear my words even if much of the time he didn't understand them. We never knew what he understood, except when he smiled or frowned or did what we asked and even then we weren't sure, because as Mother said, maybe he was obeying God's voice and not ours.

An arm's length away, where snow had melted in the sunshine, I noticed a pool of still water, the size of a saucer. The sun hung in one corner of the pool, and when I bent over the small mirror, my own face hung in the blue sky. Would those broad cheekbones ever look pretty? Across that broad face of mine I pulled my thick braid of hair as if it were a bundle of reaped wheat. But it didn't smell like wheat; it smelled like the forest where we gathered wood. I glanced at Niklas, who dangled his legs over the riverbank. Heavy boots made his feet look too big for his body. His nose was larger than mine, his eyes a lighter blue, almost the color of the stream flowing past us. Mother had cropped his hair, and I could see in his round head the fine little holes from which the white hair grew. Hair as white as snow since the lightning struck. A fly was dancing around his mouth. It was the first insect I had seen in months.

Once again I looked at myself in the pool of melted snow, but the surface trembled, and the broad cheeks and thick braid broke into pieces like river ice.

"Niklas," I said, not knowing what I would say next, but a strange thin sound from the distance stopped me from saying more. We both turned in the direction of the mill. Over the treetops we could see its thatched roof. And then the sound again, climbing into the sky darkly like smoke. It was a howl of pain.

Then we were running along the riverbank, seeing ahead of us the waterwheel. It sat in the water as big as a scaly brown beast, next to our old millhouse. Coming around the far corner of the mill were one, two, three men—armor glinting in the sunlight—and this glimpse sent me hurtling into a clump of bushes, with Niklas following.

We breathed against the ground while hearing them yell into

14

the air. They were calling to one another and laughing, but from inside the mill there were screams and clanging, as though great lengths of metal were hitting together. Holding Niklas's hand, I scrambled up and led us across the verge of bushes until we came around the mill to face its entrance. We crouched behind a large bush and stared across the snowy yard at the big door flung back. Through its empty darkness a man staggered into the sunlight and blinked.

He was a soldier in red tattered hose and tall boots with the tops turned down. He wore a long-sleeved doublet and a padded woolen jacket with a dirty breastplate strapped to it.

I would remember it all.

He held a war hammer in one hand, our father's tankard in the other. Pushing him roughly out of the way, another soldier appeared in the doorway, this one wearing a leather cape and a soft felt hat and defense armor on one leg, ankle to knee. He was laughing as he yanked the tankard out of the other soldier's hand. The three we had first seen came around the mill again. Two held pikes and the third a poleax, and they all had on bits and pieces of armor.

The five crouched in the melting snow, as if waiting, and then out of the black doorway lurched our mother, her hair down, only a torn smock below her waist. An undone kerchief hung from her neck down to her ripped bodice, but she didn't try to straighten it or hide her exposed body. She just kept shuffling along the path. She didn't seem to see anything, but breathed hard, the way she'd breathe climbing a hill. The men stood up, grinning. The one with the poleax reached her first. He wore an iron skullcap and sheepskin mittens. I would never forget that: the mittens.

When he stood in her path, our mother went around him, almost as if he weren't a man but a tree, a rock. For a moment he watched her go past, then reaching out with his free mittened hand he spun her around. With surprising strength our mother yanked the ax from him and in the same motion slashed out, so that the blade cut through his blue sleeve. Instantly a line of red swept along the blue.

The others had reached her by then. They watched her drop the poleax and go on, slowly, the way she did when sleepy in

15

the mornings. The man in the iron skullcap and mittens looked with surprise at his bloody arm.

Then another soldier took a step toward her, blocking our mother's way, and I could see the swift horrible motion of the shaft as he pulled back a long pike and shoved it tremendously forward, the tapered head disappearing into our mother, *but in the Lord there is mercy,* and it kept going in and in and in, *we must trust in the mercy of,* until when she turned slightly it came out crimson and clotted from her back.

While she gripped the shaft with both hands and sank to the ground, the soldiers stood watching like dogs.

There was a small noise close by, like wood grating against wood. I turned to see Niklas, mouth open, straining to scream.

Clamping my hand against his lips, I kept telling our mother in my mind to pull it out, pull it out, as if by doing that she could save herself, but from where we were hiding I could see her poor hands, drenched in blood, relax around the shaft. She moved no more, and the men, rubbing their chins, turned away.

Letting go of my brother, I tried to think of asking God's mercy, but words couldn't get past the sight not twenty paces away.

A pair of soldiers came out of the mill, one gaily waving a mace. The other had a pile of clothes over his arm. I recognized our father's jacket, the soft velvet one he wore to the cathedral on saints' days, and the work pants of Erich, who tended the stamping hammers.

And then another soldier emerged, holding young Erich by the neck. A long ugly gash ran from Erich's pale forehead through his eye into his cheek. He was screaming. The soldier pushed him to his knees and the watching men smirked. Then he was telling them how he knew where the miller had hoarded up gold. The soldier kicked him to the ground and nuzzled his throat with the point of a sword. Erich was silent then, as if listening to the blade.

And beside me Niklas had somehow got a sound into his throat. It was low, like a puppy whimpering in a nightmare, but loud enough perhaps for the soldiers to hear.

Taking his hand, I ran off at a crouch through the nearby

wood. We ran through brambles and against trees and crushed the snow still coldly thick in the shade and never caught our breath once, *God take her soul to His bosom,* but continued our way into a hollow, where a pond lay banked by sedges. I threw myself down against a waterlogged stump, Niklas followed, and together, panting, we looked up into the leafless trees of early spring.

It seemed to me then that Judgment Day had arrived. Words from a priest's sermon came out of memory. Stars of fire would soon be hailing down from heaven. The moon would bleed. Angels would blow trumpets so loudly that our ears would crack like bowls. Locusts with tails of scorpions would come out of the black air to sting us blind. The sun itself would turn black. I turned my head to see if it had already begun to change color. And the earth would shake and the terrible four—Famine and War and Plague and Death—would gallop down the sky on horses breathing fire. A seven-headed beast would come out of the sea, the priest had warned us that sabbath day.

The beast with seven heads would crawl through the land, along with slime-covered dragons, and the world would end. Because it had already started to end. Our mother dead in the melting snow. Erich, too, by now. And in the millhouse our father, surely. And Joanna the scullion, not a year older than I was.

"Niklas," I said, but I had to say it again before the word came out of my mouth. "Niklas."

With his legs pulled up to his chin, Niklas sat against the stump. He was shaking. It reminded me of the awful day three years ago when he had been sitting under a tree and a lightning bolt struck it and slithered down into his body like a snake, turning his face blue and his hair white and leaving him shaking, just as he shook now against the stump.

"It is God's will," I told him in the voice our mother used to explain misfortune to us. "You stay here." When I started to rise, he grabbed my hand and held on. "Brother, you stay here until I come back. Don't move from the stump. Not one foot from it until I come back. Do you understand?" I pulled free and stood up.

Cocking my head to hear a sound on the wind, I heard nothing. They might have gone by now.

Picking my way slowly through the wood, I stopped often to overhear them but heard nothing. Then I heard something snap in dead leaves. Crouching, I saw one of our hens come through the undergrowth, clucking and pecking. Farther on, I heard the grunting of a pig from the bushes. So the soldiers had let the livestock out. They must have come along the road this morning, as soldiers do these days, a hungry band of them, cold and tired from marching or fighting, perhaps some of them wounded, and all with empty purses. They must have heard the waterwheel turning and followed the sound to any-place they could loot.

Looking up to see if the sun was going black, I went on toward the mill. Each moment I braced myself for the world to end.

2

APPROACHING the edge of the yard, I paused to listen for their voices, but heard nothing save the slow creaking of the mill wheel and the tinkling splash of water from blade to rising blade. For a moment the monotonous sound from the waterwheel reassured me. Nothing had happened here. Satan had put into my mind a waking nightmare.

But then, stepping into the sunlight of the yard, I saw our mother lying with the pikeshaft protruding from her as if a limbless sapling had grown right through her body. I walked far around her, muttering a prayer for her soul. It was then I told myself not to cry, not to sit down in the yard and cry, because if I did a thing like that everything would stay the same, just as it was, the world would not move forward, the dead would lie where they were, and Niklas would remain out there, against the stump, waiting for my return. I did not cry but stepped beyond our mother, looking for Erich. He was not in the yard. Was he still alive? Had they taken him with them?

The black gaping doorway of the mill stood in front of me. It was where I had to go, though I was sure of the horror inside.

But I could not have imagined what was really there.

Nothing remained in place or upright in the havoc of the room. Our father lay to one side of the overturned table, one hand still clutching the iron candlestick with which he had brained two of the soldiers. In death they sprawled together like harvesters asleep after a long day in the fields. If it were only so, and it could have been except for the blood. Except for our father's other hand, which lay far from his body.

Don't cry, I told myself. I didn't sit down, although my legs felt too weak to support me. Instead, I righted a stool that had been thrown into a corner. I picked up a few shards of broken bowl, but let them slip out of my fingers when I saw Joanna the scullion lying in the storeroom entrance. She was naked. I couldn't look at what they had done to her.

Yet I made myself step over her into the storeroom. Don't cry, I told myself, or you'll sink down and not move and then nothing will happen here or in the forest where Niklas is waiting.

I looked around. Everything had been taken or smashed or strewn across the floor. Sacks of dried beans and peas, ale and wine kegs, the rye-flour pastries our mother had made last week, a side of bacon, such things must have been loaded into a cart by the soldiers until the axles under it creaked. I thought of such things. I made myself take note. I forced memory into my head. Kneeling, I found grain from overturned baskets, some hunks of bread hastily chewed at and thrown down, but not much more. I found myself looking at things with infinite care, studying what the soldiers had done and not done, and in this way calmed myself.

"Don't cry," I said aloud, stepping over poor Joanna's body, crossing myself quickly, *for the merciful shall have mercy,* and went out of the mill, through the terrible yard. I stopped at the pigpen, chicken coop, and stable, but all the animals were gone, either taken by the soldiers or let loose to wander.

It is God's will, I told myself, everything is His will, and with measured steps, walking in the strong way our father would have wanted me to walk, I reached the shadowy wood.

Soon I came upon one of our chickens and chased it a long while through the slushy undergrowth. But it wouldn't be caught. Niklas and I would have to eat what little was left in the storeroom. And we needed strength for what we must do, because by then I understood our lives would go on and the world not end. No trumpet had sounded, no seven-headed beast or the Four Horsemen had appeared, and the sun glowed through the trees as if nothing strange had happened today.

When I reached the pond, Niklas was sitting against the stump, just as I had told him to do, except in his arms he clutched a young rabbit. It must have escaped from the soldiers when they opened the cage.

As I approached, the rabbit's ears twitched and Niklas smiled faintly. I looked at boy and animal breathing quickly together. The rabbit had large brown eyes; its quivering fur was dark brown mixed with ashy gray above and all white underneath. It was not plump after the winter, but its young flesh would sustain us. The rabbit was a sign that God wanted us to live.

"Good for you, Niklas," I said. "How did you catch it? Did it come right up to you? In fear of the soldiers? Well, good. We'll build a fire behind the mill and cook it. We need strength for what we must do."

When I reached for the rabbit, Niklas pulled back, covering it with both forearms.

"Niklas. Give it to me."

My brother stared from his blue eyes.

"God has sent us this rabbit to eat, Niklas. For the strength to do what we must."

I waited for him to give it to me. "Niklas," I said.

Niklas's chest and the furry sides of the rabbit seemed to move in unison like a single bellows.

"Niklas."

Clearly I would have to yank the animal from his grip. It was a violence I could not then commit. "All right. We'll boil some grain and there could be onions left in the bin. But then help me do what must be done. I can't do it alone. Come along, Brother."

As we returned to the mill through the wood, I told him, "The Lord has taken our father to His bosom too. It is the will of God. We must dig a grave big enough for both our parents and Joanna, too, because she'll lie with them, and deep enough so dogs won't get them. This must be done, Brother."

Cradling the rabbit in both arms, Niklas sloshed through the melting snow beside me. Instead of going straight to the mill, I took us around to the shed where our father kept his tools. Most of them were gone, but under a length of canvas we found an old shovel, some nails, and a pickax with a broken handle.

I led Niklas to the bank of the river away from the mill yard. This would be the spot. From a grave placed here our parents and Joanna could hear the sound of water flowing along the blades of the wheel, but they wouldn't really hear it because they'd be with God, I thought. "Niklas, we dig here."

I told him to wait, not needing him with me yet, and I went around into the house, without looking at anything. I stepped over Joanna and scooped up a few handfuls of grain into a pot and picked up the half-eaten chunks of bread. In the kitchen larder I looked for a pitcher of goat's milk, but all I found was three broken pitchers and spilled gouts of cream. Everything movable, including spoons and knives and seed bags of wheat, had been taken away.

I left the house without looking toward the hearth where our father was and walked through the yard without a glance at the hideous limbless tree. From the woodpile I got kindling to make a fire and again went into the house without looking either right or left to light some twigs from embers smoldering in the hearth.

While I was blowing on the embers, my eyes turned to the dead face of our father. For an instant I stared at his curly beard, his thick brows, his large nose, his ruffled brown hair. He seemed asleep from above the shoulders. At any moment he might rise up and sing as he did in the evenings, a merry tune or a song in praise of the Lord. Or he might boom out, "Anne! See to your brother!" Or he might smile at me in a bemused way, not thinking so much of me—I was always sure of it—as of our mother, whom he said I would someday grow up to resemble.

Then I blew much harder and from a plume of flame popping out of the embers I lit some twigs. Outside, away from the mill near the river, I started the fire and when it was going well, I set the iron pot on the burning wood. Once again I entered the house without looking, this time to get some rush straw and a hunk of old mutton fat to make a candle when we needed light to dig by. It was getting late, almost the time of vespers, with the sun hovering just above the treetops, its last rays catching at the ice-littered surface of the river. In a storeroom bin I found a dozen onions, half of them sprouting, and rolled them up in the apron I wore.

While grain boiled in the pot, I told Niklas to begin digging. For a moment he stared at me, then gingerly set the rabbit down. It stayed where he set it. My brother started to loosen the earth with the pickax, and I followed behind him with the spade. After we had worked awhile, I said to Niklas, "In one thing God has been good to us today. He has brought us spring, so the earth's soft enough to dig."

When the grave was half dug, we stopped for food. It was past vespers then, and only a dull glow shimmered on the river. But the waterwheel still turned, as it had turned ever since I could remember and ever since our father could have remembered, for he was born in this mill, too, and his parents lay in graves, side by side, in the woods. Niklas and I hadn't the strength to dig separate graves, such as our grandparents lay in, but I told him as we munched pieces of bread and onion and swallowed the hot bland gruel, "Our parents will understand how we must do it. And they'll have the company too of Joanna who was a good girl. And all day long and the night too they can hear the wheel turning and then have a long sleep when the snows come. Niklas, you can keep it."

He looked at me.

"The rabbit." I nearly added, What shall you call it? But he couldn't have told me that.

That night we worked by the light of a rush candle until the grave was deep enough, well over our heads, and long enough for our father's head and feet not to touch the ends of the grave. Then, exhausted both, Niklas and I went into the toolshed, where we huddled together, along with Rabbit, and fell

22

into a deep sleep, despite the cold wind that blew through the cracks, reminding the world that everything of winter was not yet memory. . . .

3

WHEN I opened my eyes the next morning, it was past the hour of prime, for the sun was already up. What I noticed, beside me in the straw, was Niklas's white hair and the white belly of the rabbit clutched to his chest. White of the same shade. They were both asleep, as innocent as the Lamb of God.

Had I lived or dreamed yesterday? At first I didn't know where we were, but then I knew it was the toolshed and a stone's throw away was the mill yard where a limbless tree grew out of our mother, who always remembered well what the priests said and who repeated the words to me by the fire so that I could remember too. I remembered then what the priests had warned us of. *And I saw a new heaven and a new earth; for the first heaven and the first earth were passed away, and there was no more sea.* But it was not true. Here we were with a rabbit in the toolshed and so much death close by, and the old world, our world, still to live in.

I got up to fetch from the river some water in the pot and returning to the shed gently roused Niklas. He wouldn't eat the onion I gave him until the rabbit had first nibbled a crust of bread.

"Niklas," I said, "the hard thing to do is what we do now. I can't get them to the grave alone. Come along."

When I opened the shed door, a chill vapor lapped about our legs and billowed along with us as we walked. I stopped. "Put it down, Niklas."

He put the rabbit down, and it stayed where he put it.

"First we go where our mother is. Then we go to the mill. You mustn't cry. You must pull hard when I tell you."

The mist was so thick, we could hardly see the body until almost upon it. I heard my brother make a little sound, but didn't turn to look at him. Don't look too much, don't think, I told myself, and gripped one leg of our mother at the ankle. I pulled. She moved, so that the tree growing out of her swayed. He made the sound again. Turning, I said to Niklas, "Do as I do."

He bent and took hold of the other leg at the ankle and together we dragged our mother around the side of the mill to the edge of the grave. I saw him staring at the treelike thing growing out of her.

Then we went back. Father, a big man, was difficult to drag around the overturned table and through the doorway and out to the grave. When we got him there, we were sweating and had to sit awhile on the bank.

I said to my brother, "Niklas, it isn't them. By now their souls have gone to heaven, and at the white throne the Lord will judge them good people and they will hear the angels. What we bring here isn't them. But if it was, it would be nice for them to hear the waterwheel turning. Come along. Joanna now."

I had him wait at the mill entrance while I went inside and found on a hook behind the door—the soldiers mustn't have looked there—the good cloak with embroidery on it that mother wore to town on festival days. This I wrapped around the naked girl, then called in Niklas. Joanna was the lightest of the three; soon we had her at graveside, where the mist was lifting and the sunlight shone through it like a veil. "Go get Rabbit and come back here," I told Niklas, then went into the house again.

In the milling room there were great piles of linen sacking and rags and fishing nets and lengths of old rope that had been saved for the shredding beaters and the water baths and the flattening that would make the fibers into paper. I searched under them for the ax that I knew Erich used to keep there. It was there. I went back with it to the gravesite, where Niklas was waiting with Rabbit in his arms.

This would be hard to do, I thought. But it was better than trying to pull the pike out. I turned our mother on her side and after a few clumsy blows managed to hack through the spear shaft, making it short enough to fit into the grave. I felt tears in my eyes, but didn't wipe them away for fear Niklas would whimper again.

I had brought a piece of rope from the milling room and untwisted a few strands of it. With the unraveled yarn I tied together some twigs into three crosses, but the dead hands were too rigid to close around them.

"Never mind," I said, looking at Niklas. "Help me lower them in." But the bodies were too heavy for that, so we ended by letting each one drop into the grave. Stepping down into it, careful where I stepped, I fitted them side by side—Father, Mother, Joanna—and placed each cross of twigs on their chests. Crawling out, I said a prayer. I could hear my voice ringing across the riverbank, asking our Lord to take these souls into His keeping, asking for His eternal mercy.

Then I remembered something. Running back into the mill, I took a piece of sacking from the milling room and wrapped our father's hand in it. This was a terrible weight to carry. As I took it into the yard I felt as if this burden were burning through the cloth. All my life I had watched this hand at the labor that kept me alive and felt this hand touch mine in love. Now cold and stiff, with congealed blood on the clenched fingers, it was being carried by me like bread from market. When I reached the grave, my own hands were trembling violently. Leaning over the side, I dropped the wrapped object in. Standing up, I said in a loud, severe voice, "We shovel the earth in now."

Niklas and I worked silently until the grave was covered. Then I sank down on it and cried at last and cried and cried until there was no thought or feeling in me, until I felt on the back of my neck the warmth of Niklas's hand.

"Dear Brother," I said, wiping my eyes on my apron. His hand was alive and loving, but his eyes looked as empty as the sky. I got to my feet. "What we just did was the worst of it."

I started for the house, then turned to wait for him and Rabbit. "Niklas, I hope you understand what I'm saying. I cried only because we'll miss them and we loved them so, but believe me, they're with the Lord now, they're in His hands and safe."

I said the words, but for the first time in my life these words

25

said in love of God were only words. A poison was seeping through the veins of my body, working into my heart of hearts. For Niklas's sake I must pretend to believe in the mercy of God, was my thought then, but the truth was—I knew it as surely as I had seen lightning strike my brother dumb—I no longer believed in God's mercy.

Such awful knowledge did not, however, cripple me. On the contrary, I had never thought more keenly about things that must be done.

First I remembered what Erich had said when the soldiers dragged him into the yard. He had pleaded for his life in exchange for the miller's treasure. I had forgotten that. Once, maybe a year ago, I had gone with our father under the mill when he dug the small casket from its hole in the riverbank. I had watched him lift the lid and put in three coins along with the others he had begun saving long before I was born.

Erich must have watched him sometime, too, because when I scrambled down the riverbank to the hiding place, the coin box was gone.

But I could not let the loss of money stop us from leaving. Nothing must stop us from moving away from here and into the world or we would meet a fate as awful as that of our parents and perhaps as quickly. I knew what would happen to us, alone, too young to run the mill. My brother could not speak and was slow. I was almost a woman and thus game not only for wandering soldiers but for neighborhood men as well. God would not show us mercy, I thought. There was no mercy from Him. And for that matter, perhaps God and Satan were one. How could that be? The idea stunned me into halting on the way up the riverbank. Because neither God nor Satan showed mercy, because neither could be trusted, they were like each other. And so we must provide for ourselves.

When I returned to the mill, to my surprise Niklas was sitting on the floor near the two dead soldiers, holding Rabbit in his arms.

The sight of him sitting there as if grieving for them annoyed me enough to speak sharply. "Niklas!"

He didn't move. I went into the storeroom again. It was easy to do without poor Joanna lying in the doorway. After a thorough search I accumulated more than a dozen onions, half a loaf of barley bread, a quarter of old cheese, and in the kitchen larder a piece of salt pork that the soldiers had missed. They had taken the big stewpot.

When I went back into the main room, Niklas was still sitting near the hearth, staring at the dead men.

I said, "Niklas!" again, but when he didn't turn to look at me, I went through the milling room, past the hammers and gears and vats, into the storage space where our father kept the finished paper. Most of it had been sold during the winter, but I found a dozen sheets, left because surely the soldiers had no idea of their worth. Folding them carefully and rolling them in a length of canvas, I put them in a rucksack along with the food.

"Niklas," I said, going back into the main room. He wouldn't move, he and Rabbit, but remained there, staring at the crushed skulls of the soldiers. Wearily I sat on the stool.

"No, Brother," I said. "It would mean digging again. Do you want that? And these men murdered our parents. Must we give them respect?"

We remained in silence a long time. Rabbit's whiskers twitched, but Niklas never moved. Finally I got up.

"But not near the river. I won't have them disturbing our parents. So it must be in the wood. And not deep either. I don't care if the dogs do get them."

I went outside, with Niklas following. We dug at the verge of the wood until the sun was overhead, then sat sweating in the shade. The hole was only waist-high when I stood in it, but I would dig no deeper. We dragged the soldiers out and dumped them in.

"No prayers," I told Niklas, who stood there holding Rabbit, staring at the covered grave. Quickly I muttered, "God have mercy on these sinners," and crossed myself. "Come along now."

We went back to the house, at last empty of the dead, and climbed the old ladder to the place where we slept. It was like a stall with a small window. We had a straw mattress with ticking and a stool and a closet where our clothing was kept. The closet had been overturned and everything strewn around. Almost everything was still there, however, because the soldiers hadn't seen much value in what we had or hadn't been able to wear it. I told Niklas to put every bit of his clothing on, and I did the same with mine: three skirts, four bodices, two jackets, two cloaks, a battered hat of mangy beaver fur that I wore in the coldest days of winter, a heavy black hood.

I felt huge and must have looked it, because Niklas smiled. For his part, Niklas looked round and awkward, a rumpled little bear, with a stocking cap hiding the white of his head. We smiled at each other.

"We're going now," I said, but without knowing where we were going. First, however, I remembered the knife our mother kept in their room. I went there and found it under the mattress where her head had lain each evening of our lives and where sometimes I had seen her brown hair fanned out and her broad forehead pale in the candlelight and her keen blue eyes watching me as I stood in the doorway and her mouth smiling. But I had cried and must not cry again. I would not cry again.

In the corner I found a fancy linen wimple and stuffed it into the rucksack that Niklas would carry. And wedged halfway under the mattress was our mother's best pair of shoes, pointed, of leather. These, too, went into the rucksack. Strewn about the room were the torn leaves of a prayer book, its binding of boards, held by brass clasps and covered in leather, broken into pieces and flung around. The soldiers had seen nothing valuable in the old vellum book. Yet it had been our mother's most cherished possession, which she had brought to the mill as a bride. She had taught me to read with that book. On cool mornings, with the mill wheel turning steadily beneath us, she used to point out the letters and have me name them and later had me read the words of Scripture aloud. Those were our best times together.

At the doorway I looked at the empty bed for a moment, then we went down.

Outside, we stood near the waterwheel turning in the sunshine. "See the blade, Niklas? Rising on the wheel? That one rising was us yesterday. Now, Brother, see it go past the top and down into the water? Us today, at this moment. But now it's rising again. That's tomorrow. Father once told me life is like a wheel. We stood right here and he pointed as I'm doing now and said, 'Anne, life is a wheel,' and I believe it. Because that's God's plan. Now come along."

We knelt at our parents' grave and I prayed for them and for us, although in truth there was a coldness in my heart, like a piece of ice that can't melt. I said the words for my parents and for the sake of my brother, but for me they were only words.

God was not listening. Of that I was certain, even as I begged His mercy.

Shaken by the heresy of my thoughts, I told Niklas to strap his rucksack on. "We're leaving now."

When we left the mill, I didn't look back and neither did Niklas, who carried Rabbit in the crook of his arm. We started down a trail winding toward the road. Along the edge of the wood were two, three, four dandelions. Spring was here, and we were walking through it.

But where were we going?

"Niklas," I said. "People say people have gone to the Garden of Eden where Adam and Eve once lived. It's far away in the east behind mountains. There the smell of flowers never fades and they can heal you. The water flows over jeweled rocks. There's no wind or rain or cold and no sorrow and no death. Beside a blue lake is a great palace glowing like the sun and beyond it is a mountain whose peak touches the moon. They say people have seen all this. Maybe we'll go there ourselves someday. But now we are going—"

I had been thinking while we dug the soldiers' grave of where we might go and so at that moment I made the decision. "We are going to Uncle Albrecht. He lives in a village maybe a week or two north of here. He's a smith, I think. He'll be good to us."

I didn't tell Niklas that our father used to say of his brother, "Albrecht is the strangest man on God's earth," or that I had never met our uncle or that I didn't even know the name of his village.

"Come along," I said to Niklas, bending down to look hard at a dandelion. "We have a long way to go before vespers."

4

I AWOKE thinking it was not true. I would turn to Niklas and shake him and together we would go down the millhouse ladder to find Mother preparing hot gruel for us, and later, after breakfast, we would go outside to watch the great wheel turning, while Father came along the path, carrying fagots cut in the nearby wood.

But when I turned to Niklas, the truth stayed my hand. The wheel was turning, turning near the grave. I couldn't shake him until the trembling stopped.

We had found shelter last night in the haymound of a farm stable. When I turned, the straw under me crinkled and sighed. It was cold. My breath shot out thickly when I whispered Niklas's name.

"We must leave," I told him. "The farmer might not want us here."

Gathering up the rucksacks, we staggered out of the stable into a bitter dawn wind. Clouds billowed and churned above us. My brother's white hair blew back like bits of cloud as he hunched forward, clutching Rabbit to his chest.

"Niklas, God has taken good care of us so far," I said, "our feet are on the right path." For I was determined not to fill my brother with sadness at God's indifference or to shock him with my heretical fear that God as well as Satan might hurt us. What I suffered must remain a secret.

Rapidly we crossed the open space between road and stable, with an old hog, tethered to a stake, grunting fiercely when we passed. At the farmhouse entrance a big man was standing, pointing the tines of a pitchfork in our direction. When he saw what we were, the farmer went back inside. Because he'd said nothing in anger, I was encouraged to return and beg him for some warming time at his fire, where we might eat our food. But I decided against it.

Stopping beside the road in a thicket, we ate barley bread

and bits of cheese. Hearing a rushing sound, I discovered a nearby stream from which we drank icy water, cupping it in our hands and letting it slide with a sensation of burning between our reddened fingers. The cold drink thoroughly awakened us.

Before continuing, I had Niklas sit against a tree while I inspected his head for lice. He often had them, more than I did. Perhaps it was the whiteness of his hair that attracted them. Rabbit watched me hunt through the soft strands. As our mother had taught me, I cracked their hard, shiny bodies with my thumbs.

"Niklas," I said, "don't worry. Uncle Albrecht lives just up the way. It won't take many days to get there. And if we don't like staying with him, there are other places." Because I was not sure our uncle would take us in, and I had to prepare my brother for such misfortune. After all, we were strangers. Uncle Albrecht and Father hadn't seen each other since before I was born—Mother had once told me this, adding that the two brothers had parted in anger.

What I didn't tell Niklas, of course, is that we had no place to go except to our uncle—if we could find him. Like it or not, he was our hope. Of Mother's family, only she had survived the Black Death when it swept through before I was born, and of Father's family, only he and Uncle Albrecht had been spared. Now our parents were dead. And it was possible that Albrecht had died in the meantime.

But as we slung the rucksacks over our shoulders and braced against the morning wind, I said to Niklas, "We're on our way, Brother."

Were those tears in his eyes? Maybe the biting wind had caused them. But, of course, I knew better. And so in a hearty voice, as if our journey were for pleasure, I said to him, "We'll see some of the world, Niklas. Our parents would like that."

Luck was on our side. Not an hour down the road we got a ride in the wagon of a farmer who had been to a village market. We sat among bags of wheat seed, onions, and salt. Half a dozen pickled eels lay in a cask, and their aroma made me hungry. I saw Niklas sniff the air, too, while in front of us the farmer talked without ever stopping for an answer, as if he never had much chance to use his mouth for talking. He talked about an archbishop somewhere who devalued the local coinage, then raised the tax on cattle and caused rioting and looting that didn't end although he excommunicated the whole town. And the lonely farmer told us about a shrine where three consecrated wafers dripped blood last summer.

"But that's nothing," he said, whipping up his swaybacked mule. "I knew someone who once met a man who talked to the Virgin." He glanced back at us. "You two look cold. How can you be cold with so much fat on you?"

He took our clothes for fat.

"Some years ago, before your time, we had a cold spring. Froze all the streams in this neighborhood. Fish froze solid in them. You could hack them out of the ice and put them in a pot and when they thawed, they swam around." He glanced back again. "Don't believe it? Ask your parents if it isn't true. What's wrong with him?"

"Nothing," I said. "He's quiet."

"Because I don't want him in my wagon if he's sick."

"He's healthier than you and me."

Satisfied, the farmer struck the rump of his mule with the reins. He wore a sheepskin mantle like many of the travelers on the road. In spite of the cold weather and lowering clouds that could bring snow, many people were on the road, in fact crowds of them, all going from east to west. There were merchants on horseback, peddlers leading packtrains of mules, peasants hauling two-wheeled carts, and brown-robed monks walking beside their porters, who carried bundles of food and large crosses wrapped in burlap. There were even woodcutters with axes slung round their necks. And almost all of them were heading west from the east.

The farmer was talking, of course, but I interrupted a string of his words to ask why so many people were on the road, heading west.

"They think they can run." The farmer laughed. He had a weathered face, a snub nose, a shock of hair sticking out from under a dirty felt hat. "They think they can run from the Pest, but they can't."

The word *Pest* frightened me. Although there hadn't been an outbreak of plague in my lifetime, the possibility was always there, lurking in the shadows like an assassin with a dirk, as my father used to say of it.

"These people are running from plague?"

But he wasn't listening. He had pulled the reins in, halting his mule. Ahead of us people were moving into the ditch to let a large four-wheeled wagon pass. It was covered with canvas and drawn by three horses harnessed one behind another. As it approached I leaned forward to have a better look, and when it was broadside I glimpsed through its window a pale and pretty woman, surely a lady of rank, in a linen wimple and fur cloak. Her eyebrows were plucked.

Behind this wagon were others of a flat kind to which were strapped pieces of polished furniture and cooking pots and casks and boxes of silver plate, some of it sticking out because the packing had been hasty. There were half a dozen such baggage wagons and a large number of servants, who shuffled along with a haughtiness much like that of their mistress on her cushioned seat.

"Look at them," the farmer sneered, glancing back as he whipped up the mule again, clucking to it. "You can't run from the Pest. He brings peasants and kings to the same fate."

"Has the Pest come back?"

"I heard the rumor last week and from what I see today it might be true. All these people must be leaving towns in the east. But of course people need only hear the word *Pest* and they run like mad dogs. If you don't believe me, ask your parents. They'll know."

A few snowflakes fell on Niklas's hair, white on white, and on Rabbit's belly, white on white, too, while the animal lay asleep in my brother's arms.

Late in the morning, when the farmer turned into a rutted lane, he stopped for us to jump out. Studying Niklas a moment, he said, "Are you sure he's all right?"

Not getting a reply from me, the farmer clucked to his mule and rattled off down the deeply scarred road.

We kept to the main one, walked all day with only a few stops for rest and a shared piece of salt pork, which we ate in a brace of trees beyond the sight of travelers.

Toward dusk, when the main road forked, we kept to the northern branch. Only a few travelers on this road were bearing their worldly goods with them.

I asked a man why. He told me with a wink that the north road held little interest for people able to run for their lives. "If they die, they'd rather do it in the big cities," he said. "North or south you can find good places to work, but cities in the west are known for pleasure. That's why most people are heading west. To die having pleasure."

I must have looked at him doubtfully, because he added, "You weren't alive last time, child. Because that's the way it is with the Black Death. When the Pest comes galloping along, people look to their pleasure. Knights and their ladies. Merchants. Even peasants roll up what they have and set out for adventure. Even monks. Where can we go that has good food, good wine, gambling, and other delights? The Pest herds them all together for a good time. And that's why he catches them so easily."

Giving me a long look, he said, "A girl like you ought to go west too."

"Why?"

"To get the sort of work a girl gets when she goes where people want pleasure."

As I walked on he shouted at my back, "Think about it! What else can a girl do better?"

As we walked on I said to Niklas, "The Pest won't get us now. We're going north where he isn't."

5

WE spent that night in the guesthouse of a monastery. A monk at the main gate told us how to get there. We went around the monastery wall, past a vat for trampling grapes, some barrels, and a storeroom for hemp and a sheep pen, until reaching the timbered building that was the guesthouse. Actually, the guesthouse was a woodshed, hardly big enough for the ten travelers who jammed into it for the night.

When the shed was filled, a monk came in to ask for whatever we might spare in the name of the Lord, but only a peddler gave anything, a halfpence. Then the monk blew out the candle, took it away, and left us in darkness. I didn't like being there, but it was too cold to stay in the woods, and I feared a second night in a haymound. No one spoke to us, however, or touched us. The other guests talked among themselves and wriggled noisily to find comfort on a cold floor strewn with wood shavings. There was much coughing.

One man hacked terribly, but he could still complain about the nobleman from whom he rented land. He said the lord made him bring his cow to and from pasture in a roundabout way, so it would cross the lord's fields and drop manure for the manor's crops. By such a method the lord got fertilizer from his tenants free. And not only that, said the farmer, he had been forced to marry a woman who belonged to the lord's domain. And this woman hadn't borne him children, so he had no heir, not even a girl. In consequence, everything he owned would go to the lord by the lord's own law—the house he had built, the tools he had bought, the clothes he wasn't buried in, would all go to the nobleman who had robbed him his whole life long. He said he owed fees for milling his grain in the lord's mill, and baking his bread in the lord's oven, and pressing his apples in the lord's cider press.

Telling his story sent the man into a fit of coughing, but he

35

wouldn't finish. "If we don't obey this lord, we'll spend eternal life in hell."

"Who tells you that?" someone called out from the darkness.

"Our bishop. He nailed a pastoral letter to the church door."

There was scornful cackling, but that didn't stop the farmer. In a wailing voice he added, "Not only that, not only that! We are ruined everywhere we turn! We pay the bishop higher taxes than we pay the lord!"

There were scuffing and turning and other noises in the woodshed, along with so much coughing that I couldn't sleep. But with Rabbit tucked inside his tunic my brother slept soundly. I kept one hand all night on Niklas's shoulder to see that no one harmed him, because people were shifting and turning in the darkness and I had no idea what they were doing or might do.

Often I dozed off, only to jerk fully awake at the sound of terrible coughing. I heard someone whisper, "I'm burning up," and later the same gasping voice—it was a woman's—panted through the night, "I am chilled, I am burning up. Oh, burning . . ."

Toward dawn I sat straight up at the sound of violent thrashing. There was other movement then—shapes bumbling through the woodshed toward the thrashing—"Hold her, hold her down!"

When it was light enough, I peered at the sprawled bodies of sleepers, trying to discover who had passed such a terrible night. The sounds had come from the left, where a peasant lay with her head against a pile of logs. After a few travelers had roused themselves and left the woodshed, I could see her plainly: shiny red bumps on her face, her mouth twisted to one side.

Shaking Niklas, I got up and prepared to step past her. But I couldn't. I bent down because I was looking at something now as familiar as the faces of our parents: I was looking at death. The dead woman's cloak was splattered by vomit she must have coughed up last night.

"Go outside, Niklas," I told him, and he went.

"Couldn't do anything for her," an old man said gently as I knelt beside the dead woman. "Must have died of Saint Anthony's fire. There's a lot of it this season. But there used to be much more of it some years ago. One of my sons died of the fire." He smiled at me in the growing light. "Had headaches first. Said he felt weak. I thought he didn't want to work. Lazy boy, I called him. But he itched and fell asleep standing up and his arms cramped. Then his fingers turned numb and foul and the flesh stank. He felt hot and cold. Poor boy, he wasn't lazy at all. Then came the vomiting and the thrashing just like hers last night." The old man touched the sleeve of my cloak. "I'll see to her. She's had the good luck to die here. Monks will say prayers for her soul."

So I left him in the woodshed with the dead woman. Niklas was waiting outside, his eyes asquint in the heaving wind. Rabbit's brown ears appeared over the top of my brother's jacket.

Mother had once told me about Saint Anthony's fire. The illness was named for a vision of hellfire that had brought the youthful Anthony to seek salvation from wickedness. It was a lesson for us all, Mother had said.

Had the woman in the woodshed been wicked enough to deserve such suffering? Had our parents been wicked?

No. They had not. They had not been wicked.

All morning as we leaned into a cold wind, I kept asking myself, What happens to fire when it goes out? Where does it go? How do we know what happens to souls?

When snow began to fall, I pulled the stocking cap over Niklas's ears and wished I could ask him such questions. Not that he could answer them. But it would be nice to hear him say, "Ah, sister, I don't know."

The day grew warmer, so that night we stayed in a wood. I pulled branches of a thicket together and laid a blanket over them for a shelter. We snuggled beneath the other blanket I had brought in my rucksack. Rabbit stayed cozy between us.

Next day was warm, suddenly a warm spring day. Melted snow glistened in wheel ruts like tiny lakes and reflected the first cloudless sky we had seen on our journey.

A woman bending in a nearby field had gathered her skirt between her legs and fastened it to her belt. From the basket her skirt made she was taking out seeds and scattering them in furrows that two men ahead of her were gashing through the wet soil with a plow—one pushing, one pulling it.

"What a beautiful day," I said to Niklas. "Our luck is holding. It's warm now, it's really spring. It's a good day for a journey."

But for a journey so lacking in plan? We were going north simply because our uncle used to live up there. And north was big enough surely to get lost in.

Two days went by in the warming spring. Our spirits began to match the weather. We smiled at each other as memory faded in the sweet bright air.

On the third day of our journey we heard voices before we saw people. There was a murmur ahead like the stream bubbling past our watermill, then a louder anguishing sound as if we were coming to a place of battle where wounded lay.

Finally we saw them, a long file of people crossing a fork in the road. I wanted to avoid them and their cries. "Come along," I told Niklas, starting for the ditch. "We'll go into the wood over there."

But my brother headed for the marching people.

I fell in with him, knowing that Niklas seldom led, but when he did I must follow.

Coming up close to the procession, we halted to watch it pass. So did farmers who were hauling firewood on their backs. We all stood by the roadside while a few hundred people shuffled by.

Taking off his rumpled hat, a farmer said, "People of God."

Most of them were barefoot, wearing coarse trousers and blouses of horsehair that must have scratched terribly. Many of the men, all of whom marched in the front ranks, were stripped to the waist and steadily lashed themselves with leather whips. A trail of blood appeared in the dust behind them. Some of the women wore ropes tightened around their necks; others were smeared head to toe with wet ashes. All of the penitents were groaning, weeping, praying, reciting hymns of woe.

One of the farmers, witnessing the pain, bent down to dip his fingers in the spilled blood, then pressed them to his eyes and muttered a prayer.

When the flagellants had all passed, we followed them, as did some of the farmers, into a nearby village. The penitents halted at a swept area used as a threshing floor, still whipping themselves while their leader addressed the villagers who were gathering around.

These devout worshipers, he declared, would march in their suffering for thirty-three days, each day for a year of our Lord's life. They could not bathe or tend their wounds. They could not sleep in beds or touch another person in all that time. They were redeemers. By making their own blood flow they enacted the scourging of Christ. They were atoning as He had done for the sins of mankind.

I glanced at Niklas. He had removed the stocking cap long ago, and in the sunlight his lightning-struck hair was as white as Rabbit's belly. They both looked soft and gentle among the flagellants and curious villagers.

"The world is growing older," the leader told them. "In Matthew it says the sun will be darkened, and the moon will not give its light, and stars will fall from heaven, and then all the tribes of earth will mourn."

I looked again at Niklas, unable to tell what understanding there could be in his blue-eyed gaze.

"We must arm ourselves against Satan, who has broken loose. He has come again with his demons—part reptiles, part women. They lay waste to the world, bringing fires, causing famine, sowing disease. Pray for us, join us, help us in the name of the Lord."

Women were bringing sick villagers through the crowd to get to the leader for his blessing. The threshing floor was slippery from blood.

I took Niklas by the arm and firmly led him away. "Brother," I said, "We've seen too much pain. The pain we saw until now was pain no one wanted. But these people want pain. Come along."

He looked past me at the men scourging themselves.

"No," I said. "It wouldn't bring our parents back. It wouldn't help them in heaven." I said, "Niklas."

Slowly he turned to look at me.

"It wouldn't help them if you drew your own blood. God wouldn't ask that of children. Come along."

He came along then.

As we trudged down the afternoon road, for some time the sound of sorrow and fear and suffering behind us surged like an angry wind against our ears.

And when silence returned, save for the brushing of our sandaled feet across the dusty road, I told myself if God willed our failure to find Uncle Albrecht, I would turn westward to the cities. I would do what girls do there, if it would save my brother. He would have drawn blood for our parents. I would draw my own for him if God willed it.

6

THREE days later we were still drifting northward through the spring. In spite of sweating in so many clothes, I kept all of mine on. Looking into the limpid brook of a woods where we slept, I could see what an ungainly creature I'd become. Swaddled as I was, I had the look of something overgrown, a big fat child. Moreover, the battered hat of beaver fur hid my thick braid of yellow hair. A man bent on mischief would probably not think I was worth his effort. I had come to the age of caution some time ago, so that from the outset of our journey I'd been fearful. But the road itself had given me a deeper sense of womanhood, a feeling for the danger that went with it.

There was no need, however, for Niklas to wear heavy clothing. He removed his outer mantle and two of three pair of trousers and a leather jerkin. We put them in his rucksack, but when he wasn't looking, I stuffed them into my own. If the long journey had tired me, from his dragging step and haggard face I knew my brother was exhausted. We had only onions left to eat.

Our luck was not holding, but I said to him, "Good weather is good luck."

In each village I asked for Albrecht Valens the gunsmith—if

my memory was correct, gunmaking was what he did. No one had heard of him.

A week after leaving home we were on the outskirts of a village when the boys saw us. There were six of them, about my age. They were in a nearby field, throwing rocks at a skinny dog who kept circling just beyond their range. Why didn't it run away? One of the boys was holding something up—a kitten. They were tempting the dog to come closer, then throwing at it.

When they saw us hobbling along the road, they gave up on the dog and turned as one to watch us coming. I could feel them. Without meeting their gaze I felt their attention, and it made my knees weak.

"Move along," I told Niklas briskly. "Move along."

Out of the corner of my eye I saw them crossing the field. This would bring them to the road ahead of us. I felt sweat in my eyes, but not from heat: it was fear pouring out of me. Even the soldiers at the mill had not frightened me so. I glanced at Niklas. Surely my fear was as much for him as for myself. He was small, holding a rabbit, with nowhere to run.

They stood in the road, blocking our way.

One said, "Who are you?"

"We're going north," I told him as calmly as possible.

Another was looking at Niklas. "Why do you have white hair?"

"He was struck by lightning," I told the boy, who was the biggest of them. He wore torn trousers, a jerkin with one sleeve, clogs. He was beginning to have a beard, and it clouded the lower half of a big-jawed face. He was squinting hard at Niklas.

"Why do you have white hair?" he asked my brother again.

"He was struck by lightning," I repeated.

"You shouldn't eat that rabbit," he said to Niklas, ignoring me. "Your sister's too fat anyway. Give it to me." But he didn't step forward to take it.

I said in a pleading voice, "We're on our way home."

"Is he your brother?"

"I know what's wrong," another boy said, laughing. "He can't talk. He can't say a word. He's mad."

41

The biggest boy stepped in front of Niklas, studying him. "What we do in this village with mad people is carve a cross in their head."

"We're on our way home," I told him again.

"Then go home, fat girl. We'll just take the rabbit."

"And give your brother a cross on his forehead to go with his white hair," another said.

The biggest boy reached for the rabbit, but as his hand shot out, my brother flung himself on the ground. He was clutching Rabbit with both hands, curling up around the soft little body like a shell.

A boy stepped forward to swipe at Niklas with his foot, but the kick only grazed my brother's head. Before another blow could be aimed at him, I hurled myself on top of Niklas, spreading my arms over his body. And almost immediately I felt a sharp pain, another, a series of them on my arms legs neck, as the boys kicked and finally rolled me over.

I opened my eyes to see the biggest boy leaning close, his hand fisted and pulled back. I put up my arms, warding off the blow as it came down heavily, but someone else pummeled me in the stomach so hard, I couldn't breathe. Yet I managed to crawl back on top of Niklas, covering his body again and putting my hands with his around the animal, our four hands deep into the fur, keeping the boys from snatching Rabbit away. I was thinking more of holding Rabbit without squeezing him to death than I was of the blows.

Pain was everywhere except in my hands circling the soft fur. It seemed that I knew nothing but hands and what they protected, that what was happening elsewhere to me was happening to someone else. I felt the pain of my body, yet I was not where pain was. In truth I was hands. Mine and those of Niklas wrapped around the fur. Nothing could take Rabbit from us. I knew this was true in a silence of my mind even while the boys hovered screamed punched kicked.

Then quite suddenly it was over.

I heard a questioning voice, a cry of anger, a deep command followed by silence.

Opening my eyes, I looked up at a big man in a belted tunic. He held a cudgel at his chest. His broad nose was caught in sunlight beyond the shadowy rim of a hat. His thick eyebrows pinched together as he stared down at us. He looked like something carved.

Getting painfully to my feet, I didn't see the boys. A look at that cudgel must have scattered them. I lifted Niklas up; he still clutched Rabbit. There was blood, both my brother's and mine, on the rumpled brown fur, the white belly. But Rabbit wasn't hurt.

Turning to the man and holding back tears, I thanked him.

He was looking across the fields where the boys must have gone. "Godless," he said. "It's the world today."

With an old rag I washed with in streams, I wiped the blood from Niklas's face, proud of him for not crying. Then I wiped my own, aware that my lower lip was puffed out, that my right eye was almost closed. I felt a throbbing pain in my back and a sharp pain in my ribs when turning. Even so, all the clothes I wore must have saved me from worse injury. Not a tear escaped either of us. We wouldn't cry, even in front of the man who had saved us.

Surprised that he hadn't moved on, I thanked him again. He stood beside a two-wheeled wagon loaded with fagots he must have cut in the woods. There was a slow, massive look about him that I liked and in a moment trusted.

So with a boldness born of our journey I asked him if we could have something to eat.

He nodded and we fell in behind him as he pulled the wagon along. I kept wondering: If God loved us, would He give us such pain to feel?

The man's farm was in a field just beyond the village. The house, actually a hut, was built of timber with a thatched roof. Lying in the yard were some of his tools: a spade, a scythe, some hoes, a plow. He didn't have a stable, didn't have a single work animal or a chicken. A half-grown girl holding an infant in her thin arms watched us coming. A woman and a girl about my age stood in the open doorway of the hut.

When we got near, the man halted to wipe his forehead. "Godless times," he called out to the woman.

From the way she looked at us I knew we could stay for the night.

We stayed longer than that. The family took us in, although there was little space in their hut. They had a trestle table with a bench, a single chest, some iron pots and clay bowls and a washtub. There were two pallets wedged together. Blaise (for that was the farmer's name) and his wife slept on one, his three daughters on the other. The baby was laid on straw in the washtub. Niklas and I stretched out at night in front of the hearth.

For the first time since leaving home, I spent my days in thin, loose clothing. Aches and bruises disappeared. I washed my hair in a brook. As the ripples settled I looked at broad cheekbones, wide-set eyes: the ungainly creature had become a woman, one with sharper features than the girl who had taken to the road a few weeks ago. Niklas recovered quickly from his wounds, too, and it did me good to watch him run in the fields again like a boy.

So here we were—safe, with a family. No one mentioned my brother's hair, although the baby sometimes reached out to touch it. No one asked me why Niklas couldn't talk. They shared with us their dark barley bread, oat gruel, and pieces of salt herring. They asked nothing in return.

Looking at me, Blaise would often mutter, "Godless times," as if that was reason enough for such kindness.

I helped his wife at the hearth, taught her as my mother had taught me how to make mustard with vinegar and spice. They liked the herring better with my mustard, which made me proud.

After a week of living with Blaise and his family, I felt we belonged with them.

At night, listening to the steady hum of breathing in the little room, I imagined the future clearly for the first time since our parents had died.

Niklas, I'd say in my mind, we're staying right here. These are good people. We'll work for them. I'm stronger than his eldest (pale, she coughed a lot and once I saw the poor girl spit blood and wipe her lips quickly so no one would know). Soon,

Brother, you'll be big enough to work in the fields too. We'll work side by side next to Blaise. And I'll cook things that Mother taught me. Did you notice how they liked the mustard?

Of course, this was not life as we had known it at home. Our mother used to say we lived well, but until coming here I didn't know how well: the large millhouse, a variety of food, warm clothes.

Once, feeling sudden joy in my new home, I said to Blaise's wife, "My mother taught me to read, and I can teach others."

She looked at me in amazement, so I said no more. Mother had warned me not to tell people we could read. They might think it was a devilish skill for women to have. Our father was a well-known miller for miles around, but no one knew there had been priests in my mother's family who could read Latin and a wool merchant who could speak the Arabian tongue.

Now I began to wonder how to use such advantages for the benefit of Blaise and his family. I wanted to please them, to have them say, "We did right to take in Niklas and Anne."

I'd call out soundlessly to Niklas in the darkness, This is where we'll stay, Brother. The breathing of sleepers in the little room reminded me of the soft, continuous sound of insects in a meadow. I'd say to him in my mind, We might never find our uncle or he might treat us badly or turn us out. I'll make tasty dishes the way Mother taught me. That is, I'll make them after we help Blaise to do better with his farm, so he can buy all sorts of food. We won't let him pay us for our work. We'll tell him we'll always owe him, because he saved us. We'll help him plow and plant and harvest, because his daughters can't do such hard work, Niklas. And when the family has money, I'll cook them venison frumenty and pork pastry and brewet the way Mother made it, and they'll say they never ate anything better in their lives. I lay awake each night in the sweetness of the dream.

I had a secret too—not even shared with Niklas. I was going to teach the eldest daughter how to read.

One afternoon I found her behind the farm hut, trying to weave some strands of meadow grass together. "Want to learn something other girls don't know?" I asked.

She grimaced. "Will it hurt me?"

"No. Look." I drew a letter in the dust with a stick. "Do you know what that is?"

"Writing?"

"I knew you could learn. Yes, it's writing. Want to see more of it?"

When she nodded, I drew another letter in the dust.

"Don't tell anyone," I said. "It's our secret." When she nodded, I drew a dozen more letters in the dust and told her the names for each of them. She repeated them slowly. Even as she was squinting down at the letters, I was saying to Blaise in my mind, And I'm teaching your eldest to read. Before you get angry, listen to me, our dear friend Blaise. If she reads, she can go to the city and deal with merchants who buy your grain. She'll know too much for them to cheat you. She'll know how to double or triple the worth of your farm because she can read.

I was saying these words to myself, when Blaise's wife came around the hut and called my name.

Leaving the girl, I followed her mother inside.

A frail woman with a kind face, Blaise's wife smiled at me. "You're a good girl, Anne."

"I want to be."

"What was that you had her doing?"

This was not the time to reveal my secret. "Nothing," I said.

With a little sigh, she wiped her hands on a dirty apron and stooped over the fire to work up some embers. "Anne," she said, looking at them, not at me, "I think you'll have to go."

"Go? You mean, leave here? You want us to go?"

Still without looking at me, she said, "It's the food. We don't have enough."

I bent down beside her, while she kept needlessly stirring the embers. "That's what I know. You can't feed us without something in return. That's what I want to do—work in the fields with Blaise. And Niklas. Soon he'll be big enough to work too."

At last she turned my way. "Niklas will never be able to do that."

"But I can. I can push or pull the plow. Whichever Blaise wants. I can work all day." I held out both arms with hands spread wide. "See? I'm young and strong. Very, very strong."

For a moment my heart leapt with hope, because she stared thoughtfully at me and smiled. But then she said, "No."

And I knew from the sound of that "no," I could no more change her mind than change the movement of the sun.

Next morning, before leaving, I gave her our mother's pointed leather shoes as a gift. She cried and thrust them back at me, but I insisted. Then I cried and so did the girls, and Niklas stood sniffling in the doorway.

After I told our friends good-bye and we reached the road, I recalled my last look at them gathered in front of the hut, with Blaise standing apart, his big face set like stone, his big hands hanging at his sides.

And then I knew. We'd been turned out because of him. His wife had feared me.

7

A FEW days later we learned where Uncle Albrecht was or at least where he might be.

Since leaving Blaise and his family, we had been wandering northward, always northward, without a plan. Blaise's wife had given us a round of barley bread they could little afford to part with, and when that ran out, I sold our mother's linen wimple to a peddler for money to buy food. The wimple was the last thing of value we could part with.

Then I felt sick, both hot and cold, so with money in hand I inquired for lodgings at a wayside inn.

A man standing in the kitchen doorway asked to see our money. When I held it out, he took only half a pence. He was florid, fat, with kind eyes. "You better stay in the pantry, not upstairs in a room. There's a corner you can curl up in. People are always around the pantry, so you're safe. Don't show anyone that money. What's wrong with the boy?"

"Nothing. He's tired."

"Keep him out of sight. When they start drinking in there"—

he pointed toward a door leading into the dining room—"they might think a white-haired boy is amusement."

So that night we crept into a corner of the pantry among kegs and sacks, with plucked fowl hanging above us on hooks. The fat cook and his helper and two hefty serving girls came in and out, winking at us, smiling.

I felt hot and clammy, sicker than I'd been when we came to the inn, yet there was something in me that wanted to know what was happening in the dining room, from which voices started coming after nightfall. I told Niklas to stay where he was. Then I slipped out of the pantry and through the kitchen, and hid under the stairway. Between the steps I saw long dining tables with trenchers of bread set beside tankards. Men were sitting on benches, spooning meat and sauce from a big bowl onto their trenchers. The air was filled with slurping noises and laughter.

In spite of the fever I grew hungry watching them gobble up sturgeon, eel pastry, meat fritters. Most of them looked like merchants and carters—men of the road. And there were chevaliers, too, occupying a far table. They wore breastplates, mail breeches, and iron skullcaps. They kept apart from the others.

Suddenly two of them raised their voices in argument. Flinging back the benches, they faced each other. One shouted, "No man accuses me of riding a mare into battle!"

"Your mount was no stallion. You were riding a mare, a nice tame mare who wouldn't throw you into the mud."

"No man says that to me."

"It was a mare you rode that day. So you wouldn't be thrown on your back. So you wouldn't get a pike in your guts."

"No man says that to me."

"Because you never were a good rider. A nice gentle mare is right for you."

The other knight's hand went to the grip of his sword. "No man says that to me."

"And no man threatens me."

Followed by their comrades and other diners, they pushed out of the room. Someone called for torches. Through the open doorway I could see them gathering in a circle, with the chevaliers facing each other.

48

Intent on the terrible thing about to happen, I didn't notice right away a little man bending down for a better look at me.

"What are you doing in there, child?" he asked pleasantly, and poked his head into the cranny beneath the stairs. One eye looked at me, the other focused past my head. In one hand he held a tankard, in the other a clay pipe.

"Heh? Is it sport watching them insult each other?" Straightening up, he laughed. "I should think it's sport!" Then he squatted and crawled in next to me. When I moved over, both of us huddled beneath the stairs. "Have some wine?"

When I shook my head, he leaned closer. I smelled spiced wine and the odor of him. He was very dirty, with a gray rag tied around his skinny throat. On his left cheek was a large wen. Even so, I didn't mind someone being there beside me, when a nearby crowd was yelling for blood.

"They will fight," he said, drinking from his tankard.

"With swords?"

"Of course with swords."

"Will they kill each other?"

He shrugged and leaned closer, until even in torchlight I could see his veined nose, the cloudiness of an eye whose gaze shot off to the left. "I'm weary of their fighting. In every inn I come to these men-at-arms are at each other. They need war to be happy. What are you doing under here, child?"

I knew that my hiding beneath the stairway must have seemed foolish. So I had nothing to say.

He answered his own question. "I suppose you think those brutes are worth watching. Maybe they're amusing if you don't know them. You don't work here at the inn if you don't know them. Are you traveling?"

"I'm going north."

"We're all going somewhere, aren't we? Everyone of us to death?" He gave me a wink, then pursed his wet lips. "Better north these days than east. The Black Death's in the east again. They say whole villages are disappearing. They say the Pest is dancing through the countryside." He smiled as if telling me something pleasant. "I'm going north too. I sell saints at fairs." Fumbling in his jacket, he came out with a little carving of painted wood. It represented a woman in a long robe, holding a lamb. "Saint Agnes," he said. "I sell a lot of them. Do you know the story of Saint Agnes?"

He didn't wait for me to say I did.

"Agnes refused to marry a boy, so his angry father sent her to a bad place. Do you know what I mean?"

"I think so."

"Of course. You're no child. You're a pretty young woman. You know what pleasure is. I'm sure many a fellow has taught you a thing or two in the fields. Yes, I can well imagine. . . . What was I saying?"

"Saint Agnes."

"Yes, pure little Agnes. She prayed for protection from sin and her hair grew to such a length, it covered her body. They tried to burn her, but she stood unharmed in the flames. Then they struck off her head. People have seen visions of her in a robe of heavenly glory with a lamb at her side. Sells very well." He put it back in his pocket.

Then he looked at me so long, I became uncomfortable. "You're too young to understand what I have seen. I have seen the lancehead that pierced our Lord's side. I have seen a nail from the True Cross. I have seen half of the Crown of Thorns. I have held in my own hands a finger bone from Saint Bartholomew's hand." He sighed and touched my arm, looked at the sleeve thoughtfully. "Going north, you say. I know every inch of this countryside. You have to be careful, my pretty thing. Know who you're talking to. That's my advice." He drank, then ran his tongue along his upper lip. "Going alone?"

I said nothing.

"Don't pick up with just any man. Be choosy, girl. For example, you could travel with me."

"I'm traveling with my brother."

"Is he young too?"

"Oh, no," I said quickly. "He's older."

The man frowned.

"He was once a man-at-arms."

"Where is he?"

"Outside somewhere."

The man glanced around, sighed, and stood up. "What are you going north for?"

"To find our uncle."

"Where does he live?"

"In the north."

The man puffed on his pipe and smiled. "You don't know where he is."

He was bending down, studying me. "Tell me the name of this uncle. If he's known in these parts, I'll know him."

"His name is Albrecht Valens. He's a gunsmith."

"Albrecht Valens? He's more than a smith these days," said the man, looking toward the open doorway, from which came the sudden sound of metal clanging. "Is your brother going to work for him?"

"Yes, that's it."

"I wish your brother good luck." The man drained off the tankard, the wen on his face moving with the motion of his throat. After another thoughtful glance my way, he started for the door.

"You know my uncle?" I cried after him.

But he kept going toward the noise of fighting. I thought he had forgotten me altogether, but at the door, before going into the torch-lit night, he turned to say, "If he's the Albrecht Valens I know, he's more than a gunsmith."

"Where does he live? Where?" I had squirmed from under the stairway and stood with clenched fists.

He named a town and stepped toward the battle.

Next morning before dawn, wanting to avoid the peddler of saints and the other men who had reveled far into the night while one of the chevaliers lay dead (for I had heard the survivor toasted), I roused Niklas and we staggered into the darkness. Fever and chills gripped me as we walked along. Plenty of time to rest when we found Uncle Albrecht. But I felt as though I were wading through a swamp. Chest hammering, vision blurred. It was necessary to stop often beside the road. Carters were appearing on it and some of them stared curiously at us.

I said to Niklas, "Can you understand me, Brother? I'm not feeling well. Maybe I'll have to stop awhile. But you mustn't worry."

His eyes looked as blue and empty as a cloudless sky. Cradled in his arms Rabbit slept, the great eyes shut to slits but the pink nose twitching to sense the air.

I said, "Just wait till I'm better. Just a short while."

I tried to think of what to do if the fever overwhelmed me. Arriving sick at an inn would be dangerous, even more foolhardy perhaps than stopping in the countryside.

As it turned out, the choice wasn't mine to make. Soon after the sun came up, I couldn't go farther. We managed to reach a clump of woods beyond the road before I collapsed under a tree.

There is no way to tell how long I lay there. I would open my eyes to see pinecones on a branch above me, then they'd become water rushing past the mill. Unseen things were crashing wildly through the thicket. At times I saw Niklas bending toward me with our clay drinking cup in his hand. I remember the icy taste of springwater and the pudgy look of his fingers holding the cup to my lips. I remember trying to say, "So you understand," but whether I said it or not is another thing.

Faces came out of mists, hovered and burst, and I wanted to call out to someone half seen, almost known, who appeared again and again and went away until at last I knew it was Niklas bending toward me.

When I opened my eyes, the pinecones wavered but remained where they were, steady on the branch above my head. And there was someone beside me. But instead of Niklas I was looking at the thin, wrinkled face of an old man, whose eyes fixed me with such a cold wild stare that I screamed out and once again the darkness swallowed me.

When next I came into the world, Niklas was at my side. And so was the hideous old man, who cackled with glee when he saw my eyes open.

8

HE put his face close to mine and grinned. "I am Great Mortality, the Evil One. I am Pest. What do you think of that?"

I tried to see him clearly. He was standing up in the remnants of a knight's clothing: torn red doublet, torn green jacket, battered sandals, an empty dagger's sheath on a peeling leather belt, and what must have once been a beautiful white cloak, now worn and filthy, thrown across his bony frame. There was a seal of arms sewn on the breast, a temple with a cross above it. My fever enlarged the look of it.

For a moment I thought I was dreaming again, this time of an old chevalier who had traveled a great distance through forest and desert to mock me in my fever. But he was real. His long white hair—white as Niklas's hair—flowed around his shoulders.

Working my elbows, I managed to struggle into a sitting position against the tree trunk behind me.

He was limping back and forth, grimacing, talking to himself. Now and then he halted to look my way.

"I could have sat on your face. I could have killed you. You and the boy."

I tried to see him clearly through the fever.

"Do you know who am I?"

"No, sir."

"Great Mortality. The Black Death."

"Sir?"

Rather grumpily he said, "I am the Black Death. Me. Do you understand?"

"No, sir."

"I could have slit your throat when you slept. But there are other things to do. I'm heading north to bring destruction. I'm dancing the Dance of Death." He tried to whirl around with arms outspread, but staggered and nearly fell. His legs in the red hose looked twisted and bent, as if he had met with a terrible accident.

"I'm not yet at full strength, having slept all winter," he said with a grin, halting nearby. "Do you hear me?"

I nodded.

"Now I will dance every day all day through the spring. Talk to me. Say something. I'm tired of your silence," he grumbled. When the old man bent over to scratch his knee, I noticed a great hollow below it, as if the bone had been smashed in. Straightening up, he demanded again that I say something.

To appease him, I said, "Good sir, I am sick."

He chortled, as if I had told a joke. "Sick to *death*. Yes, I know, I know. I know death very well. I knew it as a Knight Templar. You look at me stupidly. You don't understand."

There was silence, then a bird rattling branches. The old man wasn't looking at me. His look roamed past me, as if other people in the wood were waiting to hear him. "We Templars were the sword arm of the Church. God's warriors. But in the Crusades we amassed riches. Now that is true. We accumulated wealth while serving the Holy See, and for it we were envied. Are you listening? Are you listening?"

The second time he asked, I said, "Yes, sir, I am listening."

"Kings and bishops brought us down. I know about death, I know, I know." He squatted among pinecones in his dirty cloak. He stared, as he spoke, at one scrawny hand; two fingers were missing. *"Quand sera ce? Tost ou tard vienne."* His eyes shifted instantly to me. "Say something. I'm tired of your silence."

"Sir," I said, "when will what be?"

But I could tell that before I asked the question, he'd forgotten me again. "So in one swift night," he said in a thoughtful voice, "they broke our blessed Order. In one treacherous night, treacherous treacherous, they brought down the warriors of Jesus. Seized such good men for heresy. They put us to the rack, pulled out teeth and fingernails, burned our feet over slow fires, hung us in chains. They broke our bones with the wedge," he said with a short laugh, slapping one of his misshapen legs. "In the name of God, Whom we served at Tripoli and Acre against the infidel, they used wedge and rack and fire."

He started to laugh, rose, and stumbled around the clearing in a sort of dance. When his laughter died, the motion of his lame legs stopped. "That was before. Now it is after."

Slumping down, he crossed his legs and gloomily stared at me. "Now it is after all that and I am Great Mortality. I am the Evil One. I am the Scourge. Do you understand? Look at me, girl. I've been waiting for you to open your eyes and say something. You haven't been listening. You believe nothing I say. Speak to me."

Getting to his feet again, he towered over me, scowling, while I tried to find speech.

"Have mercy, sir," I whispered.

"Ha! Ha! Ha!" He clapped his hands, threw himself next to me.

I had never seen such a wrinkled face. Or perhaps I thought so because of my fever.

"When I choose who will die, I put black swellings," he said, "the size of apples under their armpits and between their legs. These buboes I put there are God's tokens of displeasure. Do you know how many I killed during the Great Plague?"

I shook my head.

"Ask me."

"How many?"

With a laugh he clapped his hands again. "Thousands! Thousands upon thousands upon thousands! They lay piled in the streets. There was never such a stench of death since the beginning of time. And I did it to avenge the Order. I did it for vengeance! I did it! Me! They will torture no more Templars. They will rob us no more or put us on the rack or break our legs with the wedge."

He stopped talking and sat quietly with his thoughts.

I heard birds twittering in nearby trees and a trickling sound —perhaps the brook where Niklas had filled our drinking cup with water. Niklas. I turned slightly. Was he frightened of the old Templar? Of the Pest? My brother sat with Rabbit in his lap, caressing the long ears.

Suddenly the old man scuttled through a layer of pinecones

to reach my shoulder. He put out a bony hand and touched my arm. "Do you understand the mystery? Do you believe I'm Pest?"

"Yes, sir."

"I am bringing the world to an end. Satan is free and I am his servant."

"Yes, sir."

"Now you are listening."

Cocking his head, he seemed to be listening himself to something. "You must be careful. You must pay attention to everything. Only that way can you understand the mystery as I do. Until then simply watch the world."

Again he seemed to be listening. We sat a long time in silence before he broke it with a slow deep voice. Words came from his mouth as if each had been carved out of stone. "Priests are filled with greed," he said. "Nobility wallow in sin. Merchants practice fraud. Kings and knights glory in violence," he said. "Listen, are you listening? But don't say anything. Worms crawl through the dead, and toads sit on the eyeballs of dead men. All these things I have seen."

While he paused, perhaps to think of what he had seen, I heard birds racketing overhead. My eyes were fixed on the old man, who was rocking back and forth, his own eyes half closed.

"I have watched angels and demons hover at graves. They wait for souls rising from the ground. They fight for each soul," he said. "Are you listening? You must listen to me. For I have watched the stars falling from heaven. I have seen the hands of monsters shove whole mountains into the sea." His bony hands pushed at the air. His eyes stared past my right shoulder and his mouth parted in a smile.

"All of it is my doing," he said. "Do you understand? Well? Speak to me."

"Yes, sir."

"Then say it."

"It is all your doing."

He nodded with satisfaction. "The dance has begun again, just like the last time. Death dancing through the land. Say nothing, girl. Are you listening?"

"Yes, sir."

"All of it is my doing. Do you believe me?"

Weak and burning, I tried to look at him as clearly as possible, and it seemed in truth that the old man was just what he claimed to be.

"Yes," I murmured.

He was Pest. He was dancing his way through villages and towns, leaving horror behind.

"Yes," I told him, "I believe you."

I'd have fled had I been able, when next he howled and whirled to his feet for another spinning dance.

I must have lost consciousness, because when I awoke it was darkest night. And again I slept, waking into sunlight that slashed across my face like fire.

Beside me, Niklas was curled up with Rabbit. And Pest was there. He sat cross-legged, grinning, hands lying flat on his knees.

"See? You won't die. I could have sat on your face. I could have murdered you both. I let a few live to remember me."

How long we stayed that way, quiet in the glade, I can never know. At last I started to sweat; it poured out of me like a river. And my eyes focused clearly on the old man, who stared at the ground as if looking straight through it. Suddenly I felt hungry and thirsty but dared not disturb the silence.

Then the breaking of a twig close by broke the silence. Propped against the tree, I glanced around. To my horror I saw them even as they saw me: four men in the doublets and piecemeal armor of wandering soldiers.

And not only those four. I saw a fifth coming through the ring of trees.

It was Erich. Our Erich who had been father's helper, who in exchange for his life had betrayed our treasure to the marauders. He had left when they did.

Now he appeared in their company as one of them. He was dressed like the others, with a kettle helmet on his head. Under it his face looked young and pale and startled, too, when he saw me.

They were coming slowly into the small clearing, almost at leisure, for it was clear that we couldn't escape. Pest had also

57

heard them. Turning, he guffawed, which so surprised them, they came to a halt.

"How dare you come here!" he shouted.

One of the soldiers raised a war ax.

"Ha! Ha! Ha! What do you think you're doing? Can you fight Pest? Can you stand against Plague? Can you stand against Great Mortality? Can you do battle with the Evil One? Fools? Can you? Speak to me, say something!" He was on his feet, waving his hands.

All but the soldier with the ax started to back off. The loud, wild voice of the old man had agitated birds in a tree, and they beat noisily away.

Pest, with a sweeping gesture, drew the white cloak around his thin body, hiding the torn garments that hung on him. "Listen, you contemptible fools," he said to the astonished soldiers. "I have struck down better than you a thousand times with this good arm." He raised one skinny arm above his head.

"I do the same work now with breath. Yes, with *breath*. You," Pest said, beckoning to the soldier with the ax. "Come strike, if you will. But meanwhile I've been breathing on you, on you all, and this is a poisoned breath." He turned in a slow arc to look at each one.

"You will die of it, every one. For I bring the Black Death. I bring the poison. Listen and learn of evil. You feel the poison in your gizzard first—it brings on a fear deep in your bowels. You sweat foully. Yes yes yes. That's as sure as the sun coming up. The air about you grows foul, believe me, when your skin is full of plague. Your droppings turn black, your water too. Boils spread, fester, burn burn burn. There's no escape from it. *Listen to me!* You spit up your heart's blood. You burn like wood. You scream in the agony. That's as sure as the sun coming up. You die because I breathed on you."

These words were followed by shrieking laughter that echoed through the trees, raising more birds to flap darkly upward. The laughter bellied out of him like something alive, like winged things from a cave into a terrible darkness, until the earth itself seemed to shake from the motion.

Yelling in terror, the soldiers turned and ran—all save the one with the ax. Leaping forward, he swiped at Pest with force enough to sever a hand. Standing above the old man where he fell from the blow, the soldier lifted his ax high.

Pest howled like a wolf, though it seemed more of a battle cry than a cry of pain, and then, quite beyond understanding, he started to laugh again, wildly, as if in great joy.

The soldier lowered the ax, his eyes round and desperate. The laughter seemed to have a force of its own, pushing him backward step by step. Then, turning, he rushed to join his companions in crashing through the undergrowth.

Pest slumped forward, wrapping his gushing wrist in the bottom folds of the cloak. Blood was turning the dirty white cloth into a field of crimson.

I tried to get up, but fell back against the tree.

"No, you can't help me," he said quietly. His lips trembled, but otherwise his face was calm. "Get out of here. Go now. Quickly."

There was something new in his voice, a briskness, as if he had come out of a deep and terrible dream. "They might come back. Take the boy and hide. Quickly!"

Perhaps his commanding manner gave me strength to rise. I inched my way along the tree trunk to a standing position and leaned gasping against it.

"Niklas," I said.

Cowering nearby with Rabbit clutched in his arms, Niklas stood up.

"Hide," the old man said. "Quickly." The cloth twisted around his wrist was leaking blood. His wrinkled face was ashen.

I took one step toward him, but in his new voice he demanded that I go. Then in the wild old voice he said, "Ha, they are deadmen. Sure as the sun coming up. Yes, deadmen. Nothing can save them." He was chuckling. "I have breathed death into their blood."

Gripping the rucksack and calling Niklas, I staggered into the undergrowth, hearing at my back the old man's final words: "Believe me, I am Pest! Hope never to meet me again!"

9

I AWOKE to stare up at pinecones—not at the ones I had seen above me during the nightmares of fever, but at cones on trees deeper in the wood where I had staggered with Niklas, plunging and stumbling through the undergrowth, as far as we could go before faintness threw me down.

When I came to my senses again, it was early morning, birds singing. My brother was sitting against a stump, his blue eyes fixed at a spot somewhere above my head. When he saw that I was awake, Niklas scuttled forward with the clay cup. It was brimming with cold water, which I drank greedily.

"I'm all right, Brother. See? The fever's gone." Hungry as I'd ever been, I reached for my rucksack, hoping that he'd saved a few bits of the meat pie I had put in it when we left the inn—how many days ago? Two, three? Even four?

So I was amazed and saddened when I found the entire pie, not a piece of it gone. "Ah, Niklas," I said, "you should have eaten at least *some* of it." I broke the pie in two pieces and gave him his half. Instead of gobbling it down, he looked at me, waiting. "No, I don't need it. I have enough. Dear Brother, *eat.*"

When we were finished, to test my strength I stood up and took a few steps through the crackling pinecones. "See, I'm fine. A little weak—" As I tottered forward Niklas ran up, gripped my arm, and whirled me around in another direction.

His eyes were round, his lips trembling. "What's wrong, Niklas?"

He stared hard at the undergrowth.

"Is that the way, Brother, back to the clearing?" I couldn't remember how we got to this place. Had yesterday happened? Had the old man been there? Was he there in a clearing beyond the undergrowth? I hadn't thought about him since waking, except as a shadow in my mind. Now I thought of him sitting on the ground with his arm wrapped in a bloody cloak.

By forcing me to get up and move, maybe he had saved our lives, because Erich and the others might have returned. The clearing must be nearby; surely I hadn't had the strength to run far. Was he still there? If so, had he bled to death?

Or worse still—yes, worse—had he survived the terrible wound? Had he simply made the blood stop flowing by saying the magic words of a demon and then danced his way out of the forest?

If he lay dead in the clearing, that was proof he'd been human. But if he was gone, nowhere to be seen on the bloody ground, the old Templar might have been the Pest as he'd claimed and as I'd believed in the fever.

"No, Niklas, we won't go back there," I said.

It was better not to know. I couldn't bear it either way: finding an old man dead or a demon vanished.

Picking up my rucksack, I motioned for Niklas to get Rabbit, who was nibbling some grass, and we set out through the wood to find the road again.

By noon, when we stopped to rest beside the road, I could see in the distance a forest of spires rising through the sunlight.

"It won't be long," I told my brother. "We could be in Uncle's house before nightfall."

I was not faking such confidence, because throughout the morning, as the townward traffic grew brisker, I believed our luck would change. The world seemed too bright and clear and busy to hold more bad luck for us. Who were we, but a girl and her small brother looking for safety? If God was not willing to help us, at least He wouldn't seek out such weak creatures for punishment undeserved. That was my hope. And my hope grew, for I took it as a favorable sign that nobody bothered us on the road: the merchants on their donkeys and the carters pulling their wagons and all the travelers shuffling alongside us made no attempt to do harm. We saw ladies carried on litters and knights mounted on chargers—all headed as we were in the same direction.

One old chevalier reminded me of the Templar: he sat tall and thin on a white stallion, a sword clanking against his armored thigh, the visor of his sallet raised so his weathered face was turned to the sun.

Dust swirled around us as we walked. On either side of the road were pastures where sheep grazed or green fields where farmers bent to do their weeding. Blackbirds fluttered up out of hedges, dotting the cloudless sky with dancing black spots. We passed by the low stone buildings of monasteries, and monks in their brown habits looked up from their hoeing to smile. A few even waved at us—surely at Niklas.

No, God would not waste His time harming a small boy and his sister. Surely He had forgotten us and in this way His forgetfulness was a kind of mercy.

During the frequent rests I was forced to take, we sat alongside the road and watched the packtrains plodding by: the round flanks of mules loaded with baskets of geese and grain, with casks of wine and fish, with bundles of cloth and leather goods. The line of animals and their drivers stretched as far as we could see.

"Niklas," I said, taking his small hand in mine, "we're going to town. Isn't it wonderful?"

I had been to a town before—to the town near our mill, sometimes as often as three or four times a year, but it was very small compared to the town we now entered. We shouldered our way along with other travelers across a drawbridge over a dry moat. Two guards stood at the double-leaf iron door at the town wall, but they stopped no one.

On either side of the gate were watchtowers with an overhead passageway connecting them. "Look, Niklas," I said, but he was too busy protecting Rabbit from the jostling crowd. The towers, chimneys, and spires rose above us in such a jumble that I felt dizzy.

After entering a cobbled thoroughfare, almost instantly we were surrounded by loud noise, by an uproar coming from a big muddy yard filled with tents. Vendors were selling boots and pots and knives and belts and rosaries. Honking geese were scudding beneath the feet of passersby. Pigeons rose and fell in frantic blue groups among the stalls, where women in hooded mantles were haggling with merchants. I stopped a moment to watch a knife-grinder send sparks flying from his stone. Everyone was screaming his wares, but the loudest voices belonged to a seated row of money changers who shouted out currencies I had never heard of.

Surely we were walking through the busiest place in the world. I turned to Niklas, but when I saw how fiercely he held Rabbit to his chest, how his lower lip was folded against his teeth in determination, I said nothing of my excitement.

The uproar continued, increased, as we started down a warren of lanes. Carpenters banged hammers and carters unloaded wagons of spices, cloths, sacks, and bales. Colored banners on iron poles were hanging above storefronts, hiding the way. It was like being lost in an unfamiliar wood.

To Niklas I said, "You and Rabbit mustn't worry. We'll find Uncle soon."

To prove it, I stopped a man to ask the whereabouts of Albrecht Valens, gunsmith. He cupped his ear because of the din, and shook his head when I repeated the name. I asked two more workmen with the same result.

We can't lose hope, I told myself. God has forgotten us and restored our luck.

The next workman I asked gave me that hope. "I heard of Albrecht Valens." Strung on a line he carried over his shoulder were pots and pans. He was a tinker.

"Where can I find him, sir?"

The tinker smiled at the respectful *sir*, then scratched his head. "I wouldn't know that."

We continued through the narrow warrens until reaching a muddy, wagon-choked square. At the end of it was a squat gray mass of stone—an abbey. Masons were standing on a scaffold along the wall. When I shouted up Albrecht's name, one of them shouted down, "I heard of the man," and another added "me too," but neither knew where our uncle lived.

"I know where you can find him."

Turning, I faced a friar in the black robe of a preaching Dominican. He was short with an angry-looking boil on his nose.

"Yes, I know where Albrecht Valens lives," he said. Standing in the road, the good friar gave us precise directions. Having made sure I had them, he cocked his head curiously. "What do you want with Master Albrecht, child?"

"I am his niece."

The friar put his head back and laughed. "Albrecht? A niece?" He patted my arm. "Well, go with God's blessing. You will need it."

When at last we found the street he had described, night was almost upon us. Houses in the dusk leaned darkly toward each other, toward a garbage-filled gutter running the narrow lane's length. As the friar had described it, midway down the lane was a house faced with red and blue tile. From somewhere nearby came the slow tolling of a bell, and it seemed at that moment the sound was telling us we had come home.

Across from the tiled house was another house described by the friar: half timbered, half stone, of four narrow stories, each projecting over the one below.

"Niklas, stand straight," I said in a commanding voice, though I could hear the trembling in it. "This is our uncle's house."

I stepped up and lifted the iron door-knocker. Firmly I brought it down against the thick wooden panel, again, again, again.

After a while the door opened a crack and I saw a tiny person within, staring out with a large round eye.

"What in God's name is the racket for?" It was a woman's voice.

"I am . . ." Mustering courage, I started again. "I am the niece of Albrecht Valens and this is his nephew."

"What?"

"We have come to see our uncle."

The door swung open slightly and I could see a wizened little woman gawking at us. After a moment she began to smile. "Niece and nephew?"

I smiled back.

"Well, then, come in come in. It's almost nightfall. You can't be on the street now. Don't you hear vespers tolling? Cutthroats have the town all night. It's ours again with the ringing of prime at sunrise. That's the way of this town, girl. Come in quickly."

Part II

10

WE were not taken directly to our uncle, but through the front chambers and an open court to the back half of the house. In a small room littered with bits of iron, the old housekeeper, for that's who she was, set a lit candle on a barrel and looked at us carefully. Then she brought a basin of water. I washed my face, then Niklas's, and with a rag she gave me I brushed the clothes we had lived in for weeks.

Margaret, for that was her name, waited patiently, her tiny hands knotted against her stomach as she stood watching. She wore a kerchief around her head. The skin of her face was blotched with small brown circles, like the whorls on a tree trunk. There were only a few teeth in her mouth, but that didn't prevent her from smiling when I rubbed Niklas's jacket and trousers as clean as I could.

"You smell better," she said. "I put rosemary in the water. But the clothes need more than a brushing. You must have come a long way."

Here was a woman who had treated us well. So while scrubbing our clogs, I told her what had happened at the mill.

"God in heaven," she said. "Poor child." Glancing at Niklas, who was stroking Rabbit's ears, she said, "Children."

Then I told her how long we'd been traveling, how hard it had been for us to get here.

Her tongue clucked in surprise. "Hard enough to bring yourself so far, but him too . . ."

When she hesitated to say more, I looked up from Niklas's clogs. "He was born right. But a few years ago he was sitting under a tree," I told her, "when a bolt of lightning stretched him out. He turned blue. His eyes rolled back. Father shook him and breathed into his mouth till his chest moved again.

67

When we got him home, Mother put him to bed. For days he stayed like that. All we could keep down his throat was gruel. But he came out of it." And I added, "We used to say Niklas was one of God's chosen. The lightning was a sign from God that he was blessed somehow. He never did get his speech back though, and not all of his knowing either, but he can dress himself and eat without help and he loves me."

"Then he's a fine boy," Margaret declared. "I'll go tell your uncle you're here."

At the door she turned back. "The rabbit. Is that a gift for your uncle? He likes a rabbit brewet with cameline sauce."

"No, no," I said in alarm. "The rabbit's not for eating. He's our friend."

She nodded solemnly. "So be it. Wait for me."

We waited a long time, it seemed, before Margaret returned for us.

"Come, child," she said to me, and stared a moment at Niklas. "If he comes along, will he be quiet?"

"Niklas is always quiet."

"So be it then."

She brought us through the middle court to the front rooms. In one of them a fire was roaring, though it was not cold. At a large table sat a large man over a trencher of bread, with a steaming bowl of meat next to it. Immediately I knew who he was, for in his fleshy nose and heavy brows and ample mouth I saw the features of his brother, our father. He was much older than our father and in his quilted jacket seemed much heavier, but when he looked at us from those deep-set eyes I nearly cried at the resemblance.

To Margaret our uncle said, "Tell Cook I want carp for tomorrow. If he hasn't realized it, this is carp season. You," he said to me. Then he poured some stew meat on the trencher. "You say you're my niece?"

"I *am* your niece, Uncle."

He ate with lusty appetite, all the while fixing us with eyes that reminded me so achingly of our father. "You say your parents are dead?"

"They *are* dead, Uncle." And as I had told Margaret, I told him all.

At first he continued to eat while I talked, but then he shoved the trencher away and sat with both elbows on the table, his big red face braced against fisted hands. When I had finished telling him everything, he said quietly, "Your mother suffered greatly?"

I said through tears, "She did."

"And my brother fought hard?"

"He killed two."

"You look like her," he said thoughtfully. Framed by the huge hands, Uncle Albrecht's face looked suddenly younger but sad, almost like a boy's when you've taken something from him.

"Yes," he said with a sigh. "I believe you." He dropped both hands to the table. "I see her in you. You're my niece." He stared at Niklas hard. "Margaret told me about the boy." This was said in a gruff, almost angry voice. Then he broke off a piece of the trencher and loudly munched it. "You and the boy can stay here tonight," he said to me, and to Margaret he said, "Tell Cook about the carp. Don't let him pick one with yellow scales. That's from muddy water. Carp from good water has white scales. He knows it but gets careless with fish."

And as Margaret led us out of the room, he shouted at her tiny back, "Have him carry it belly-up from the market in damp hay. Belly-up! Belly-up or it won't stay fresh! If you can't trust him to remember, go with him yourself!"

In the hallway I turned to the old woman. Unable to keep panic from my voice, I said, "What did Uncle mean, 'tonight'? We can stay only tonight? Can't we stay longer?"

She did not come up to my shoulder, yet Margaret seemed like a big woman when she gripped my wrist tightly. "Listen, child. Pay no attention to him. Tonight *and* the nights that follow. You'll stay, is that clear? Good, it's clear. So be it."

She let me go and moved on. "Now come to the kitchen for salt eels if you like or for some of that stew your uncle was gobbling down while you children stood there starving."

As we crossed the courtyard, Margaret halted a moment to give full meaning to what she said. "It's not that your uncle is mean. He's just a thoughtless man. These days he thinks of two things only: his belly and his clock."

The first thing I learned about Uncle Albrecht was the truth of her claim that he was not mean, just thoughtless. Indeed, from the next morning on there was no doubt of our staying. That first night he had simply not spoken of his decision to take us in. Carp had been on his mind. Though he felt sorry for what had happened to his brother and sister-in-law and for what might happen to their children if he didn't take them in, Albrecht Valens had been thinking of his belly, too, just as Margaret claimed.

We knew about the clock from the sound it seemed to make when we awoke the next morning. Beyond the door of our little room there was a frightful banging.

I said to Niklas, "I know what a clock is. I've heard of sand running through a bottle and shadows from the sun that tell you somehow the same thing that bells tolling from a church tell you: the hours for prayer, the vespers, matins, and all. I've heard of this thing, the clock, that tells time without priests telling it when to. Because it's not like the bell keeper of a church. It's not a man. It's a kind of thing that works by itself, I think. That banging must be the clock, Niklas."

I was not satisfied with what I'd told my brother, because it seemed that the more I said, the less I knew. I hoped to see the clock.

Later, when we went to the kitchen for a bowl of gruel, our uncle passed through, heading in the direction of the banging. He scarcely noticed us, carrying as he did a long black rod of iron. I decided it was better not to ask him then about clocks, because maybe he was worried about his own clock. Surely he looked glum—like a friar at prayer. That was the way our father used to describe glumness.

In following days we saw little of Uncle, except as he waddled from room to room with merchants in fur-lined cloaks or workmen in smithy aprons at his heels. The big house, I soon discovered, was almost a town in itself—and he ruled it.

There was a banquet hall upstairs where he entertained visitors who spoke different tongues and whose clothes suggested far-off lands. Often such men stayed for days, as if this were an inn, and from our room at night we could hear them up there laughing and talking.

Others tramped in daily with sacks and bales and left with sacks and bales.

"Niklas," I said as we stood to the side, watching, "this uncle of ours is a busy man." Sniffing the hot, oily air of the house, I said, "He has more here than clocks."

What he had, I learned, was an iron foundry and an armorer shop. The banging we heard that first morning had nothing to do with clocks. Smiths were at work here, shaping the raw ore of iron into long bars and then shaping the long bars into armor, weapons.

Many rooms were used for storage, and when these chambers were opened by workmen, we had glimpses inside of pikes and helmets and breastplates stacked in piles.

At first we only peeked in the doorway of the iron foundry at the rear of the great house. Workmen in there were hammering on hot metal against anvils. Then, good-humoredly, they invited us in, where we could feel for ourselves the dry heat of the blazing forge. The smelter, wearing a leather apron and a wet rag over his face, plied the tongs that held the ore. Blooms of iron glowed in the furnace fire like spring flowers. It was beautiful to watch, and so were the hands of workers who hammered the heated blooms. The thick, knotted fingers reminded me of our father at tasks around the mill.

I came to love the sight of metal changing shape, just as I had always loved the way old rags turned into paper by the pounding of mill hammers. The noise was different here, though: not wood, but metal hitting against metal. The clanging made a higher and colder sound than wood thumping against wood and cloth. But here at the foundry, as at the mill, a thing was always becoming something else. It was like a miracle.

In the armorer shop the crash of hammers seemed even sharper. The armorers were welding together sheets of iron, joining layers of them into single fagots. This took a long time. Indeed, time meant nothing there. Metal had lain in the earth so long, it had no time itself, no mercy on the men with their hammers who struggled to give it new shape. Again and again a

71

fagot of iron was heated and then beaten, as the Demons of Hell are said to beat a sinner. There was a constant din, and blasts of heat, and the sparks flying in air turned sunset-red from the forge.

Truly, the power shaking those walls seemed ready to burst forth and rip open the house, but I was never frightened by anything in there. What held me was the change in things. I never tired of watching when a heated fagot grew soft enough to fold and shape—like the dough our mother kneaded into bread. I stood sweating against a wall with Niklas alongside me (often clamping his hands to his ears), while thick slabs of iron took the form of a battle-ax or sword.

I learned not only the names for what men wear into battle but how such things are fashioned: the brimmed kettle hats; the brigandines of canvas with rows of iron plates riveted between them; and the cuisse, greave, and kneecap armor; the steel defenses for both the bridle and striking arms of a mounted knight; the lance rests bolted onto breastplates; gauntlets, sabbatons, couters—each object heated and hammered and cooled within the confines of our uncle's house. Hanging on the foundry walls were steel-stave crossbows, ax blades, hammerheads and spikes mounted on shafts as tall as I was. Long after leaving the armorer shop my ears would ring from noise as loud and terrible as battle itself must sound.

In such a house my brother and I were forgotten, and had we been smaller the porters and carters, foundrymen and armor merchants, might have trod us underfoot. We could have been living in the bustle of great Paris, Milan, or London, as I had heard of such places from our mother's lips. In this house we were at the heart of a whirlwind, yet free of danger.

Niklas began to spend much of his time in the courtyard with Rabbit. The two of them sat on flagstones in the sun. When a friendly workman gave him a knife, Niklas whittled on pieces of wood, one after another, until each stout branch was reduced to a thin rod, which he then snapped and put aside to begin another.

He was safe, and so was Rabbit, and their safety gave me a chance to explore the world of my uncle's house.

I dogged the footsteps of Margaret, who took me on her

housekeeping rounds. She taught me things as our mother used to do. I learned how to make a great-sized bed, such as Uncle Albrecht slept in, by using a long hook to turn the coverlet. She taught me to take grease spots from cloth by soaking it in hot wine. And if wine becomes muddy, Margaret explained, you can clear it by hanging cooked eggs inside the wine cask. She taught me to make glue by boiling holly bark and wrapping it in elder leaves for a fortnight, then pounding it into cakes to keep in a covered pot.

Margaret took me along when she and Cook went to market. She taught me to choose fresh plaice: the skin must be soft to the touch, Margaret said, whispering to me that sometimes Cook was careless in selecting fish. A good eel should have a small head, loose mouth, shiny skin. And she knew about butcher meat, about fowl too. In the markets she'd stop and tell me things. She told me that a good mallard has feather quills well joined to the flesh; ruffled feathers, easily pulled out, mean that a bird's been long dead.

Cook, a scrawny little man, let me watch him prepare special dishes. This was at Margaret's prompting, for otherwise he'd have run me from his kitchen with its toothed racks and skimmers and pincers and spits and kettles on the boil above logs the length of Niklas. In this place of heat and noise, not unlike the foundry, Cook set out to please our uncle. He worked long days on dishes most people taste rarely in a lifetime: mortrews and blacmanger, savory rice and boar's tail with hot sauce, hare in black civey, salt goose and chines.

All of these dishes our uncle ate with the hunger of four men, washing down huge portions with tankards of red wine, for as he told me one night, when we met accidentally in the courtyard and he seemed in the mood to say something, a man in good health never drinks spiced wine or eats uncooked fruit or onion sauce ever or sleeps on his stomach.

Once in a hallway—I squeezed flat against the wall so he could pass—Uncle Albrecht looked down suddenly and said, "How old are you? Time to be thinking of marriage?" But these questions, once uttered, were forgotten before he'd stepped three paces down the hall.

Of course, we never ate with him, but Margaret showed me

how to prepare scented water for his hands when he'd finished with sauces at the table. In this manner I could show him I was part of the household. I put bits of sage and rosemary along with boiled orange peel in warm water.

This I brought one evening to the dining room, where he sat in deep thought, belching. I placed the bowl beside his trencher of bread. Perhaps this action brought me to his attention, because he turned those deep-set eyes my way.

He seemed in a trance, as slowly he pronounced the Latin: *"Ruat coelum, fiat voluntas tua."*

He hadn't really meant the words for me, yet I smiled and nodded.

"What, girl, are you smiling at?" he asked with a sudden frown.

"Your words, Uncle. They are fine, brave words."

Putting one sauce-soaked hand in the water bowl, he grinned at me. "Oh, are they? And what, girl, could they possibly mean?"

"Though heaven should fall, do what you must do."

Uncle Albrecht stopped grinning. His wet hand, raised from the bowl, seemed suspended in air. "How do you know that?"

"Through study, sir."

"You?" Then his big red face broke into a smile. "Of course. She taught you."

"Yes, she did. Our mother taught me."

"She taught you," he murmured, gazing at me for a moment with such tenderness that I felt tomorrow I'd be remembered by him.

74

11

BUT the next day he walked past me in the courtyard without so much as a glance.

Accompanying him was a short, wide, black-bearded man in a loose-fitting, brightly colored tabard. On the chest of it was sown a nobleman's badge of arms: this one a red dragon eating a chained white hart. He wore pointed shoes of red leather, a silver-hilted dagger in its silver sheath, a belt hung with little bronze bells, a puffed green velvet hat shaped at the back into a curlicue. He was very grand.

They were headed for the foundry.

From an open doorway, later that afternoon, I saw the powerful little man clanking round in full battle dress, while Uncle Albrecht, along with an assistant, inspected the riveting of each plate in each section of armor.

That night, long after supper, I strolled into the courtyard for some air, as it was very warm. The sound of revelry reached me from the second floor, where Uncle Albrecht and the visiting knight were dining.

Margaret sat against the courtyard wall, her face dimly outlined in candlelight spilling from the upstairs window. As usual, she relaxed by puffing on a long clay pipe.

She invited Niklas and me to sit with her. For a while we listened to the laughter from above.

Then she said, "He made a good sale today. That's a famous warrior up there with him and a rich one too."

I said nothing.

"Your uncle," she continued, "makes very fine armor. I never knew about such things till he bought this place and I came with it as housekeeper. Now I know as much about weaponry, I venture, as most men who use it. Enough to know the value of his armor."

I said nothing.

"To become rich, though, is not his purpose."

I said nothing.

Perhaps my cautious silence challenged her to say more. Because then she said, "Don't think you see the full man. You won't understand your uncle easily. He is not like others."

"What is he like?"

Margaret did not answer immediately but puffed until the pipe went out. Setting it aside on the flagstone, while above us the men kept at their revels, the old housekeeper told me the history of Albrecht Valens.

He had been an ordinary blacksmith for a while, having learned the trade with his brother from an uncle of theirs. The brothers had run a smithy together.

This I had never known. I had known that our father had been a blacksmith at the time of marrying our mother. I had not known of his owning a smithy with Uncle Albrecht.

But they soon went their own ways, having quarreled about something, Margaret continued. Albrecht joined the household of a duke who spent his days at war. In the employ of such a man Albrecht learned the arts of military siege. He built catapults and battering rams and assault towers. His reputation grew wherever men fought. With time he became a renowned inventor of arms. His missile engine, a trebuchet, could throw an iron ball of a hundred pounds the distance of four hundred yards with accuracy. And he designed a crossbow that was cocked by means of a stirrup, making it load faster. Then suddenly he vanished.

"Do you know what your uncle did, child?"

I heard her cackle with pleasure at the sound of her own question.

"He did a most remarkable thing. He became a Black Monk. Gave up everything and went into a Benedictine monastery. He'd seen enough slaughter for any man, that is true, and so for two years your uncle renounced the world. He studied God's words and obeyed the Rule and hoed in the garden and practiced humility. But such a life was not really for him. He went into the world again as an armorer. And today, this is no empty claim, none make better weapons or defenses than your uncle."

"Why did he leave the monastery?"

"Such a man obeys no one but himself." After a pause so long, I believed she was thinking of something else, Margaret asked me, "And so, do you judge him?"

"I have no right."

"But you judge him. You smell the oil and hear the hammering and feel the blazing heat and know its goal is to kill people. And for helping to meet this goal, your uncle is paid well enough to live in a fine house and eat good food. So you judge him, don't you, girl?"

"I know men go to war and fight for the Lord."

"Not always for the Lord."

"No," I admitted, "not always."

"You're a cunning thing," Margaret said with a laugh. "Would you have wanted your father to be an armorer?"

"No."

"Not even if you could have lived in such a fine house?"

"No."

"Therefore you judge your uncle. You needn't say it. I know. You think if he lives by death, he lives godlessly. Just like the soldiers wandering the countryside, who took the lives of those dear to you. Is that it?"

"Uncle is not like them."

"But he makes the weapons they carry."

"I have no right to judge my uncle." Even so, it was true that in recent days, living near armor and swords, I had wondered if God looked down with displeasure on me for being here. This place of fire and hot metal could be where demons dwelt. And sometimes I awoke from nightmares, carrying from dreams before they faded the sound of pain and death, of steel beating against steel.

I felt the hand of Margaret on my arm.

"What you don't know," the old housekeeper said gently, "is why he went back to making weapons. It wasn't for love of war or money. It wasn't even to fill his belly, though God knows he loves to do that well enough. The truth is, your uncle came back into the world to learn about the world. Yes, child. To learn."

Margaret refilled her pipe and put it, unlit, into her mouth. "To learn, yes, that's true of him. Scholars come to teach him about strange machines and a thing called a crank and coiled pieces of wire called springs and how to make harder brass. They show him how to cut holes in iron, God's truth—right through iron—with a thing called a 'throw' that goes round and round on a belt. It's not like a belt we wear, but a long one of canvas attached to the ceiling. Is that clear?"

"No, ma'am."

"Anyway, these men teach him things. Even about the strangeness of mercury. Do you know what that is?"

"No," I admitted sheepishly.

"Anyway, he travels great distances to study with wise men. Great men who know about wheels with teeth in them and rods all moving in such ways as to make other wheels with teeth in them and rods start moving in other directions. All of it connected somehow and moving. I don't have to ask you if that's clear. It isn't."

With a sigh the old woman rose to her feet. Stretching a moment, she looked up at the lighted window. "You can't learn something, child, without paying for it one way or another. Your uncle works at what he knows best—arming men for battle. It pays for the learning."

As she turned to go back inside the house, I said to Margaret, "Is the learning for his clock?"

Margaret squinted at me a moment. "You're no fool, are you, girl. Yes, that's it. For his clock."

In following days I thought about our uncle in a different way. His gruffness and faraway look and indifference had nothing to do with me, everything to do with the clock. Margaret was right about that too: The clock claimed his attention.

And now it claimed mine.

The clock was a thing I had to see, and as time passed, with the bustling excitement of the great house everywhere around me, with my brother safe and his rabbit safe, too, with good Margaret to give me a smile each waking day, I had the time and assurance to think only of the clock.

From Margaret I learned that behind the foundry was yet another small room. It was here that some of the workmen labored with Uncle Albrecht on the mysterious thing that had captured my attention. Sometimes they worked at night, and I could hear banging and filing—not as loud as the brassy noise coming all day from the main foundry, but thoughtful-sounding in its way of often starting up and the next moment stopping. It was so powerful in my mind that sometimes I fell asleep to dream of a great fire stoked by the blast of a bellows until it reached higher than mountains. In its flames immense wheels were glowing white-hot. They were turned when hammers as large as the house itself came down against their metal sides with a clang as stupefying as the final trumpet at the world's end. I'd awaken in a sweat, as if my own body had been heated at that forge.

It was after such a dream one night that I awakened to the sound of hammering. Nothing as awesome as in my dreams, the pounding nonetheless excited me—enough so that I got up and left our tiny room for the hallway leading to the foundry. I went on in the darkness, drawn by the wild banging.

At the foundry door I hesitated, then opened it and went in. A blush of crimson from the banked-down fire led me past the workbenches and stacks of armorplate to the back door. I opened that too. Never before had I gone so far through the house. There was an open passageway between the foundry and another small building, which stood by itself near the rear wall of the property. From this shed came the noise. Then abruptly it stopped. Candlelight slanted under the shed door.

He was in there. Uncle Albrecht was in there.

I did not hesitate. Crossing the dark passage to the shed, I knocked once, twice, three times on the door, then stood back, waiting. In the silence I heard my heart pounding as if it, too, were struck metal.

Then the door opened and he stood outlined in the shed's light: a tall heavy man gripping a hammer, his breathing loud and fast.

Having made this moment happen, I had no idea what to do next. So I said, "Uncle." I said, "I dreamed of a noise and when I woke up it was still there and I came out to see what it was."

"What it was?" He grunted scornfully. "It was the sound of failure." He tossed the hammer down. "Girl, I'm not a patient man. I can be an angry one."

79

Not knowing what to say, I said nothing.

"When something goes wrong and you become angry, what do you do?"

At first I wasn't sure I understood. Then I stamped the ground.

He laughed at this. "That's what I mean. It's in our blood, girl—not to take failure easily. I nearly wrecked the workshop just now. Are you trying to see inside?"

In truth, I was—craning my neck to look around his huge body at the candle-lit room. Straightening up, I said boldly, "Yes, Uncle."

"Are you curious about something?"

Framed as he was in front of the light, I couldn't tell from his shadowed face what he was thinking. But there was no good in lying to this man. I felt as though he could look into my heart.

"Yes, sir. I'm curious about the clock."

"I see. Curiosity is idle or it comes from a true desire to know. Which is it with you, girl?"

All I could think of at such a moment was something our mother had taught me in Latin.

So I said the words: *"Ad astra per aspera."*

For moments he was silent, and I wondered, had I offended him some way. Mother used to be knitting by the riverbank or preparing a meal when suddenly she'd turn to me and say those words and tell me that anything good in life is earned by trouble.

"Ad astra per aspera. Do you know what that means, child?" he asked finally.

"To the stars with difficulty."

"She told you that?"

"Yes. Often."

"What do you know about clocks?"

Looking down at my feet, I said, "Nothing."

Uncle Albrecht stepped back, so that I had a sudden view of workbenches, a small forge, a strip of canvas stretched from the ceiling to the end of a machine that surely must be the throw, and forests of black rods attached together and wheels with teeth in them turning, slowly, each in its own direction—just as Margaret had described.

"So you want to see a clock?" he asked in a strangely gentle voice.

"Yes, sir."

"Then come inside."

12

BUT when I went inside, I didn't see much of the clock. Uncle Albrecht sat me on a stool beside a workbench (littered with files and tongs and hammers and objects of metal I didn't recognize) in such manner that the iron assembly, about as tall as a broom, was moving and clicking behind my back.

He sat beside me on another stool and for a long time, while I listened to the raspy whirr of the clock I had had no more than a glimpse of, our uncle stared thoughtfully at me.

Finally, pursing his lips, he said, *"Deus vult."*

I took him to mean that God had willed our meeting tonight.

"Tell me what time is, girl."

"Time?"

"Yes, time. You feel time happening, don't you?"

"Happening?"

"You feel here and you feel here and between them is time."

I smiled at him. What did all of this mean?

"Time," he said, "is the order in which things happen."

I tried to glance over my shoulder at the clock, but his voice called me back to him. "Don't worry about the clock till you know something about time."

"Yes, sir."

"What did I tell you time was?"

"It's the order. Isn't it?"

"Of what?"

"Of things happening."

"If things don't happen together but happen separately, the space between them is a part of time." Again he studied me.

81

Surely he wondered if I could understand, if talking to me was worth his effort.

"What measures a part of time?" he asked.

Without hesitating, I said, "Your clock."

"All kinds of clocks. There have been water clocks and candle clocks and sandglasses and the shadow reckoning of sundials to measure time, but none of them has done what men really want."

He paused. "Well, ask me what men really want."

"What do they want, Uncle?"

"To measure time in a special way."

I knew what he wanted, so I asked, "In what way?"

"In such a way that we always know where we are. I mean, where we are in time. Do you understand?"

I said, "Men want the comfort of knowing."

Reaching across the workbench, Uncle Albrecht picked up a silver flask, from which he drank. I smelled the pungent odor of strong liquor.

"Toothache," he said with a grimace. "It's a malady of mine." He raised the flask again. "The comfort of knowing. Yes, I suppose you're right about that." Uncle Albrecht continued to look at me uncertainly.

"Time is nothing if it isn't measured," he said after a long silence. "An easy way of measuring it is to follow the course of the sun. But we can't use the sun if we want the comfort you speak of."

"Why not, sir?"

"Good. I think you finally asked a question of your own. Because the day as measured by sunlight changes. Daylight in winter is shorter than daylight in summer. Some winter nights are almost twice as long as winter days. You know that, of course."

"I never thought of it."

My confession made him smile. He was not a man who tolerated lies. Or evasions.

"To order time, that's our task."

"Yes, sir."

"We must even out the hours of each day into parts of equal length. We must average the time. Do you understand?"

"I do sums and divide them. I know what average means."

"She taught you."

"My father taught me."

Again he fell silent, as if struggling with the idea of going farther in his explanation. I must say that our uncle puzzled me. I had come into the shed to see the clock, not to talk of the sun or sums.

After a while he said, "Margaret told you something about my life."

"Yes, sir."

"About the Rule?"

"She mentioned it."

"Benedictines admire timekeeping—strict timekeeping. Do you know why?"

I shook my head.

"Because prayer must be regular. It's an act of faith." Again he reached for the flask, again drank, again grimaced. "We used a small water clock to alert the sacristan. When a hammer struck a brass plate, he rang the abbey bell. Every day he called us to the offices of worship."

Uncle sighed, as if remembering those days.

"No one," he continued, "can know the meaning of time like a monk. Time brings him into communion with God: the measure of chant, the constancy of prayer—such things have the rhythm of time. Yet what we relied on—that water clock—was most imperfect. Of course, in daylight we could use the sun to judge by, but before dawn or on cloudy days or for the night offices we had only the water clock. The poor old sacristan and his water clock!"

Our uncle chuckled, then drank. Whenever his mouth opened, I saw blackened teeth, broken stumps.

"I don't know which was less reliable: the old monk or the water clock. Maybe the clock. As the level of water changed in the pot, so did its rate of flow through a funnel. As inconstant as a man of little faith: that's what we called it. God in heaven— sometimes it failed completely."

He paused, as if waiting for my question, so I asked it. "How can water fail completely? It's a simple thing." I was thinking of water as it struck each blade of the mill wheel. "Water just flows."

"In winter, Anne? Can a miller's daughter say that?"

I thought of the wheel fixed solid in ice. I smiled. "So water in the water clock freezes too."

Uncle reached for the flask again. "The Rule has no interest in comfort. There's no heating a monastery. The old sacristan overslept when the clock failed because of freezing, and our prayers were thrown off schedule. We were defeated by time. Time—the very thing we used to gather us so we could praise God. *Cucullus non facit monachum.* Do you know what that means?"

"Something about a monk."

"The cowl does not make the monk. It didn't make me one," he said with a smile. "Yet the calm life enabled me to find my thoughts. And they led to this conclusion: The world we live in is nothing less than a great clock set in motion by God." He looked severely at me. "If you want to know the world, understand time. Because the world *is* time." Uncle spread out his brawny arms as if encompassing more than the room we sat in. "All of this around you and in the heavens is the space between *now here* and *now here*. I was convinced that this space is what God feels."

Dropping his arms, Uncle sighed and looked at me, as if unsure of my understanding. "That idea of interval took hold. It was with me in the hallways of the abbey. Instead of concentrating on prayers I concentrated on the time we took to chant them. I wasn't praying, I was asking. Was there a better way to mark the canonical hours? And not only the canonical hours but the other hours as well and the minutes and the seconds of each day down to a hair of time so thin it could not be split farther? What do you say of such questions?"

I didn't know what to say.

Uncle stared hard at me, then continued. "The questions led to another thought: Creation for us is not complete. As agents of God we bring Him pleasure by discovering for ourselves some part of His creation. That is *our* creation. Do you understand?"

"Is it why you left the monastery? To learn about time?"

"You understand." He drank again. "Now go to bed, child."

Nodding, I went to the door, but turned when he called to me.

"Is your curiosity satisfied? Be truthful."

"No, sir."

"Why not?"

"I haven't yet looked at the clock."

"Would you learn about clocks?"

"Yes, sir." I didn't try to keep the eagerness from my voice. "I would like that, sir, very much."

"Do you know why?"

Without an answer to give him, I said nothing.

"Never mind. Come here tomorrow."

I left him sitting at the workbench, staring at some pieces of metal that seemed to have been broken and flung in a corner. Perhaps he'd been hammering at them earlier in his rage. My last backward glimpse was of him tilting the flask.

Returning to our room, I saw the gentle moonlit sleeping face of my brother. Rabbit was snuggled in his arms.

Lying down, I whispered into the night, "Ah, Niklas, if only you could know. The world is a clock."

And so it began.

Each day I went to the workshop behind the foundry where Uncle Albrecht sat me down on a stool, my back to the clock, while his assistants filed and pounded on pieces of metal or used the throw to cut through iron wheels.

What he told me was not always easy to understand. His clock did not depend on the seasonal movement of the sun or the temperature of water or the consistency of sand but on pieces of metal fixed to perform in the same way again and again. His clock was a machine. It had power that had to be controlled in definite amounts at a definite speed. I did not understand much of it at the time, but to my surprise Uncle Albrecht proved so patient in his explanations that finally I began to think of his clock (with only a rare glimpse of it) as a machine.

This was the idea: Its power came from a weight being lowered; then wheels and rods took this power to the part that measured time.

At last he let me look closely at the clock. It sat high on blocks of brick. This allowed the stone weight unwinding from a drum to drop on its rope below the machine.

"Don't look yet at all those wheels and rods." Uncle pointed to a thin metal rod swinging one way, then the other. "Look at that," he said. "That's the foliot, that's the secret of accuracy. It's the heartbeat of the clock."

He showed me how the speed of the foliot could be changed by moving little weights at both ends of it. Bringing them closer increased the swing; pushing them apart decreased it.

"In this way we make the machine go fast or slow," he said. "When your father and I were boys, such a thing did not exist."

The foliot was attached by a shaft to an iron circle whose toothed upper edge looked like a crown of thorns. The crown wheel rocked back and forth with a faint clicking sound. A small bead of metal on the shaft allowed only one tooth at a time to escape and move the wheel along.

"Watch closely," said Uncle Albrecht.

I did.

I watched with all my power until it occurred to me that one tooth escaping at a time was the reason for watching. Because one tooth escaping was the way of keeping the motion exact. And by such exact motion the other wheels and rods, fixed to one another, were turned in their own right, and by such turning the stone weight unreeled from the drum and fell slowly earthward on its rope, bit by bit by bit, as the sun falls steadily from the noonday sky.

"The foliot and crown wheel," Uncle said, "are the escapement. Escapement means power escaping little by little."

He leaned toward me—it was his way when he spoke of something important. "Few people in this world have seen such a thing, Anne. The escapement is a great creation. A great man showed it to me, and I show it now to my niece. It's very beautiful."

Understanding the explanation was hard, made doubly so because part of my attention—indeed I think most of it at the time—was on my uncle, on his look of wonder. Perhaps the way the escapement worked was for him a glimpse of God at work. I was beginning to understand.

At night I'd say to my sleeping brother, "Today he showed me the trains of a clock. A train is a group of wheels and rods. A clock has two of them." I tried to sound like Uncle. I wanted to be as precise as the motion of gears. "The going train measures time and the striking train announces it by striking a bell. He also explained the count wheel, Niklas. The count wheel has notches cut in its edge. When a lever rides along this edge, a hammer strikes. The striking continues until the lever comes to a notch and falls into it. Then the striking stops. It is that and nothing more or nothing less. The widest distance between notches is at noon and midnight. Why? Because those hours require the most blows, twelve. To strike them, the lever rides longest on the edge. And Niklas, if I had one wish at this very moment, I'd wish for you to know the beauty of a count wheel."

I lay awake, the new knowledge burning in me like the steady fire of a forge.

During those days, Niklas spent much of his time in the courtyard. He whittled sticks but no longer threw them away. He kept them stacked in neat piles in a corner of our room.

Half the courtyard was laid out in a little vegetable garden that a scullery girl tended. Niklas began to help her with the weeding and the transplanting into pots of young marjoram and tufts of fennel. He watered the pumpkin pips and manured the earth with sheep dung. From the foundry doorway I'd watch him bending toward a plant, regarding it as if it had a soul that he could take to himself with a look.

Lines of contentment on his browned little face reminded me of home. He'd had the same faint smile when he sat near the mill wheel and listened to the music of water dropping from blade to blade. He was happy like that again, happy and safe.

I spent most of my own days in the workshop, although our uncle began to ignore my presence. It was clear that nothing interested him for long, except time. He had enjoyed teaching me, but the more I learned, the more his enthusiasm for teaching faded. His attention was given fully then to the construction of a new clock for which he was designing a new way to drive it—by something he called a spring instead of the stone weight.

I slipped into the background of the workshop—welcome to be there but largely forgotten. Yet I was grateful to Uncle Albrecht, and always would be, because through him I had found a new world.

After a while I turned to his chief assistant for help with questions.

Justin was a small, narrow man of middle age who had come to clocks from lockmaking. He was a master smith like Uncle Albrecht and they shared a passion for work. On the broad leather belt that Justin wore were incised the words *Orare est laborare, laborare est orare*. Since Justin didn't read Latin, I knew that our uncle had provided him with the motto—to pray is to work, to work is to pray—which they both seemed to believe in. They rarely talked to each other, but simply smiled when an axle fitted into a wheel, or grimaced together when it did not.

One day I found Justin with a length of parchment spread out on a bench. He explained that it was a diagram for parts of the clock. Next to drawings of wheels and pinions were numbers for the thickness of metal, the length of studs, the diameter of pins.

"Teach me to make the drawings," I pleaded, and Justin, in his own stolid way as eager to teach as Uncle Albrecht had been, sat me down then and there to a piece of parchment.

I went at it every day, dreamed of it nights. I had a pair of compasses, a ruling pen, a semicircle of horn, a chunk of india rubber, a stick of ink, a boxwood scale.

In the darkness on my pallet, I'd say to myself (not to Niklas) the admonitions and instructions of Master Justin: "Turn the compasses lightly, always in one direction. Keep the central leg upright or the point prick will widen, destroying the parchment. Ink the curves in first before inking in the straight lines. Start with those of the smallest radius. Ink the curves in first. Ink the curves in . . ." Until falling asleep.

For a week our uncle never looked at my efforts at drawing an arbor, a pallet, a click—at least not in my presence. While I was so preoccupied with drawing a flywheel that even he went unnoticed, Uncle Albrecht looked down one afternoon over my shoulder.

He said stiffly, "You have a talent for it."

Thenceforth his interest in me returned, for I had once again stepped into his world.

Since neither he nor Justin had talent for drawing, I became by default a true member of the workshop, though I was only a girl. Their lessons then included not only the forging of wrought iron and the use of wire gauges, but also mathematics and the shape of things, geometry.

Early one morning I walked into the workshop with a length of canvas under my arm. Under the curious stare of the two men, I unrolled it and smoothed out the dozen pieces of paper brought from the mill. During the journey I had never thought of selling one sheet for shelter or food. Because this was paper our father had pounded and flattened and cut. This was memory.

The two men fingered the paper, so much finer than parchment, with obvious admiration.

"I'm giving it to the clock."

When Uncle Albrecht looked up from the paper, his eyes widening, I said, "Yes. I'm giving this paper to the clock. It will make good drawings. Our father would want the clock to have it."

Rarely in life have I been as happy as when they nodded silently and both touched my hand.

A few days later as I was passing Margaret's room, something —perhaps a faint smell—encouraged me to peek inside, for the door was ajar.

Margaret was lying on her pallet. I nearly walked by, but then I really smelled something. Pushing the door open, I felt my nostrils fill with a rotting stench. As I stepped into the twilight murk of the room, what I saw of Margaret drew from me a cry of horror.

Her brow was blotched, her face twitching, her mouth drooling a thick black liquid.

I could not help myself but ran into the hall, screaming, "He is here! He has come! He danced here as he said he would! Pest is here! He is here!"

13

IT was evening when Uncle Albrecht finally came out of Margaret's room.

Until then everyone in the great house waited in the courtyard: Niklas, Justin, Cook, porters, scullions, and foundrymen. I was ashamed of my outburst, which could have brought the whole neighborhood down on us, Cook angrily pointed out. Indeed, my cries of terror were the last loud sounds heard in the house. When the news got around, a sudden deep silence prevailed: no pounding at the forge, no banging in the kitchen, no arguing among the servants.

In muted voices the household speculated about poor Margaret. Perhaps it wasn't pestilence, only a stuffing of the lungs, common enough in winter.

But when a low, terrible sound came from behind the closed door of Margaret's room, Cook leaned forward and said in a whisper, "That's the boils, the buboes. They blacken and burst and give you a pain unknown in hell."

A foundryman said, "I had a brother who was a scholar of the stars. He told me what causes plague. Plague happens when Saturn and Jupiter meet in Aries. Anger in heaven causes it."

"Did your brother die of the Black Death?" someone asked.

"He did. His knowledge couldn't save him."

"They say you get it by a victim's looking at you," a scullery girl said.

"Nonsense," Cook said. "Earthquakes cause it. Their fumes poison the air."

They all fell silent, absorbed by what was happening to poor Margaret, by what might happen to themselves. None of them knew that I'd met the Pest in human form, that formerly he'd been a Templar, that he'd saved our lives in the wood, that he'd dragged off somewhere to recover from a wound, and that since then he'd danced his way here as promised. Hope never to see me again, he'd warned. I trembled at the possibility.

After nightfall someone fixed a torch in the wall bracket of the courtyard. We sat in silence until at last Uncle Albrecht came out of the room.

"She is gone," he said, motioning for us to gather round. When we had, he said, "Nothing happens we're not fitted by nature to bear. A Roman emperor said that, and I believe him. If the plague runs a full course, we may all follow Margaret. But in this house we'll do what we can to live."

"So it's the Black Death," someone muttered.

Uncle Albrecht said, "I want bolts set on both the front and back doors and steel bars put across them. No one will leave or enter without my permission."

"So she died of the Black Death," a foundryman said.

"And more will follow in this town within hours," Uncle told him. "Within a week there won't be food for sale. Farmers won't bring goods into town. Looting will start. To protect ourselves, we must barricade the house."

"What if some of us, God forbid, come down with plague?" asked Cook.

"They must leave," said our uncle.

"You would throw them out?"

"If anyone has a better plan, speak."

It was a measure of our uncle's strength of will that none spoke. At that moment a score of people placed their lives in his hands.

Or so we thought.

The next morning Margaret's room was empty. In deepest night Uncle Albrecht and some men had taken her away. Before dawn they were headed for market and returned not long after sunrise, hauling a wagon piled high with sacks of broad beans, with slabs of salt fish, blocks of cheese and bags of nuts, kegs of cider, hard biscuit, spice, and honey.

By then the bolts had been fitted, the steel rods placed across them. Guards were posted at both entrances and one at the backyard well—no one was allowed to drink from it without Uncle's permission.

It was when we lined up for inspection in front of the foundry door that a count of heads revealed three people missing: one housekeeping girl, two porters. They had chosen to go their own ways.

One by one we entered the foundry and closed the door. Sitting on a stool, our uncle bent forward to inspect each arm-pit, each groin, for in those places the buboes of plague have their beginning. At first I burned with shame to bare my body to a man's look. Yet he managed his study of me with such solemnity that I came to accept it each morning as part of the day.

By noon of the first day a cone of black smoke drifted out of our compound. Everything owned by poor Margaret went into a bonfire in the courtyard. Every floor in the house was sprin-kled with vinegar.

No one replied when neighbors shouted out of windows at us. "What's happening in there? Is it Pest? Rumors are flying. Do you have him there? Speak up! They say he's come again. Do you have him?"

At both doors the guards were equipped with pikes, war hammers, and swords made in the foundry. All the men wore daggers on their belts. As Cook grimly described our house, "We're a fortress under siege."

The second day, after inspection, Uncle ordered a young foundryman pushed out into the street. For an hour he sobbed piteously and banged on the door, swearing by his mother's soul that there was not a buboe under his arm, not a buboe not a buboe, until trembling we clapped hands over our ears.

I knew if our uncle found one of the swelling black sores on Niklas or me some morning, he'd not show mercy. If it hap-pened to Niklas and not to me, I'd leave with my brother. I would, I thought. But would I? The empty streets came to mind, where the steady tolling of church bells already reported the mounting deaths. To die in the street alone. I could not bear the thought of it.

At the end of a week I sat dumbly in the courtyard, listening to neighborhood voices that carried from window to window.

"They say a girl lets him in."

"How?"

"It's a demon in the shape of a girl. She opens the door and Pest creeps in to do his filthy work."

"It's no girl that lets him in," someone said from another nearby house. "What lets him in is a flame coming from the mouth of the dead."

"Are they burying them?"

"Piling them outside of town. There's no time for burying now."

"They'll be dumped in the river if it's like last time. I should know. My little girl was one of them."

As I was sitting there, our uncle came along and halted to stare at me, as if not sure who I was.

"Come with me," he said.

I followed him through the foundry, where a few men were listlessly shaping pieces of armor on anvils, then into the clockmaking shop, where Justin was busily filing a wrought-iron arbor.

Uncle said to me, "Sit down."

I did.

"Why haven't you come to the shop these last days?"

"Sir, the plague—"

"Do you have it? No? Then why not come here? You have work to do."

"Yes, sir."

"Now I want you to tell me."

"Tell you what, sir?"

"What has made an old woman of a girl? You sat in the courtyard like someone without hope."

"I know that, Uncle." Hesitating, I glanced over at Justin, whose foxlike face was bent over the workbench. His hands were moving a long file rapidly over the edge of a toothed wheel. Taking a deep breath, I said, "Uncle, does God love us?"

"So that's it."

Once started, I could not stop revealing my thoughts. "How can He love us? He wouldn't let the Pest dance through town if He loved us."

"You doubt God's love. Well, why not. Who can be sure of any love? Can ever know, for that matter, what love really is? Don't worry about God's love. Don't question Him. Question what He has put before you. Power, for example. The power to drive clocks. Someday we'll free clocks from stone buildings. Power of some kind will let each man keep a clock on his body."

"Why would he want that?"

"So he'll know the time at all times."

"All men will want this?"

"All men, I think."

"But why, Uncle?"

"That's something I don't know. And yet I believe someday men will have reasons for knowing the time each click of the crown wheel day or night."

I smiled at our uncle's strange ideas.

"Let me show you something."

He picked up a thin coil of hammered brass, pulled it out to its full length, then let one end of it go. It sprang toward the other end with force, shivering down its length the way Rabbit shivers.

"That's power," Uncle said. "If you could use such power to run a clock, you could get rid of that . . ." He looked over his shoulder at the clock stone's weight unwinding from its drum. "Without a heavy driving weight, you could make a smaller clock. Perhaps one small enough to put in your pocket."

Holding up the wire again, he said, "The tighter it's coiled, the greater the power. As it uncoils, it loses power. What would that do to the clock?"

"I don't know."

"Think."

Under his brooding look I tried to think. "Would it slow the clock down?"

"You have it. As the spring unwinds, its power changes. If it ran a clock, the clock would slow down as the spring unwound. You really do see that?"

"I do, sir," I said. And I did.

"So here is my problem. I need to keep power constant as the spring unwinds. For months I've looked for a way." He pointed to a workbench scattered with coils of brass, gears, spindles. While he heated and hammered a new length of brass, I watched intently.

A clock small enough to carry?

It was as strange as his saying we can't know if God loves us. All this time I'd been harboring my own secret doubt, and today, in the midst of plague, our uncle discussed it as calmly as the weather.

Should a monk, even one no longer in the Rule, talk of God in such a way? Which was stranger, a clock that could be carried on the body of a man or the doubting of God's love?

Days passed slowly, like the turning of geared wheels. Town criers came down our narrow street and called out unceasingly the names of recent dead.

Then the day came when they stopped coming.

Buboes were found on another maid, another porter. When a strapping foundryman was told to go, he drew his dagger, and only when the guards came running with pikes and war hammers did he finally back through the door to curse us wildly from beyond it.

Then the church bells stopped tolling, and in the barricaded house we knew nothing until *he* came along.

From the piping sound of his voice, we knew he was a boy. He came each day and stood at the back wall, which was far too high to look over, and he shouted the news at us.

"Hey, in there! There were a hundred died yesterday. The rich are running to the country, but there's no one there to help them and they die, too, in ditches, in fields. The bodies piled up out of town are being dumped in the river. I saw a fat dog gnawing a man's carcass this morning. People don't help one another. You inside, hear me? They say a man will run from his brother!"

And the next day: "Wolves came down from the hills last night. They fought dogs for the dead. No one wears any color but black. We have all lost someone. And food is scarce. Even if you break into a house where they're all dead, you can be sure someone's been there before you. Can you drop a piece of bread over the wall?"

95

To this request, which all of us wished to meet, our uncle said, "Give to one, give to all. You'll be forced to."

We all stared at Uncle Albrecht.

"Because," he explained, "one will tell another and he'll tell someone else and soon a starving town will be at the door, shoulder against it."

Even though we gave him nothing, each day the boy returned to shout in his shrill voice, "There's no priests to hear confession. They have died or fled. It's said whole villages have gone. They say men with dog heads are coming and snakes with eyes of emerald."

I spent much of each day in the workshop. In rages our uncle often swept spindles and coils off the workbench. He drank from his flask, muttering, "Constancy." Justin filed and hammered hot metal on the anvil. Uncle said, "The power we want is midway between a coil's tightest point and loosest point."

Looking at his red face pinched in thought, I didn't know what to make of him. Plague was at the door, yet in this hot little room he gave himself to the study of hammered brass, how it coiled around spindles. Almost every night he smashed what he'd made by day. Was he mad?

Yet hour after hour his other clock, the finished one, whirred and clicked with its wheels and rods as steady as the sun.

Weeks passed. No one else failed the morning inspection, although a porter climbed the wall one night and disappeared. He wanted freedom rather than life in the confines of our fortress.

Work shut down completely in the foundry. People wandered through the rooms, sleeping anytime, anywhere. Smoke drifted across the compound each day, carrying the rotting stench of Black Death. We held pomanders wrapped in rags against our noses.

And each day the boy came, cheerfully relating the news, though in return he received nothing. "Men are stabbing one another in the streets. They're all drunk. Girls are murdered in the alleys. Hogs are running wild, the corpses craze them, people say. They say the whole world's dying."

"Niklas," I said, looking at him one morning as he weeded the garden, for he'd never stopped working on it.

He turned toward me, his blue eyes empty.

"Let me ask you, dear Brother," I said, "do you know what's happening outside?"

Not that I wanted him to know.

He turned back to the weeding. His plump hands darted quickly among the plants. They were such quick, quick hands that I couldn't think of them belonging to Niklas. And at his whittling they showed the same uncommon speed: his knife moved with the surety of being wielded by a man of skill.

I was watching him one afternoon, when a servant girl came along. She was very pregnant and leaned back to carry her belly.

"I've been in the front of the house, seeing that fool who got me this way," she said. "He loves being a guard, wearing a sword. Huh." She wiped a big forearm across her sweaty brow. "Across the street a few soldiers are sitting. Nasty-looking fellows."

"Will they attack us?"

She laughed. Her face was broad, weathered, red. "They won't attack anyone. You should go see."

I went to the front part of the house, up the stairway to the second floor, where the windows had not been boarded. Looking out across the narrow street, I saw half a dozen men slumped against the wall of the opposite house. Plainly they were sick, dying. As I turned away, one of them caught my eye.

He was breathing heavily, his face marked by the telltale blotches of plague. Though the young soldier wore a breastplate and a sword strapped to his belt, he was in rags. There was scarcely enough hose and doublet left to cover his body.

It was Erich.

I had last seen him running from the woods with the Pest's laughing curse at his back.

Ah, Erich. Memories of home.

Pest had said, "I have killed them, I have breathed on them."

I shouted to Erich in dismay. The sight of him returned me to the mill, and I saw him coming through mists of morning with a load of kindling across his shoulders, and he smiled.

"Erich! Erich! Here! Across the street!"

Lifting his head feebly, he couldn't see me in the window. After a moment he slumped down, closing his eyes. His tongue, swollen in his mouth, searched the air like a thick worm.

I retched.

The next day the boy did not come with news.

Or the next.

On the third day all of us, excluding Uncle and Justin, stood by the wall in late afternoon when the boy usually came.

On the fourth day only a few watched for him.

By the end of the week even I didn't bother.

One night I heard Uncle Albrecht crashing around in the workshop, and I said to my sleeping brother, "Niklas, I love you." I said it defiantly. "I do know what love is and I love you. I love the clock too. But I love you more than the clock. And if he sends you out, I'll go with you."

14

"THE pestilence is gone, Niece, but the clock remains. And we still have the problem of releasing the spring's power."

This was how Uncle Albrecht summed up the end of that terrible time.

For him, of course, each day ran with the regularity of a clock, and his plan scarcely changed, even when the street beyond our house grew loud with people returning from the countryside where they had fled during the plague.

Some of the adjoining houses, where everyone had died, were broken into by looters, who stayed until all the wine casks were empty, all the stores pilfered, all the household treasures duly piled in wagons for a trek to the next neighborhood.

The sound of voices, even those of drunken foragers, was like a chorus of angels when we listened from our house. We

CAPTIVES OF TIME

were accustomed to cries of fear, moans of anguish, and had almost forgotten in the last three months what laughter could sound like, drifting through open windows.

We survived in our fortress, but one of the scullery girls had gone mad. She babbled about the end of the world and sometimes danced in circles, telling us she was Death's Maiden.

Yet on the day that our uncle ordered both doors unbarred, the pregnant housekeeper gave birth to a healthy boy with the ease of a cow dropping its calf. Perhaps it was a sign that God no longer wished to punish us. The open door drew us toward it with slow and careful steps, as if we approached the threshold of heaven itself.

Peering into the street, I realized that the possibility of seeing the outside world again had long since faded from hope. I had expected to live and die in our fortress, close to the whirring of a clock that seemed eternal.

"Come, Niklas," I said, holding out my hand to him. "We're going into the world."

Once he had tucked Rabbit securely under his arm, we ventured into the streets as everyone else did (except Uncle and Justin, who kept at their labors).

It was not the same place we had passed through months ago in search of our uncle. Gone were the crowds and wagons, gone the marketplace noise, gone the clutter of things moving so quickly, I had seen only bits of them.

Even so, the town was coming back to life. Merchants were setting out in stalls what merchandise they still had. Porters with rope slings draped on their arms were looking for work. Horse-drawn canopied wagons were clopping through the streets, hauling home the wealthy who'd escaped the plague in distant lands. People trudged in from villages, sacks on their shoulders, carrying tools they must have collected from empty farms.

Everyone was smiling, for we had triumphed over Pest. But there was something else in the faces too: a far-off look in the eyes. God had spared us death but left us memory.

"Come, Niklas," I said, beckoning him on. "Let's go to the country."

It was a windy day with clouds shredding in the blue. I

breathed in deeply the green smell of grass. On a canal there were small mills already working again. We stopped to look at the floating hulls with millstones seated midway on platforms. A wheel turned; stones ground; the milled grain trickled into a sack.

Our mill at home had been much larger, yet it had followed the same principle. It had done the same work. As canal water flowed across the small paddles of the mills, I could see in my mind a man bending, a woman standing, our dear parents, and in my mind I could hear, as if it were actually happening, the steady splash of water against the blades of our mill wheel as Niklas and I lay up in the loft on a warm morning.

I turned to Niklas, but said nothing because I could see memory in his look—jaw thrust forward, mouth opened, blue eyes fixed on the mills. I hoped he was remembering home in a good way.

We found a field to lie in. Above us the clouds ripped silently like pieces of silk and around us the weeds were swaying. Rabbit hopped up to crouch on my chest. His whiskers twitched, feeling the warm breeze. Within the great circles of his pink eyes I saw my brother's head, where it lay beside my own, with blue eyes staring back at Rabbit.

I said to Niklas, "We must thank God for this." Even as the words came, I was not sure I meant them. But of this I was sure: We were alive because our uncle had taken ruthless control of every life in the house.

But did he care if any of us was alive? Did he care for anything save the clock?

Looking up, I imagined in the clouds the swing of a huge foliot on its endless journey between two points. The plague was gone and with it the lives of countless people. The clock still clicked away, as he had said. Here, perhaps, was what he wanted me to believe: The clock was better than we were because it remained untouched by things that happened to people.

After the unpleasant shock of such a thought faded, I let it stay with me awhile.

The clock had a life of its own, was that what he meant? But without people to know what it did, the clock was worthless, wasn't it? What, really, did our uncle mean? All I knew was what he'd done—saved us for this moment in a windblown field.

Approaching town, I saw billows of smoke rising.

"Ah, Niklas," I said, without completing the thought—maybe Pest had returned!

Hurrying through the streets, we were halted by a procession. It was familiar enough from the past—a line of flagellants, leaving behind them a trail of blood. They chanted mournfully, coming from the direction of a fire that leapt above the rooftops. The sight of them, haggard and bloody, frightened me into a run.

"Quickly, Niklas! Get home!"

When we arrived at the great house, what I feared might happen had happened: The door was barred. Screaming for them inside to open it, I stepped back and waited in despair, for it seemed unlikely that the bar would be lifted again.

In a short time, with a clang, the door opened.

"Get in here," the guard said.

I heard angry voices long before reaching the foundry. Rounding the corner, I saw Uncle Albrecht facing three of his ironfounders.

"He stays," Uncle declared.

One of the men, stocky and dark, shook his finger threateningly. Never had I seen anyone, even during the worst days of pestilence, behave in such manner to our uncle.

"You're harboring a child killer!" the workman cried.

Calmly, Uncle said, "What child did he kill?"

"You're letting demons into the house! He's a son of Satan!"

Another, bigger man pushed him aside and came within arm's length of our uncle. He was the hammerman who stamped *AV,* for Albrecht Valens, on each piece of armor. "The leader said—"

"What leader?" Uncle asked.

"The one who leads the People of God."

"The flagellants." Uncle shook his head scornfully.

"I heard them in the square. Their leader said the Jews brought poison here and dumped it in the wells. The Jews brought plague in leather bags. And when children died in the streets, the Jews took their bodies home. They did things with the little Christian dead to celebrate the devil."

"I know nothing of that. The man stays."

"People will come here looking for him. They've burned most of the Jew houses already. They want blood for blood."

"They won't come here if you don't tell them." Uncle looked the big hammerman in the eye. "If you tell them, they'll blame you as well."

The third man stepped forward. "The Jew brought two sacks of goods in here with him. At least confiscate them. In the name of the Lord."

Uncle looked at each man carefully. I could tell he was weighing their determination.

"Very well," he said finally. "I'll confiscate them. One sack is yours. The other holds books that mean nothing to you or to God. I'll dispose of that one. Agreed?"

"You say one sack is ours. Did you look in it?"

"I asked him what's in it. Silver plate. Silver goblets. And other valuables."

"You want the books. But those other things—"

"Yours in the name of the Lord."

The men looked at one another thoughtfully. The hammerman, speaking for them, said, "Agreed."

"But say nothing about him or the sack and don't harm him. Hear me?"

The trio hesitated. The hammerman said, "People should know a Jew is in the house."

"Without his patch who will know?"

The hammerman rubbed his chin. "A Jew in the house."

"Why should we keep silent for a Jew?" the small, dark foundryman said.

I held my breath, for they seemed as ready to attack Uncle as to obey him.

"I have work for the Jew," Uncle added. "If he helps me, then he helps the foundry and in that way helps you."

The idea seemed to pacify them. They stood a moment longer, scuffing their shoes in the dust, looking at it whirling round their feet.

When they walked back into the foundry, Uncle turned to me and said, "Take food to him. His name is Jacob. He's in the fuel bin next to your room."

In my whole life I had never seen a Jew, and the prospect of seeing one then filled me with dread. As a small child, when I had done something bad, our mother used to say, "Be good or I'll give you to the Jews." The threat would follow me for days. I had visions of a cauldron boiling, of creatures with pointed tails grinning with pleasure as they lowered me into it.

Going into the kitchen, I asked Cook why a Jew had come here. With a grimace, he told me that the Jew had escaped the day's massacre and had come running here to Uncle, who had known him a long time.

"Take this to him." Cook gave me the wooden bowl; it was only half filled with gruel. "Jews don't eat much," he said.

Hesitantly I took the bowl. "There weren't Jews where I come from."

When he ignored me and went back to work, I kept standing there. "I don't think I saw any on the road either." After a pause, I added, "What do they look like?"

Cook turned with a grin. "Go see for yourself."

Trembling, I went to the doorway of the fuel bin and stood there holding the steaming bowl of gruel. The bin was dimly lit by a small candle. On a big chunk of charcoal sat a heavyset man, darkly bearded, with hollow eyes that stared at me questioningly. He was about the same age as our uncle.

Relieved by his human appearance, I entered and said, "This is for you."

He took the bowl silently and began eating. I had never seen hands like his: big, bigger even than our father's and our uncle's, and gnarled like an old tree. The knuckles seemed as though at one time they'd all been broken. The thumbs were outsized compared to the fingers. I couldn't take my eyes off those hands.

He slurped up everything quickly and then licked the bowl clean, never taking his eyes off me. His eyes, like his hands, were big, too big for his long, thin face, and in the candlelight had the shine of still water.

"Next time," I said without thinking, "I'll bring a trencher with the gruel."

He nodded and wiped one of those huge hands across his soft mouth. I noticed a yellow circle sewn to his jacket. When I reached for the bowl, he gave it to me with a smile.

"You're pretty," he said.

I carried away his remark on my face, for I could not help smiling. No one had said that to me, not even our mother and surely not our father, who never even said such a thing to our mother. During the day I found myself touching my hair.

In the workshop there was a chunk of glass used to inspect the clock from below. When the workshop was empty (I waited until both Justin and Uncle were gone), I slipped in and found the piece of mirror under some rags. Shifting it around to catch light in the doorway, I studied myself.

Pretty? Was it true? Surely I looked older than I had looked at home. The braids of my hair were long. I touched them. And soft. And my eyes were set far apart, as blue as my brother's. But my mouth was wide, too wide, and my lips big. I had a big enough nose, surely, and large cheekbones. What sort of face was it? Pretty?

I felt sudden despair and wondered if the Jew was trying to seduce me—not as a man with a woman, but as a heathen with a Christian: to bring me to Satan, as they say Jews are paid by the Antichrist to do.

But then I thought, no. Nothing bad had been in his eyes. And hadn't our uncle protected him?

Next day, after giving Jacob bread with his gruel, I went to Justin in the workshop.

"The Jew," I said. "Why did Uncle take him in and protect him?"

"Jacob's a fine copier," Justin said. "He copied books for a nobleman until the nobleman died of plague. No one has returned for the books—dead, too, I suppose—so Jacob has them. Your uncle would like one of those books. Lucky for Jacob." Justin sighted along the edge of a wheel he was chasing. "In return for staying in this house Jacob will make a copy of it for your uncle."

"Then Uncle didn't protect him out of friendship?"

Justin looked up in astonishment. "Friendship?"

"Because Jacob was in danger. Because he hadn't done anything to be punished for."

"Master Albrecht Valens a friend of Jews?" Justin, a somber man who rarely smiled, laughed outright at the idea.

In following weeks I spent as much time with Jacob as I did with our uncle. The yellow patch came off his jacket, and with its removal the people of the house seemed to forget about him. Of course, no one went close to him except me. Perhaps if Uncle hadn't said, "Learn from him, Anne," I might have stayed away from him too.

In a small room given to him for the purpose, Jacob did the copying that earned him sanctuary. First he prepared the parchment by cleaning and smoothing it with pumice. Then he marked his lines with a rule and an awl. He sat in a chair with a writing board on his lap. Within a hole in the board he put an oxhorn for ink.

For hours on end I watched him dip a quill into the oxhorn and after a moment press it against the parchment. Letters emerged, then lines of them swirled across a page. He showed me how to make the letters gracefully and taught me more about making diagrams for the clock than Uncle or Justin ever did.

He also told me things about his strange religion. From him I learned the words *synagogue, bimah, Mishnah.* He taught me *Eretz Israel,* and laughed when I said the words.

"So you'll go some day to the land promised by God, will you," he said, shaking his head in amusement. "A fine girl in Palestine you'd be."

From Jacob I heard of Jewish work besides copying. He told me how they painted cards, dyed silk, tailored. He taught me riddles, chess, card games. I watched him pray, facing east with the round piece of cloth on his head.

His task for our uncle was to copy *De ratione ponderis.* Jordanus de Nemorarius wrote in it that things keep moving not because of outside forces but because of forces found within themselves: *Vis impressa.*

"Is it for his clock?" I asked.

Jacob shrugged. "For learning."

"Do you like my uncle?"

"I work for your uncle."

"Do you think he's a great man?"

Jacob turned from the parchment to look at me. "At least he's a curious one. He's interested in the cause of motion, how it continues. He thinks you can build a machine to run forever."

"Do you agree?"

Jacob dipped the quill again. "It isn't for me to agree or disagree."

"Tell me what you believe."

"What interest could that have for you?"

"You copy books, so you know things."

Jacob put down the quill and turned to look directly at me. "I believe everything you see is full of meaning. This is because everything proceeds from God. Everything points to the establishment of his rule for the sons of men."

"Not only for Jews?"

"Why only for Jews? For all men. There is one God," he said gravely. "The Hebrew people were chosen to be the bearers of this news."

"I don't believe that."

Jacob laughed. "I know you don't."

Another time I asked him about his family.

"What family? There's no family."

"Did the flagellants burn them?"

"They burned themselves."

"How could they do such a thing?"

"It's our custom. When there's no longer hope, die in your own house."

"But you're alive."

"I could have stayed and burned too, but I asked myself, 'Why let such bastards have the satisfaction of watching us burn?' When my brother didn't see it that way, I left him and his family in the house. 'Escape and live and don't give satisfaction,' I told them, but they stood there so I jumped from a back window."

"Did you have a wife and children of your own?"

"Long ago." He dismissed further talk with a wave of his hand. His big knobbed fingers took up the quill again. And with a delicacy I think of when I think of a butterfly in flowers, he moved the quill across the parchment.

It was not a long book and within two months Jacob had finished the copy.

With Uncle Albrecht and Justin and myself watching, he folded the single vellum sheets and gathered them into sections, which he sowed together with thread. He placed them in a binder of wooden boards held by brass clasps that our uncle made for them. The binder was covered with brown leather that he himself tooled.

The day after everything was completed, Jacob left.

I said good-bye at the back door. Uncle, I knew, had paid him well, and that morning Jacob was smiling. He was not wearing his peaked hat, nor had he sewn the yellow badge back on his jacket. With the memory of plague still fresh among the people, it was probably more dangerous than usual for a Jew on the road. I hoped he'd not be accosted and examined. I knew from our conversations that if Jacob was questioned, he would not deny being a Jew.

He had a bundle of food in one hand, a bag carrying books in the other. Although Jews weren't allowed to carry daggers, Jacob had one, concealed under his tunic. I knew this because I asked him was he armed.

"Good-bye, Jacob," I said. I was ashamed of the tears in my eyes. Here was a Christian girl crying at the departure of a Jew.

Jacob was holding up a lump of wood. "Look," he commanded.

I could make out the outlines of something on it.

"Your brother gave this to me."

For a moment I was surprised that Niklas had even met Jacob.

"What is it?" I asked.

"His rabbit. He carved a likeness for me."

"Niklas did that?"

"Mark what I say. He will make you proud."

107

I waved as Jacob turned away and started down the street. I dared not wipe the tears away.

"Shalom aleichem," he called out, vanishing around the corner.

We had never spoken of the danger that would face him when he left our sanctuary. Once when I asked him where he would go and what he would do, Jacob had simply waved his big hand—so typical of him. It meant, I suppose, that the world was large and he had books with him for copying. The world and his books would combine somehow to bring him a new life.

It was too bad that Jacob was a Jew. He would have made a fine Christian man. No sooner had the thought occurred to me than I realized how much I wanted him to stay. What a danger he had been to me! Only when he was gone did I understand the nature and extent of that danger. Because if Jacob had asked me to go with him, perhaps I might have said yes, and thus committed a mortal sin.

Late vegetables still grew in the garden. I stopped on my way through the courtyard to watch Niklas pulling up weeds with his quick plump hands.

So he had carved a likeness of Rabbit. The thing Jacob had held wasn't a lump of wood at all, but a rabbit in wood. With tiny strokes my brother had fashioned an ear, an eye, a paw.

"Good for you, Brother," I said to myself, waving to him as I passed, proud of him already.

15

THE foundry was soon back in full operation, making armor. In the workshop the little clock bell struck each hour, although a few times weekly either Uncle or Justin had to reset the foliot according to a sundial. Work proceeded steadily on the new model they were building, although the problem of the spring remained.

The garden, having yielded up its vegetables, was plowed

under, so Niklas gave most of his time to whittling. The madwoman drifted away one morning never to return. The housekeeper suckled her child contentedly in the courtyard. Clients for armor began arriving again, and the second-floor dining hall echoed with laughter as our uncle entertained his guests.

Often I served wine for them and was allowed to stand in the corner and listen. According to Uncle this was the best way for me to learn of the world. I marveled at how swiftly we all forgot Pest, who had danced through town and dragged from it more than half the people. We had survived; and we lived as we had lived before.

Twice a week the entire household went to church. Our uncle led the procession, turning in his thick fingers the worn beads of a monk. Secretly I feared entering the church: within its walls God had His residence; and being so close to me when I knelt on the cold stone floor and clasped my hands in prayer, He must have felt keenly my suspicion of His love.

Often I glanced at Niklas with his own hands steepled, for he had learned it when our parents used to walk in from the mill to the village church. What did he know of God? What did I know?

One Sunday I trembled when the priest gave us the words of the Lesson: "Doomed are they only who die in a state of mortal sin, while blessed are they who have done God's holy will." If God shows no mercy, why must we do His will? I felt myself grow cold in horror at asking such a question in His house.

Were my thoughts drawing me into mortal sin? How could I suspect God and yet do His holy will?

Such questions hammered in my mind as we filed out of the church. Uncle came alongside me. "Is something wrong?"

"Nothing's wrong."

"Each time we leave the church you look sad—or is it frightened?"

"Nothing's wrong," I insisted.

But the next time we left the church, he suggested we walk along the river. When Niklas came, too, my uncle scarcely glanced his way. I could never forgive him for ignoring my brother.

Yet as we strolled I considered how much in frame and gesture our uncle resembled our father. The similarity put me at ease. When he asked again what was bothering me, I confessed: God's world was without justice. Why had my parents died so horribly?

We had reached the river, where boats spread their sails in the noon air.

Uncle stared at the water a long time without speaking. "A man once said if he had been present at Creation, he would have offered advice for a better ordering of the world."

When he looked hard at me, I knew Uncle was demanding a response. So I said, "The man was criticizing God."

"Exactly. Would you do the same?"

"No."

"But you would, Anne. You do. How could a God of mercy allow my parents to die that way—"

"I have no right to ask."

"But you ask."

This time when he looked at me, I turned from him and fixed my eyes on the river. I hoped he would stop talking. He was looming over me in judgment like a prince of the Church.

"I think you ask such questions in terror of your soul."

"Please, Uncle—"

"I think you hate your thoughts, they terrify you. Yet in a kind of silent fury you keep asking why all of this is so."

"I have no right to ask such things."

"In the monastery we asked such things."

"But you were men of God."

"None of us on earth can help asking. It's because we think."

"Then I don't want to think."

"You think because God gave you reason."

"I don't want reason."

"It's yours through Him, and if you refuse it, you go against His law. Do you understand?"

I was not looking at him, but at the wharf and some kegs stowed upon it and boats on blue water. I would not turn to look at him. He was hurting me to the bone.

"I think you question God's love even while you pray for his mercy."

What he said was terrible to hear. He was describing a doomed heretic.

"So you can't help using reason because reason comes from God and yet you are using it against Him."

I would not look at him, I would not. At this moment I hated him.

"What you haven't thought of yet is how to use it as He intended. Can you understand that?"

I would not turn and look at him. He might see deeply into my soul.

"You are angry, Anne."

I would not look at him, even when he said it again: "You are angry, Anne. Look at me."

I would not look at him.

"I love reason, Anne. But I don't trust it."

The strangeness of his words caused me to glance his way. He was smiling.

"Yes. Reason can't tell us what lies beyond measurement. To understand hidden things we take on beliefs we can't prove."

"Hidden things?"

"What we can't see."

"Like the heavens and the angels?"

"And God Himself. But they exist, even if we can't prove it. We say this is so and it is so. And that is faith. Reason brings you the world. Faith brings you the eternal."

I frowned at him.

Looking at me closely, Uncle said, "No. You don't have a feeling about faith yet. But then you've suffered a great deal." He cleared his throat. "Well, I have done it. I have spoken like a monk, and that is strange. Because in the abbey I never did. I'm not given to tedious homily, Anne, though from my behavior today you might think so. I will say no more," he added gruffly. "Let's go home."

As we walked I turned to him, feeling the corners of my mouth turn down in further despair. "And you, Uncle? Would you have offered advice at Creation?"

"No, none. The more I know of the world, the more I believe it's as it should be. We have only to discover what that is."

He would never again speak to me of such matters. Long

afterward I would understand how difficult it had been for him to speak in this way to a despairing girl—as difficult as it had been painful for me to hear him repeat out loud the blasphemy that I had nurtured in secrecy.

One day I saw a tall man in a surcoat of fine wool emerge from the foundry. He was horribly scarred, one eye closed in a lump of flesh. It seemed as if the entire left side of his face had been burned. I watched him bid good-bye to Uncle Albrecht with curt formality.

"That," Uncle said to me, looking thoughtfully after the scarred man, "is a goldsmith from the city. He's an Officer of the Corporation." Looking down at me, Uncle said, "Do you know what that means?"

"No, sir."

"He's head of the inner council of the goldsmiths' guild. He represents the city. He wants me to build a clock to go into a tower they're building."

"As big as a church tower?"

"As big or bigger. The clock would belong to the city. It would be a symbol of the city's strength."

"Will you make the clock?"

He shrugged. "It would take time from my work on the spring. And yet—I suppose making a clock for a city is no waste of time."

Each day I went to my drawings in a cubby behind the workshop, hearing from my high stool the annealing and pounding and scraping that so occupied our uncle and Justin. Uncle did not use the flask for his toothache as much now, and there were fewer midnight rages. Often from the cubby I heard them discussing the spring of hammered brass and ways to turn it with a spindle—they called the whole thing a fusee. From my Latin I understood what they meant: *fusata,* a spindle wound with thread. Proud of my knowledge, I tried to show it off to Uncle, but he paid no attention.

Once I overheard him say to Justin, "Man learns most from war. I have just solved our problem because of it."

Pausing from my own work, I heard him tell Justin something strange. What Uncle had learned from making war machines, he was applying to the clock. He was convinced that war had given him the answer to the spring. He explained to Justin how he had designed catapults for sieges—they shot seventy-pound stones, so they were large. He had wanted to save men from tiring when they cocked such a machine. A twisted horse-hair spring and a windlass had been used to cock it. The tighter the spring, the harder it was to turn the windlass. So he described to Justin how he had attached a rope to the spring and pulled that rope around a barrel shaped like a cone. The barrel had a spiral groove that the rope fit into. Men cocking the catapult pulled on the rope. When the spring was tight, the rope moved around the smallest diameter of the conelike barrel. When the spring was loose, it moved around the largest diameter of the conelike barrel.

"You see, Justin? That way they pulled at the same rate no matter how tight or loose the spring was wound. The answer to our problem with the spring-wound clock, Justin, is the same I used for the catapult: a changing diameter. Our fusee has to be shaped like a cone."

And a little later, when I had gone back to my drawing, I heard him say with a laugh, "Ah, war! It's the master we men learn from."

A few weeks after the city official came to our house, a great event occurred: The bishop paid us a surprise visit.

When someone rushed into the workshop with the exciting news, Uncle said to me, "Go back to your work in the cubby."

"Shouldn't I leave while you talk to his lordship?"

"Go back to your work."

So I sat in the cubby, where I could hear everything.

I heard them exchange solemn greetings—the bishop had a high voice, as if metal were scraped.

"It's come to our attention," he said, "you've been asked to build a clock for a city tower."

"That's true."

"The abbey could also use a clock. A reliable timepiece for the sacristan. As a former monk, surely you appreciate his need of one."

"I do, Eminence."

113

There was a long silence, which seemed to be used by the bishop to think in. Because when he spoke again, he spoke very carefully. "I assume you would build us a clock?"

"My Christian duty. A great honor, Eminence."

"And you will refuse to build the city clock?"

"Oh, I don't know yet. I haven't given it much thought."

"Master Albrecht, what do the Children of God really need? To know when to pray, isn't that so? Surely you remember from your own days serving God. And the time for prayer we have always given them, seven times each day. But when they are told by the city that the hour is this or this or this—having nothing to do with prayer—what could be the purpose of it?"

"People would know where they are."

"Where they are?"

"In time, Eminence. They'd be free to plan their day by the clock."

"Free? Isn't that the problem?" The bishop's voice went higher. "Isn't freedom an occasion for mischief? For deviation from the rules of Christian life? We must secure men from danger on the way to God. Isn't that so?"

"Yes, Eminence. We must help men avoid danger."

"That's not exactly what I said. Please follow my reasoning, Master Albrecht. Canonical hours call men for the best of reasons—to worship our Lord. Isn't that so?"

"Yes, Eminence. That's what the canonical hours do."

"What need then do men have of profane time provided from a tower built by merchants? I beg you to refuse. Please don't fail in your duty once again."

Instead of answering, Uncle offered him a glass of wine.

When the bishop next spoke, his voice was lower, less of metal scraping metal. He talked of a recent visit to the great monastery of Saint-Denis. He praised the liturgical chanting. It filled eight or nine hours a day, to the glory of God.

"As our Saint Benedict said, 'When we sing psalms, we stand before the Godhead and the angels.' "

Uncle Albrecht did not reply.

"It's a pity you never saw Saint-Denis. Abbot Suger conceived of it as a monument to the magnificence of our Lord.

And to our eternal gratitude, he succeeded. Have you read *Of the Celestial Hiararchy—Of the Ecclesiastical Hierarchy?*"

I heard no reply from our uncle, but he must have nodded, because the bishop said, "So then you know the heart of that treatise: God is light. And through divine inspiration the abbot planned the abbey on such a truth. You come from the cloisters into a tall place of air and light. Bays are open to catch the light. By replacing heavy walls with slim pillars, the abbot has allowed the light to come in everywhere. It is an irradiation of the perfection of form. It pours in through the great rose window, pours in like milk. Washed by such light, the abbey suggests heaven. And at Holy Mass the gold vessels and precious stones are bathed in such light, in the divinity of God."

The bishop paused, I supposed, from the vision his words gave him.

In my cubby they surely gave me a picture of light coming down like a rain shower, too much dazzle for us to look at straight on.

"On the high altar, Master Albrecht, there was a porphyry vase, a chalice of priceless carnelian, and another vase of, I think, beryl. All exquisite beyond measure."

Our uncle said nothing.

Then I heard someone clearing his throat. It must have been the bishop, for he'd been talking a long time. Then I heard rustling, as if the men were rising, and I couldn't resist the temptation to peer around the door.

I had a glimpse of the lord bishop, and I must say his appearance matched his voice. He was exceedingly tall, a head taller than our uncle, and as thin as men were after the plague. He had a hooked nose, keen eyes, a broad expanse of forehead. In his purple cassock he moved slowly to the door, as if weighing each step. The pompon of his biretta shone brightly when he bent under the sunlit doorway.

That afternoon, as I was drawing a line on vellum with my awl, Uncle Albrecht appeared in the doorway. I kept working as he bent over my shoulder to inspect the work.

"I want you to do them smaller now. When you're ready, I want you to do plans on that paper you brought from the mill."

Filled with pride, I simply nodded.

"I know the principle of the fusee now," Uncle continued. "What remains is to work it out mechanically. Then we'll have a clock such as the world has never seen. And my niece will do the plans for it."

Our eyes met. I had never felt closer to him.

"Did you hear the bishop?" he asked.

"Yes, sir."

"Do you agree with him about who should and should not have a clock?"

"I have no right to such opinions."

"Do you have a right to think?" He was glaring with a severity that frightened me.

"Sir, I would give him a clock for the church and make another clock for the city."

"Oh, you would, would you." With these gruff words, he left.

That he wished me to draw plans on our father's precious paper was more than I could hope for. The honor forced me to work harder than ever in the cubby.

But in the workshop matters were not going well. Uncle's flask came out again—the toothache had grown worse—and the midnight bouts of rage were heard through the house.

Although our uncle was sure of the principle, he could not produce at the forge a coil of brass smooth enough to uncoil with a steady motion. Until he solved that problem, the tests of his fusee could not proceed. Although I heard him discuss with Justin the idea of building the city clock, no decision seemed possible as long as the fusee obsessed his days and nights.

And then another great event took place—this one prepared for long in advance. The duke of this province wished to visit our workshop.

I was told by Uncle to get better clothes for serving wine in the dining hall. The idea of going to a dressmaker frightened me, as if someone at the height of plague had told me to go shopping at the market. But, having to go, I went.

With an old dressmaker's gentle help I finally managed to outfit myself in a linen chemise and blue skirt and green tunic with sleeves laced from wrist to elbow. I wore over the tunic a deep red surcoat with full sleeves that revealed the tunic underneath. The coat was bunched at the waist. My shoes were of soft brown leather.

Dressed for that evening, I whirled around the room for Niklas to see. His lips parted in a little smile that let me know I looked different, perhaps even a bit pretty to him. I kissed his forehead and went to the dining hall, where the servants had set up silver bowls of soup, knives for cutting meat, and trenchers of bread for the two diners.

Uncle and the duke came in chuckling about something. When they were seated, I poured wine and Uncle explained that I was his niece. The duke turned to look directly at me, up and down in a way that made me feel uncomfortable. Indeed, through the long evening I found him staring often at me in this boldly appraising way.

He was a short, broad man of middle age, with sunken but alert eyes, full lips, a mustache turning gray. He wore a linen coif on his head, tied by strings under his chin. His tunic was decorated with fine embroidery and tiny blood-red tassels. On his damask mantle he wore strings of pearls. Even in my new finery I felt like a clod in his elegant presence.

As they worked through the soup and blancmanger custard and a course of boiled plaice and fresh pork with mustard sauce, they talked of distant lands and battles. As they drank and ate they talked of assault towers and catapult artillery, rams, trebuchets, and mangonels with the easy familiarity of men who had either built or used such weapons. They laughed about tunnels collapsing in a siege. They cursed men who fled, extolled men who died in the breach.

I filled their glasses often and stopped listening, for their tales of warfare held no interest for me.

And then suddenly the duke said, "About the clock."

"Which clock?" Both men were slurring from the wine.

"That one the merchants want for their city. You won't build it, will you?"

Uncle laughed. "That's what his Eminence asked too."

"Well?"

"I don't know."

The duke tossed off his wine and smiled at me. When I'd filled his glass, the duke glared across the table. "From what I hear, Albrecht, your clock is a fine new treasure. Don't throw it away on fools."

"I told you, my lord, I haven't decided. A clock big enough for a tower would require a great deal of work."

"The clock you showed me tonight—the one already built—is quite big enough. It would fit nicely in a corner of my great hall."

"His Eminence wants it too."

"Treasures aren't treasures if you find too many of them. Such a thing as your clock belongs in the right setting. In the repository it deserves. In my castle." He drank and shrugged. "The clergy have their relics. Lords should have their own treasures like jewelry and horses. And clocks." He smiled with satisfaction at the idea. "Priests have too much already. Do you think the king likes that?"

"No, I don't imagine he does."

"Build your beautiful dreams for *me*. And, of course, for the king as well. When I see him next, I'll explain what you're doing here. Believe me, Albrecht, he'll want one too. But he won't like the idea of clocks appearing everywhere. These merchants, even the porters in the street, would get the idea they can have what royalty has. And where would we be then?"

Uncle nodded without replying.

This did not satisfy the duke, who thrust his chin out and leaned forward. There was a fierceness in his movements that let me see him in another place: dressed in full armor, swinging a war hammer, leading a charge through the breach made by one of those siege machines they had spoken of all evening.

"I want a clock from you," the duke said tensely.

"I am honored," Uncle said.

"But damn you, refuse those merchants. Put clocks in cities, these arrogant money-mad bastards will think themselves great. Already they wear the clothes of noblemen. They buy the same jewelry, ride the same carriages. Next the carters will be doing it. Next the common swine on the street will think they can bugger princesses. We won't stand for it, Albrecht. We won't let you puff up their filthy vanity. Believe me—we won't."

Uncle laughed. "My lord, you're a persuasive man."

The duke took this as a promise of some kind, I think, because he laughed too. I rushed forward to pour more wine, and soon both men were back to the subject of war—of cranks to wind crossbows.

Finally, when the duke staggered from the house, I stood alongside Uncle and waved with him until the horse-drawn wagon rattled off into the night. Turning to me, Uncle said, "The man is dangerous."

16

NEXT morning I laid out the rag paper brought from our father's mill and began the diagramming of our uncle's clock: the escapement, the three-spoked winding wheel, the ratchets, clicks, pulleys, oval gears and each triangular tooth on them, the wrought-iron frame held by wedges driven into rect-angular slots, the bell above the foliot and the sounding ham-mer. Measurements and ratios were first jotted down on parch-ment, then checked by Uncle for accuracy. Rule, compass, ink. Extensions of hand, eye. A jumble of shapes moving in har-mony brought to the silence and fixity of paper. Back and front, side and overhead views of the going and the striking trains.

Slowly each part of the clock emerged on the precious paper, like someone coming out of a mist, while every instant at the drawing board I trembled in fear of blotting.

Without the garden to care for, Niklas stayed with me in the cubby. Servants and foundrymen had brought him all kinds of wood, and with a quiet intensity I had come to expect of my brother, he carved from these chunks of oak and pine the image of Rabbit.

Holding a knife in his plump hand, his hair falling like a cascade of snow toward the held wood as he bent over it, Niklas carved with a motion reminding me of the way he caressed Rabbit, and Rabbit, crouched motionlessly on his lap, received a brown mantle of tiny shavings by each day's end. My brother worked slowly, steadily, until a corner of our room was piled with carved rabbits.

And then one day he carved a bird. And then he made a cat. He made these carvings while I labored on paper our father had created out of water moving across blades and the motion of hammers.

In the workshop Uncle Albrecht put away his flask along with work on the coiled spring. Demands for his clock had shifted his attention to what he'd already built.

A week after the duke's visit, some men came to the house, bearing on their jackets his seal: a white unicorn leaping toward a sunburst. After a long conversation with Uncle, they left, and on the same day a couple of foundry apprentices, under Justin's supervision, began dismantling the finished clock.

Two days later a mule train arrived at the back gate and the clockworks, wrapped in burlap, were strapped to the beasts. Justin went along to reassemble the clock in the duke's castle. When the caravan left, I stood with Uncle and watched the swirling dust cover the burdened flanks of the mules.

"So the duke will be happy," Uncle said with a sigh.

"But will the bishop?"

"The other clock, when finished, is his. The duke was more insistent than the bishop, and so he came first. You see, Niece? War before worship. And, of course, *bis dat qui cito dat,* or so I hope."

Surely it was true that Uncle had wasted no time in giving the duke what he wanted and by so doing had pacified that dangerous man. What I had not understood was then revealed to me: When a man like our uncle created something, he was not done with it. How to dispose of the thing such men made was perhaps the hardest part of creation.

Curiosity drove me, as it has always driven me, to do a bold thing. I knew that a master foundryman, Hugh, had been born and raised on the ducal lands of this region. When he was smoking a clay pipe in the courtyard one afternoon, I went up to him.

"Please, Hugh, since you once lived on the great manor, tell me about the duke."

"What interest has a girl like you in the duke?"

"I want to know why he got the clock."

"He got it because he wanted it."

"Because he's dangerous?"

"You're a curious thing, Anne."

"Yes, I am a curious thing." And gave him a bright smile.

Hugh took the pipe from his mouth. "My brother served the duke in three campaigns, died in the fourth. Yes, I do know the duke and am not better for it. Some years ago, in a rage, he stabbed his son to death—his only legitimate son. Once after taking a town, he found two of his men fighting over a woman. To settle the dispute, he cut her in half with his own sword."

"No."

"He said, 'I have done what Solomon only threatened to do.'"

"No."

"He did that and said that. And in front of another besieged town, he swore on God's name and the salvation of his own soul that if they surrendered, he'd offer the citizens no violence. When they opened the gates, for three days his men raped and looted and murdered, until nothing moved in the streets but carrion birds. That is the duke who got the clock. Even the king fears him, though he looks like an ordinary man and drinks like one and laughs just like you and me." The foundryman puffed contentedly on his pipe. "So I hope I have satisfied your curiosity." Hugh added thoughtfully, "And he'll pay too. Not well—he's miserly—but something. He might pay for the metal. That's more than the bishop will do."

Work continued on the other clock. I wondered if Uncle was giving it to the Church in penance for having left the Rule.

To complicate matters, three men arrived from the city and stayed with us a week. Our uncle had asked the city council to send them here to study the clock, because someday they'd be assembling one for the city.

So our uncle was going to build the city clock too.

Meanwhile, I continued work on the drawings—Uncle wanted two sets of them. One of the city men used to come into the cubby and stare over my shoulder at the diagrams.

"How can a girl know to do such things?" he asked.

121

In all modesty I could not reply. Nevertheless I could not help but feel pride. Of course, had I not been Master Albrecht's niece, he'd have taught me nothing. And had my brother been capable, Uncle would have turned from me to him.

But the fact remained that I could make these drawings with greater care and precision than either Uncle or Justin.

I tried to keep arrogance from my look, yet surely the flush of my cheeks must have betrayed a sinful pride.

The day that the three workmen returned to the city, Uncle Albrecht called me to the workshop, where he and Justin were adjusting the foliot on the bishop's clock.

"We'll be done in a few days with this one. Then all of us will go to the city and build a great clock." He smiled at me. "You too."

"And Niklas?"

As always when my brother was mentioned, Uncle frowned —the thought of his imperfect nephew must have pained him. "The boy too."

"Why will you build the city clock? I thought a spring-wound clock was on your mind."

"Vox populi vox Dei."

Having curtly pronounced these words, Uncle returned to the foliot.

It was then I realized that what drove him even more than the desire to learn was the desire to do God's will. As he understood that will. If God spoke through the people and the people wanted a clock, our uncle felt obliged to build one for them. But the bishop had warned that the people would be corrupted by such things. Was our uncle disobedient? Was his view of duty to God rebellious? Was our uncle's independence of mind as sinful as my own doubt of divine love? Perhaps the bond between us was more than blood. Perhaps we were allies in heresy.

When the banging roused me from sleep, I thought at first it was Uncle in another midnight rage, throwing spindles and failed springs against the workshop wall. But the din persisted and grew louder and became mixed with the sound of voices. Getting up, I hurried from our room to the foundry, where several apprentices who boarded in the house were gathered around the entrance, peering in. I joined them.

Half a dozen men, wearing black hoods, were smashing the workbenches with sledgehammers. On their jackets I saw the emblem of a unicorn rushing toward a sunburst, and through holes cut in the hoods I saw their eyes intent on destruction. In the stoked forge, they threw whatever was combustible. What they couldn't break, they tossed into big sacks.

Where was Uncle?

I suddenly feared for him, and indeed, no sooner had the fear entered me than I saw him coming from the workshop in the grasp of three hooded men. He tried to pull free, his head twisting to see what was happening back in the workshop. His cry of anger was matched by the shouted threats of his captors, who had trouble holding him.

I had never realized how strong our uncle was—perhaps as strong as our father had been. Struggling like a bull, he got free and felled one of the men with a single blow. But another man struck him across the neck with a thick staff. Two others hurried from the workshop, and with all of us—the entire household—watching from the entrance, they beat him to his knees and kicked him to the earthen floor.

I rushed toward him, getting a blow from one of them that sent me sprawling. Then the hooded band, dragging their bulging sacks, shouldered past the onlookers who crowded at the foundry door.

When I lifted up Uncle's bleeding head, from beside me a small hand reached out to help too. Turning, I looked into the blue eyes of my brother.

Uncle Albrecht, it was soon apparent, had suffered more than a beating. Lying on his bed, he gasped for breath, with a hand fisted against his chest.

I stayed beside him all night and by morning he seemed to feel better. Both hands lay quietly at his sides, a clammy sweat dried on his pale face, his breath grew calmer. Then he slept for a long time.

I dozed off myself, but before he opened his eyes, mine were opened again.

"Niece," he said weakly.

I put my hand on top of his.

"The duke."

"I understand." And I did. The duke had made good on his threat to stop our uncle from building a clock for the city. Moreover, he had smashed the clock meant for the bishop. Only one man in the region would have a mechanical clock: the duke himself.

During the next week Justin and the foundrymen did what they could to repair the damage, but in truth both the workshop and the foundry were in ruins. Bits of the bishop's clock lay about like men fallen in battle—it's what Justin, wringing his hands, went around saying.

I had once taken Justin's commitment to hard work as a sign of strength, without realizing that he was strong only when led by someone else. Without our uncle in command, I understood that clocks and armor would never be made in the house.

And it seemed that he would never again be in command, for with the passing of each day Uncle Albrecht grew weaker. At times his hand fisted at his chest and his breath came in thready gusts.

But at other times he rallied to speak of strange things. He talked of a time when every big city would have a clock. On the face of each tower a large metal circle would be fixed, so that from the street below a passing citizen could glance up and read from a long pointer the hours from one through twelve. And instead of a simple hammer striking the bell, a figure of oak, perhaps a man-at-arms, would swing sword or battle-ax and so sound the hours.

Such visions gave him momentary strength, as if the boastful words themselves were medicine. He'd raise his head from the pillow with a start of such vigor that for a moment I hoped for him to throw off the coverlet and jump to his feet.

During such times, our uncle gave orders to the household; then for a short time it would hum again with life.

His order for me one morning was both abrupt and sternly plain: I must finish the two sets of drawings immediately.

Straight from the sickroom I went to the cubby. Next to the

smashed stool I found the scattered drawings, which I suppose the Duke's men had taken for worthless scratchings.

So began a time of intense work, inspired by my love for Uncle Albrecht. I worked, ate, and slept in the cubby. The only times I left it were to check on his condition.

When the two sets were finished at last, I went to my own room, lay down, and fell into a dreamless sleep. A rough hand drew me from it.

"Quick." It was a scullery girl. "Get up. He's calling for you." She added, "He's dying."

But when I reached his room, Uncle Albrecht was breathing calmly. He turned toward me, his eyes shining with a new light, an uncommon gentleness.

"Uncle," I said, taking his hand and sitting on the bed.

"Say nothing. There's no time. You must know certain things. You must forgive me."

"I have nothing to forgive."

"I loved your mother."

"Then we both did."

"I loved her with the lust of a man."

His hand was trembling in mine.

"But never in word or deed, I swear it, did I let her know. She never knew it, never. But your father suspected. We quarreled. I went out of their lives. Your mother thought we quarreled about something else. She never knew, never. I have come to love you as if you were my own daughter."

"And I have come to love you."

"Forgive me."

"Dear Uncle, there is nothing I should forgive. You have only been good to me."

"At first I hated the thought of you being here, of seeing her in you. With time I saw you as you are. You've made me happy, Anne."

When he fell silent, I thought he'd fallen asleep, but he started up and reached for my hand.

"Listen," he said. "Go to the city."

"She never knew?"

"Listen, you're not listening. Go to the city. I have arranged it, hired a soldier to get you there. Listen. Take one set of drawings. Your offering to goldsmith. Remember him? With the scarred face?"

He was gripping my hand hard. "Give Justin the other set. Wait now—" But he started to gasp and choke. Holding his hand, I sat there till he slept again.

Toward dawn he awoke.

"Anne? Are you here?"

"Right here." I went from a chair to the bed and sat beside him.

"You have forgiven me?"

It was what he wanted to hear, so I said, "Yes, I've forgiven you."

"You don't hate me?"

"No, Uncle, I don't hate you." How could I hate him for loving the mother I loved? Even if he loved her with the lust of a man? I had hated him but once—when he looked into my soul and told me of my heretical terror.

"Look under the pillow, Anne."

I did what he commanded, and pulled out from under it a fat leather purse.

"Take it."

"No, Uncle."

"Take it. It's yours. The clock—"

I leaned forward to hear him clearly.

"Drawings must get to city. I have made a pact. They must get there."

"Yes, Uncle. Justin and I—"

"No, no, no. Don't go to the city with Justin. Let him leave first. Don't trust him—the man is not brave." Uncle raised up from the pillow, his eyes round and wild. "Let him go first. Then wait a day before you go. Promise!"

I promised.

He lay back, seeming after a while to have forgotten me. When he spoke again, his words came slowly and quietly, as if taken from a dream, and I knew at last he was dying.

"I regret not making a spring-wound clock. I could have done it with more time. I know I am right."

When he paused, I said, "You're surely right."

"Secret of fusee is cone-shaped barrel. Cone-shaped. No

126

doubt of it. We'll have clocks you can hold in your hand." He swallowed thickly and smiled. "Nothing too strange."

"Uncle?"

"We will make anything. Nothing too strange to make. It is the wish of God. Ships will run by machine. Believe me."

"I believe you, Uncle." But surely his words came from fever.

"And machines will fly. Their wings will beat the air like birds. And machines won't tire. They'll turn forever. And someday," he said in the frenzy of illness, "machines will go to the bottom of the sea."

He muttered for a long time, slept, returned to consciousness, and talked in such a way, I could not follow his mind. But I heard him speak my mother's name and my father's, too, in tones of such anguish that I wept.

It was during a spell of my own weeping that I felt his hand stiffen in mine. When I looked up, I saw him staring a final moment at visions only such a man might have.

17

WHILE he lived, our uncle's wishes had always been respected, so I felt certain they would be respected after his death. In the next week I learned otherwise.

The household scarcely knew of his death before things started disappearing: armor from storerooms, furnishings from chambers, tools from the foundry. Justin put a padlock on the foundry. The housekeeper who had replaced Margaret locked all the rooms, so even the domestics needed permission to enter them. Uncle hadn't been in his grave but a day before people appeared at the gate, waving bills and demanding payment. Rumors flew. A number of clergy and nobles were bringing lawsuits against the estate of Albrecht Valens for clocks and armor paid for but not delivered. People leaned from the windows of neighboring houses to say that the entire estate had been left to an old mistress or to an abbey. Others asked from the street if it was true that old Valens had written a strange will: Each member of the household, foundryman and domestic, would receive a portion of the estate.

Justin told me the last rumor was true.

"When will they get their share?"

"Never. They won't wait for the court to settle things. That will take much too long. They'll drift away—other jobs, other towns."

"So his wishes won't be respected."

Justin laughed. This was suddenly a new Justin. "What do his wishes matter now? Look to yourself, Anne."

I said nothing more. Instead I walked away and sat against the courtyard wall, nurturing a melancholy thought: Justin had already forgotten the man he had worked with for years.

Our uncle must have guessed this would be so. It was why he warned me to go alone to the city. A man without a memory can't be trusted.

The next day I saw Justin off. A load of clockwork, salvaged from the ruin left by the duke's raid, was strapped to some mules. Justin on horseback held a canvas containing one set of drawings. Pointing out the dangers of travel, he pleaded to take my set too. His eagerness strengthened my desire to take it myself.

Watching the mule train depart, I felt eyes on me. It was unnecessary to turn and see whose eyes they were. They belonged to the man hired by Uncle to get Niklas and me to the city.

His name was Hubert, and he had appeared the day of the funeral. He was young, only a few years older than me. He was tall and big-chested, with big feet and big hands. In a dirty blue tunic pouched over a girdle and wrinkled hose and dusty sandals and a brown woolen hood spread at the throat like a short cape across his wide shoulders, Hubert slouched against walls, waiting for me to set the time of departure. I never saw his features. Whenever I turned toward him, the closed hood was facing my way. In the shadows of it his lips—they alone visible—were always parted. He seemed to be studying what his hidden eyes saw. And what I imagined they saw was me.

128

When Justin and the pack mules had turned the corner beyond our sight, I finally turned to Hubert. "In the morning we leave."

Shortly after dawn I put what clothes I had in a leather bag, wrapped my set of drawings in a canvas that I slung on my back with thongs, and tied the money pouch to my belt. I wore a plain tunic, loose hose, and a hood with a liripipe hiding most of my hair.

Niklas was ready when I called him. He had built a cage of wood in which to carry Rabbit. Each strut of the cage was slotted into another, so the entire thing held together without a nail.

"It's a fine cage, Brother," I told him.

He didn't smile, didn't give me a sign from his blue eyes that he understood. Niklas was growing. He had filled out enough to remind me of our father's powerful frame. I vowed to spend more time with him: in a few years Niklas would reach manhood. And what then?

But it wasn't a question for our journey. We left our room and walked to the backyard, where people from the household, gathered there, were peering into the street. They were grinning and tittering.

"What's happened?" I asked when we reached them.

A foundryman said, "You better look for yourself."

Mounted on a swaybacked horse was a handsome young man with brown hair and limpid brown eyes. His features in a white face were square and prominent without being brutal. Although seated, he was obviously tall—leggings of mail encased his long legs—and wide-shouldered and his chest looked huge within a shiny breastplate. One big hand gripped the reins, the other cradled a plumed helmet. As I reached the back door of the house, his set lips suddenly parted.

I recognized those parted lips. The handsome young man ahorseback was Hubert. He had been transformed by armor.

I turned to the snickering crowd for explanation, but none came. In minutes I was waving at them over my shoulder—seated on the horse, with Hubert in his knightly armor leading it and Niklas, cage in hand, following.

129

Once we had left town (every eye on us) and reached the road eastward, Hubert said, "My lady." He called me that.

He said, "My lady, pay no attention to those people. It's no business of theirs how I spend my money. If I chose to spend it on armor, every coin I earn for escorting you, lady, every single coin on helmet and sword and horse because of the honor of owning them, why then, that is my business and mine alone."

Throughout the morning I sat on the ambling horse and listened to Hubert. Who would have thought he could talk so much? But then, who would have thought that within the hood there had been hidden such a handsome face, brown eyes, soft curly hair?

As we plodded in the growing heat past granaries, barns, wine vats, orchards, and wheat fields, Hubert told me about the thing that meant most to him in life—about knighthood. Young squires learn to hit swinging dummies with lances, he told me. They hold their knights' horses when the fighting continues on foot. He taught me that knights banneret carry banners and knights bachelor carry pennons that are forked but unlike the streamered pencels carried by squires. He spoke eagerly and at length of accolades, vows, formalities of homage, the significance of blazonry, until my head felt like bursting from such facts and glory.

Hubert stopped talking long enough to remove his arm defenses and mail leggings. Then he continued with stories of great and bloody knights like the "Archpriest" Arnaut de Cervole, and the "Man of Few Words" Robert Knollys, and Fra Monreale, and Hugh of Calveley.

He stopped in midroad to demonstrate how dubbing was done, using Niklas for the ceremony. Hubert had him kneel in the road and with a sparkling new sword tapped my brother three times on the shoulder, crying out, "Protect the king, praise God, and rise!" so loudly that peasants hauling their wagons along the road jumped into ditches from fright.

Having tied his helmet to the saddlebag on the horse's flank and the breastplate, too, so that finally he'd removed all of that hot armor under the noonday sun, Hubert plunged forward, one big hand pulling the reins, his head down, those soft brown eyes fixed on the rutted road.

"For a knight," he said, "there should be no taxes. Paying them is ignoble," he said in his grave, measured way. "A knight must prove himself with sword and lance and nothing more. On the field of battle"—Hubert glanced around at me—"he pays his debts and there alone and no place else. Nothing should matter," Hubert said with a proud frown, "except his lady and his God and the warhorse he rides."

I said, "Yes."

"Then you agree, my lady?"

"Oh, I do." It seemed my heart had come loose within my breast and was surging like a leaf in a stream. I cared nothing for his knights, but perhaps nothing he'd have said would have mattered then. I watched him lead us down the road, a strong and vigorous fellow with his soft hair stirring and his shoulders looking broad enough to carry Niklas, me, and the horse too, all at once, while he talked and talked and talked so sweetly of battlefields littered with torn silk and gold belts and bright tunics and robes lined with precious fur—the wealth of fighting men left behind with their lifeblood.

When we stopped in a village for food, he looked into his purse and found it empty. I asked him if Uncle had given him money to pay for the journey.

His lips parted in surprise, as if the thought had never occurred to him before.

So he had indeed spent everything on the armor—bought in Uncle's foundry (I had noticed the *AV* stamped on his breast-plate).

"Never mind," I said, and paid from my own money pouch.

On the road again he insisted on carrying the pouch for me. There were bandits everywhere, though I need not worry about them with him around, Hubert said. He wanted me to feel safe.

I handed over the pouch. But I would not part with the rolled canvas strapped to my back, not even to honor his courage and determination.

"My lady," he said, walking down the road that seemed longer because of lengthening shadows, "I know my ancestors must have been valiant. My father surely was. He started as a squire to a knight." Hubert halted a moment and looked at me to emphasize the importance of this fact.

I smiled in fierce appreciation.

"But his lord died in battle before my father was truly grown. So he spent his life as a man-at-arms." Again he halted to look at me.

I frowned sadly.

Hubert shrugged. "He accepted his fate. He was merry to the last, dying in his bed after years of campaign in the lands of the heathen. He was a true knight—generous and loyal." Glancing back as he led the horse, Hubert added, "True knights must protect the weak and oppose tyranny."

"Will you be a knight, Hubert?"

He seemed to grow taller. "I will be," he declared. "Now at last I have the armor. Next I'll prove myself at arms. Today, lady, knights are dubbed in the field, you see. Property's no longer required. The Crusades gave many a brave man the chance to make his mark. And I'll make mine. I believe knighthood is my destiny. What do you think, lady?"

"Oh, I think so too."

He had halted and was looking at me as intently as I was looking at him. The sky and earth became motionless, I swear it, at that moment, and for the first time in my life I looked upon a man with the full-born desire of a woman, such as that railed against by priests, who considered it the road to damnation.

18

WE trudged through a hot afternoon, past fields and forests, scarcely meeting a traveler on the way. Hubert said there were so few people because of the pestilence—like a rampaging army it had laid waste the countryside.

I told him of meeting Pest. It never occurred to me to show caution—such a confession might convince some people I was either mad or under the spell of Satan. All I thought of was making myself important in Hubert's eyes. What could be more important than meeting Pest? That was how I thought.

Hubert listened solemnly, then turned from leading the horse to squint up through the white afternoon at me.

"No," he said. "That wasn't Pest you met. That was a Knight Templar who had forgotten his true self. He didn't scream when they cut off his hand?"

"He cried out, but like a battle cry."

"A knight, surely. In pain a knight won't scream. It's part of his rule."

"Would Pest scream?"

"Of course he would," Hubert declared. "They say demons scream terribly when hurt."

Shortly after this conversation Hubert turned northward at a fork in the road, although the city lay eastward. I said nothing about this detour, I asked nothing, but watched him leading the horse, his hair flowing in the hot breeze. From a trapper on the road Hubert bought two partridge, freshly killed. He dug grandly into my money pouch, unwilling to haggle over the price, though it did seem high to me. Hubert gave the grinning trapper some coins and strapped the stiffened birds to the pummel, his hand grazing my saddle-warm thigh in a way that brought blood to my cheeks.

We decided to camp in the woods that night, because Hubert said it was safer than staying at an inn. I agreed, remembering that inn where the two knights fought over the sex of a horse. The one I now rode was a stallion, if a rather old and sway-backed animal. I didn't need to ask Hubert his opinion of mares for battle horses. I knew. Yet I asked anyway.

He stopped in his tracks. "Ride a mare into battle? Never," he said.

I was cheered by his reply. How reliable he was! Hubert would not step one inch from the path he had chosen to follow. His firmness of mind thrilled me.

Some distance from the road, in a little forest, we made camp for the night. Niklas and I gathered kindling while Hubert plucked and dressed the partridges.

Clearly he knew how to prepare and cook food. As the birds turned on a spit, Hubert told me of a childhood spent with two younger brothers and their sick mother. When not planting and plowing their own farmland, he hired out as a herdsman and a carpenter. Infrequently his father returned from campaigns to tell stories of high adventure.

"So you learned from him about knighthood," I said as we ate the cooked birds.

"It was wonderful to hear. Battles start in the dew. Lines advance through woodlands and you can smell the strong smell of green bushes. They never smell the same as when you go into battle, father said. And at midday at the height of battle you feel the sunlight warming your sword arm. You feel God looking down. He told us such things, but my brothers were impatient. I could have listened forever."

We were both silent a while.

Then Hubert looked at me with a shy smile. "Someday, lady, I'll keep hunting dogs and falcons and for you, I swear it, I'll buy ermine-collared robes and gowns of velvet."

I could feel myself blushing, though I was growing accustomed to his calling me a lady. He was a dear young man, and I smiled at him as brightly as I could, feeling the corners of my mouth turn up, knowing my eyes must shine.

But he was no longer looking my way. His eyes were fixed on the red coals. Across the fire from me his mouth had become a tight brooding line. He was thinking hard. Was he thinking of me?

It had been a long, punishing day, but though I was tired I didn't feel sleepy, not even after Niklas curled up and went to sleep, with Rabbit's cage within reach. Hubert and I sat opposite each other, staring into the fire.

Then suddenly he looked up at me in such an anguished way, I knew that his brooding had been about me.

He spoke quietly, softly, his words reaching me across the glowing coals. He spoke of a knight's love, which is to serve his lady to the end of his days. Love exalts a knight and makes him capable of great deeds of valor. Such love can never fade,

because the lady's beauty has merged with the idea of eternal beauty in his soul.

I said nothing, but the day's fatigue had left me and in its place I felt the quickness in my body felt by someone braced to run.

Hubert had known a man in a nearby village who could read. This man had known how to recite poetry and had taught some to Hubert. These poems, Hubert said, tell of the pain of love and the glory of youth, the loss of self and the final ecstasy of love.

I said nothing, but drew my legs up and rested my chin upon my knees, feeling my heart beat.

It beat faster when Hubert scuttled around the fire and sat so close to me, I could feel the heat of his body next to mine. We looked at each other in the last glow; his face was a pale moon.

And then softly, quietly, he was telling me poems. They were about lovers: the cruel lady, the pleading knight. And then he was describing her beauty, only I knew he was speaking to me as if I possessed it. He said my hair was like a burnished bowl of brass, my nose saucy, my rose-red lips as sweet as perfume, my throat whiter than a swan or snow freshly fallen on a branch. He said his hands could easily circle my waist. My form was as straight and slender as a tree. He said my flesh (I felt heat in my cheeks at the word) was as clear as dew. And then, in the singsong voice of recitation, he called my breasts white little birds stirring in their nest, reminding me of his daylong gaze fixed steadily on them, as they wobbled a little—oh, I knew this —from the swaying motion of the horse.

I was still considering his words when Hubert leaned forward and put his lips to mine. His hands traveled from my face to my neck, and they trembled on my flesh as if touching something easily crushed, like a small animal, like a rabbit, and as he touched me I felt like Rabbit must feel, safe and warm, when we stroked his sides. I felt then a warmth unlike any I had known. It flowed through me, a warmth that was something like drowsiness, except it was not the desire to sleep that filled me, oh, no. I pulled away.

"What's wrong, dear lady?" he asked gently.

"I don't know."

"Of course you know. You're afraid of love."

"I don't know."

He let me alone then, scuttling to the opposite side of the fire again. I do believe had he pressed me a while longer I'd have given myself then and there. And all the next day, whenever I glanced at him, the memory of the drowsy warmth returned.

We traveled slowly, meandering north and then a short way east before heading north again. At this rate our journey to the city would take twice as long as it should. But I didn't think about that. I let Hubert lead us where he pleased. Niklas rode behind me on the horse sometimes, but at others, restless from the swaying pace, he walked alongside Hubert.

By afternoon of this second day he had put his hand in Hubert's. I hadn't seen Niklas do such a thing with a man since the death of our father. Watching him walk hand in hand with Hubert, I remembered painfully the old times when our father would take him down to inspect the mill wheel. I'd see them stand by the turning wheel, watching the water drip from blade to blade, while they held hands, father and son. And now my brother had placed his trust in Hubert with the ease that I had. It went to my heart. For surely my brother must have seen in my face the feeling I had for this young man. Instead of anger and jealousy Niklas felt gladness in Hubert's presence too. I had them both with me on this journey and my pleasure in it was great.

We stopped that night in a forest again. From the saddlebag strapped to the horse's rump Hubert took a small iron kettle. Soon there was gruel boiling and while it cooked, we chewed on bread bought in the last village. The sun went down before we ate. I heard cows lowing in the distance, birds cheeping in branches overhead.

While we ate, Rabbit munched on grass and I could see my reflection in his big eyes glowing from firelight. Then Niklas put him back into the cage.

I felt myself thinking, Go to sleep now, Brother, go to sleep now.

Neither Hubert nor I said anything as the fire lowered and collapsed in on itself. There were other noises now that the darkness had come: the whirr of insects through the black air, the crackling of undergrowth made by scurrying small animals.

Finally, with a yawn, Niklas moved away from the fire and curled up, putting Rabbit's cage within reach.

Hubert and I sat in silence for some time, both of us staring at the boy's face, which slowly relaxed and went blank in sleep.

Finally Hubert got up and beckoned to me. Without a word I followed him away from the faint glow of the campfire and into the brush. We said nothing as he led me a few dozen paces into the woods. Then he stopped on the pathless ground and turned. There was enough moonlight for me to see the shape of his face. He said, "Lady, it's time."

I said nothing.

"It's time, isn't it, for us to love each other? Surely you know that, lady? Do you agree?" he asked in a voice of such tender pleading that I reached for the cord binding my tunic. Our pleasure flowed outward, like the warmth of winter coals from a hearth, and I cried from joy.

The next morning we set out on the northward road again. Hubert was taking me away from my duty out of love. Had the rolled canvas not been strapped to my back, I would have forgotten there was such a thing as a clock. What mattered to me was not time but timelessness. I wanted this journey to last forever, as the three of us and Rabbit headed north or south or west—anywhere but toward the city. I wanted to be caught with Hubert and with Niklas, too, in a single changeless moment until God called us all home.

19

FOR the next two days we meandered northward and slightly eastward, halting early to make camp and wait for Niklas to fall asleep. Then came love on the pathless ground under oak trees and wild cherry and alder, with woodcock and small deer skulking in the undergrowth.

I learned that our secret pleasure in the dark became another sort of pleasure in daylight. Out in the sunswept world I felt far from Hubert's body but close to his thoughts, as if they were small things, like rabbits in a hutch I tended, and when he turned from leading the horse to smile up at me and I smiled down at him, we were speaking of love the way troubadours spoke of it in words.

On his deathbed Uncle had muttered something that I had put my ear close to his lips to hear.

"Saint Jerome," he had said. "Love knows nothing of order."

I realized Uncle was thinking of Mother, of a love withstanding reason and time. Love knows nothing of order, said Saint Jerome.

Surely there was no order in my life then—no order in the presence of Hubert, only a whirling around of things and beneath them, hidden, a slow deep churning of delight.

On the third day while we rested beside the road and Niklas played with Rabbit in the grass, I turned, so full of love, both mind and body ached from it, and I said to Hubert, "You can't love me as I love you."

"But I do," he declared. "Aucassin said"—I didn't know who Aucassin was—"'Woman can't love man as much as man loves woman. The love of woman is in her eye and the nipple of her breast, whereas the love of man is planted so deep in his heart it can't escape.'"

Sweat from the summer heat prickled his sunburned face. I wanted to run the back of my hand down his cheek. And I did so, my hand accepting the wetness of his skin while our eyes met in a burning that only nighttime would quench.

" 'Then they lived for many days,' " Hubert recited, " 'and much pleasure did they have. Now has Aucassin his joy and Nicolette hers likewise.' "

"You've read so much," I told him happily. "More than I have."

"You read?" He drew back in surprise. "I don't read. The man in our village was once a troubadour and he could read, but I can't read. He wouldn't teach me because I used the plow. He said a farmboy didn't deserve to learn reading. I put to memory what he told me. Nothing more."

"I can teach you to read."

"You would do that? Would you? Good sweet lady, would you?" His pleading to learn was like his pleading to have my love.

"I promise you what I know, you'll know." And I blessed my mother for having taught me the thing that Hubert wanted so much—perhaps as much as knighthood, perhaps more than my love.

So we continued our timeless journey through the hot summer days. If it ended by me being with child, I didn't care. Nothing mattered but the moonlit nights after Niklas fell asleep.

During the day Niklas sometimes walked with his hand in Hubert's, and though my brother had rarely smiled since lightning struck him, on this journey he smiled often, as if lost in a happiness that must have come somehow from my own.

My suspicion of divine love and mercy seemed at that time more foolish than sinful. I had questioned God out of impatience and ignorance. The massacre at the mill faded in the sunlight through which my beloved led us, as I told myself that God had His reasons for taking our parents to His bosom. God knew best why they had died so violently. I no longer wanted to question the divine purpose, for I lived within a joy only God could provide.

On the morning of our fifth day, while climbing a steep hill, we heard a town before seeing it. Heard shouting and whinnying and the hard sound of axles turning and a flute wailing and the hollow sound of a beaten drum and more shouting and sudden laughter, before reaching the top of the hill from which we could see a broad jumble of red-tiled roofs beside a river. Dismounting, I walked beside Hubert; protecting Rabbit's cage with both hands, Niklas stayed close to me; and in this manner we descended into town.

Swiftly we found ourselves engulfed in a boisterous crowd that had gathered for a "hot fair" at the peak of summer. I had no idea that the pestilence had left so many people in the countryside. Perhaps the world for great distances around had come to this place.

Stalls were everywhere with produce for sale. I saw curing herbs my mother used to buy at such fairs: althaea root and elder bark and juniper and wood sorrel root and gentian. Hawkers carried blood pudding, broad beans, and dumplings on wooden trays. Through the crowd trudged porters hauling loads of malt and beehives filled with honey and tubs of lard. Lining the street were tinkers and basket weavers and knife grinders. I took Hubert's hand, even as Niklas took mine, and we passed groups of people staring at jugglers, dancing bears, acrobats, while musicians played flutes and two-sided drums.

Coming to the town square, we saw a stage erected beside the church. Hubert hoisted Niklas up on his shoulders to see over the crowd. On the wooden stage there was a little house made of canvas and wooden struts. Potted plants stood around, so the place must have been a garden, and a woman was strolling among them, glancing in every direction, looking for the Lord, she explained.

"I am Mary Magdalen," she told us, and peeked into the house that she called a cave. Two children wearing wings of carved wood on their backs came out of the cave. They were angels, they told us.

"Christ has risen," they told Mary Magdalen, who then looked everywhere for Him. But when Jesus Crucified appeared, she called Him a gardener, although in His white leather tunic He was plainly divine.

Discovering her error, Mary Magdalen cried out in joy and

rushed toward Him, but the Lord said, "Touch me not," and drew away, telling her to spread the word of His rising.

What did Christ mean by "Touch me not?" I wondered. Perhaps he was saying, "Don't cling, don't hold me, let me go to my Father." As she hastened off to spread the news, Mary Magdalen said in a joyful voice, "I will see the risen Christ in heaven!" But if in heaven he chose to say again: "Touch me not"? And rushed away? A terrible thought, a sinful thought. I quaked at having it.

Pulling Hubert's sleeve, I coaxed him away from the stage into another thoroughfare where at a weighing station men were culling through bags of pepper for fake grains. At fairs, our father once told me, there were merchants who mixed grains of black clay and oil with pepper to make heavier than they should be the bags of precious spice.

I explained this to Hubert, who nodded solemnly. "That's the way of merchants. Not the way of chevaliers."

Spread out on the cobblestone were trays of mace, salt, sugar, alum, dyes. And in the next street there were animal skins for sale, and iron and copper. Guarded by armed men were stalls displaying ambergris, pearls, and ivory tusks. My breath came in gusts from the excitement, and I squeezed Niklas's hand. But he stared emptily at the merchants yelling beside their goods.

Following a line of peasants into an open hall, we looked at the colored bolts of cloth stacked like cordwood along the walls: the countless ells of silk and wool and flax and cotton. It made me dizzy, and I pulled on Hubert's hand so that his glance my way held us for a moment in secret darkness.

On the street again, we pushed along to a field at the edge of town. A crush of people had formed a circle there and from within it we could hear a whacking sound repeated many times, then a cry of pain, a shout from the spectators.

"They're playing at quarterstaves," Hubert said, leaning forward with interest.

"Is that play?" I was looking at a man being helped out of the circle. As the wall of onlookers parted I saw through his fingers, clenched to his forehead, a stream of blood.

"Look." Hubert was staring at a man on horseback making

his way through the crowd. "That is a knight." He said it again. "A knight."

What I saw was a rumpled bearded man in a breastplate and dusty clothing. He looked like someone who had traveled a long time.

"See his coat of arms?"

I recognized it then: Painted on the breast and sleeves of the man's torn tabard were crimson falcons.

And he sat his horse well; even I could see that.

The spectators saw it, too, for they gave way to his slow but steady progress toward the circle. Reaching it, he reined in his horse. Looking down, he said, "You are the champion here?"

From where we stood, we couldn't see the man to whom he spoke, but we heard the reply.

"I am."

"Will you fight my squire?"

"I will."

Turning, the knight waved from horseback and a heavyset man pushed roughly forward. With a smile the knight bent low and whispered to him.

"Now you peasants will see something," the knight called out, giving the reins a jerk that had the horse dancing sideways, threatening the crowd.

We didn't see but we could hear, and I shuddered at the sound of wood against flesh, a roar of delight from onlookers. It lasted but a short time. Three men carried the loser—it was not the squire—past the jeering mob.

"You peasants," said the knight, glancing around with a thin smile. "You think you own the quarterstaff. My man here can beat any of you—and I can beat him. Who will try him next? No brave peasant among you? Not one?"

I saw Hubert move forward in his mind before his body moved forward. I saw the sneering challenge go to his heart, and there was nothing I could do to stop him when he shouted, "I'll try your man!"

When Hubert gave me the reins, I gave them in turn to Niklas with the command to stay well away and hold on.

Then, as Hubert strode past curious stares, I followed in his wake to the first rank of the circle. The robust squire stood there in a collarless leather doublet, holding a staff as tall as a man, with its oaken ends shod in iron. He smiled when Hubert stepped forward to pick up the staff dropped by the last fighter.

The contest would be brutal. I knew that, and I hated it. Yet something kept me there, jostled by a crowd moving in waves like a great shaken rope. My mother used to say, "Anne, you see everything." And it was true that I have ever been compelled to look at what happens, whatever it might be, just as I had watched in horror but watched indeed the slaughter of my mother.

Here now my beloved man had taken up a challenge he could not win. Though tall and strong, compared to the squire he seemed like a willowy boy, and as they circled each other, each grasping a staff, I nearly ran into the circle to throw myself at the squire's feet and beg for mercy, so unequal the contest appeared before they closed.

Yet as they circled I plainly saw that Hubert held his staff with a strange ease. His left hand clutched it in the middle, his right hand nearer one end. And when he moved the staff gracefully through the air, it seemed as if this stick of oak were nothing more than his hands made long.

Suddenly the squire rushed in, swinging his staff with such force, I let out a cry of dismay; but Hubert caught the swing in midair, twisting his own staff in such a way that the squire's weapon leapt from his grip. The crowd, roaring, urged Hubert forward. Instead, he backed away and let the squire pick up the fallen staff.

Once he had it again, the squire lunged without caution. This time Hubert hit him on the shoulder, throwing him off-balance, and then jabbed the iron-covered end of the staff into the squire's stomach, knocking him down.

Furious, his face as red from shame as from exertion, the squire yelled out, "You'll die, you bastard!"

Once again I wanted to run between them, but they joined before I could move—joined and smashed their staves together with a tremendous woody noise, like a forest ringing from timber cutters. The long rods whistled through the air and sometimes they locked, so that the two men faced each other in a still moment—Hubert expressionless and pale, his opponent grimacing, crimson.

Then without warning Hubert drew back, as though to retreat, bringing the squire forward at him, and with a long smooth horrible motion my beloved brought the full force of his oaken staff against the man's head. The dull thud of the blow was followed by gasps from the crowd, as others understood immediately what it took me a while to realize: that the squire would not get up.

He lay with his legs jerking, like an animal with its neck snapped in a trap. He was not dead, but drool trickled from his mouth, and his eyes reminded me of Niklas's eyes as they fixed upward.

In the following silence the knight leaned forward from his horse. "Get up," he said to his man. "Get up!" he shouted. Dismounting, he strode across the circle to kneel beside the squire. He slapped the fallen man's face, slapped it again. Then, turning, he scowled at Hubert.

"Waiting for a reward? Think I'll reward you for this?"

"No, sir. I am content."

"You are content," the knight repeated bitterly, and turned again to his squire. Other men were pushing through the circle. The knight ordered them to pick up the squire and bear him away. "You are content," he muttered at Hubert with a smile that frightened me. Then, remounting his horse, the knight galloped toward town, scattering people from his path.

We had walked far from town before I said to Hubert, "You angered me."

"What have I done, lady?"

"You shouldn't have taken the challenge."

"In my neighborhood we played at staves from childhood. I am good at it. That's why your uncle hired me."

Hiding my pride in his skill, I said, "You should not have fought such a man."

We walked in silence awhile, giving my fear a chance to build again into anger. I said grimly, "I thought you loved me."

Hubert stopped and held the reins taut. "I love you more than life itself."

"You were ready to throw your life away—and with it my love."

"But," he said, his brown eyes widening, "it was a challenge."

Again we walked in silence. Finally I said, "You could have been hurt."

"Ah, lady," he replied with a wan smile, "I have been."

We were coming to a wood, so I ordered him angrily off the road. Alongside a stream I had him remove his tunic and there indeed was the hurt he confessed to: The squire's stave had opened up a deep gash across his chest; already it had turned an ugly blue-gray, and when I touched it, he winced.

"There," I said. "I was right. You must never accept such a challenge again. Promise me."

He was silent, and his silence told me that that was a promise he would never make.

Having cleaned the wound with springwater, I sat beside Hubert and called myself a fool. My beloved was surely a knight in his mind, so he must be taken for one: ready for combat, headstrong, free. I vowed never to interfere again.

While Niklas strolled downstream, I leaned forward to kiss the black gash on Hubert's naked chest. "I can hardly wait till darkness," I told him shamelessly.

So finally we had our secret darkness. Except that the darkness was filled with moonlight when we stole away from my sleeping brother and made our way to the stream.

We slipped out of our clothes silently. The air was warm, but the water, as it touched my feet when we held hands and stepped from the bank, was cold enough to make me gasp. Both of us raised our arms as the coldness rose to our thighs, stomachs. In the moonlight I saw my breasts lie on the gray surface of water, shiny globes, like fruit after rain. He reached and touched and the burning went from nipple to groin.

I said, "Love me."

We came dripping from the stream and lay down on the bank. I heard an owl hooting as my beloved held me, and it seemed that everything fit together in God's world—the cold of the stream, the sound of the bird, the feel of him, were all somehow connected like roots to a tree.

Later, Hubert turned to me and said, "When I'm too old for battle, we'll go to the cities of Paris and Rome, where books are plentiful. You'll have taught me to read by then. And like a troubadour I'll make songs to your beauty."

I smiled and sighed, thinking my man was a boy, thinking I wanted him to be that way forever.

20

WHEN the sun was overhead, we stopped at a swiftly moving river. From his saddle pommel Hubert cut loose one of the three dangling geese we'd bought at the town fair. Holding the squawking bird by its neck, Hubert severed its head with one motion of his dagger. He began plucking the feathers.

We were going to roast and eat it there on the riverbank with the rushing water in our ears like the sound of voices. While Hubert worked on the goose, Niklas and I went into a nearby wood to gather kindling for a fire.

We had not been gone long before hearing above the river the sound of real voices. Curious, I peered from the edge of the wood at the broad, flat approach to the riverbank where we'd halted.

A man on horseback was talking to Hubert, who held the half-plucked carcass, while a half dozen other men, on foot, circled around him.

The man on horseback was the bearded knight with red falcons on his dusty tabard. The knight and his men were smiling in a way that chilled me. Taking Niklas's hand, I moved at a crouch beyond the wood into the tall marsh grass near the clearing where they faced Hubert.

"If you swear it's really yours," the knight said, looking at the shiny pieces of metal lashed to the flank of Hubert's horse, "I believe you. And if you say you earned that armor honorably, I believe that too. Any man who could do what you did to my squire is an honorable man. You broke his head. Now he says 'la, la, la' instead of his name."

Squatting on the ground a few feet from the bank, Hubert squinted up at the knight, whose dull armor in the sunlight had a sheen, like polished iron pieces of a clock.

"I wonder," continued the knight in a voice so pleasant I felt a chill again, "where you learned to use a quarterstaff like that."

Hubert smiled and plucked a few feathers from the bird. "My father taught me."

No, I thought, no stories now.

"Your father was a man-at-arms?"

"A knight," Hubert lied impulsively. "A knight like you."

The man on horseback laughed, and at this signal so did the other men, who were squatting around Hubert.

Hubert glanced at them and put the bird down.

"Of the peerage?" asked the knight, grinning.

"My father was not princely. He was dubbed on the battlefield."

"Ah, a celebrated warrior." The knight looked from Hubert to the circle of his men, who were grinning like him.

They confused Hubert; I could see his face redden. I thought, Dear boy, say nothing more.

"And you are the heir of that man of mark," the knight said, pulling the reins slightly, so that his mount pranced in place. "Do you know what I think, young man? I think you learned the quarterstaff in the stables. You must have killed a man of real rank in his sleep and then stolen his armor. I think your father was a thief and a whoremonger like yourself."

Hubert stared at the sun-shadowed face of the knight while I thought, No, dear boy, no.

Getting slowly to his feet, Hubert stood with his eyes fixed on the ground, as if weighing in a single instant all the decisions of his life.

"Are you wondering if my insult is worth your challenging me to combat?" The knight yanked the reins so sharply that his horse reared. "You needn't wonder. It is."

147

Hubert glanced from side to side. He turned to look at the men squatting behind him.

"Don't worry about them," said the knight in his pleasant voice. "This is between you and me, honorable chevaliers. Prepare yourself."

Again Hubert hesitated, and in this moment I understood—surely the knight knew too—that though Hubert knew how to use the quarterstaff, he was not trained for a fight on horseback.

"Pray for him," I told Niklas, glancing at my brother, who watched with me from the parted grass. "Pray for him," I demanded, having forgotten that Niklas could not.

A small warm hand slipped into mine, while Hubert, plainly with reluctance, fastened on the shiny breastplate over his shirt of mail and then the cuisse, greave, and kneecap armor similar to those parts I had seen hammered and shaped in the foundry of my uncle.

Finally, with a faint smile of courage, Hubert put on his helmet, shoving the visor up on its hinges, so that I had a glimpse of his eyes: confused, hurt-looking.

I said to myself, Dear Lord, I have sinned, but I swear if You help this boy I will be Your devoted servant evermore, Holy Spirit, because he means no harm, he's foolish like me and young, and if You do help him, dear God do, and if You have mercy, almighty Holy Spirit in heaven, I swear, I swear it . . .

The words went out of me then, for, having shoved gauntlets on his hands, Hubert approached his horse. With those heavy gauntlets on, he tried untying the battle-ax from a saddlebag, but couldn't do it. I heard men chuckling. After removing both gauntlets, he untied the ax and arced it slowly through the air, as if testing the balance of something strange. Then he shoved the gauntlets back on and held the battle-ax awkwardly.

"Holy of Holies, I beg I swear—" But I was watching the unthinkable: Hubert mounting his horse to do battle with a knight.

The knight's men were on their feet, holding pikes and hammers, but none of them offered him violence. They stood grinning, and I recalled the self-satisfied way the soldiers had grinned at the mill when my mother died.

"Well, sir. You look the part," said the knight with a nod of his grizzled head.

Surely it was true: in the shiny armor Hubert looked glorious.

The real knight, unkempt, without armor save a breastplate, slouched on his stallion like a weary traveler. "Too bad we don't have pennons flying or heralds announcing our lineage, but we must do without formalities. Ready, sir?"

I could see Hubert's eyes peering from the bright metal; they squinted and fluttered so that I knew what he must have looked like as a boy of Niklas's age when punished: fear, pride, uncertainty, and still more pride were in them.

Christ our Savior, intercede for him now, I beg You, sweet Jesus, make him stop, make him climb down from the horse, Lord, *make him climb down*, I pleaded in my mind. Suddenly I felt hope. If he climbed down, there would be a halt. If persuaded by our Savior to confess the error of his boasting, Hubert would be spared. The knight would laugh cruelly but let him go.

Should I run out there myself, beg him to stop, tell him God ordered him down?

Hubert lowered his visor and took up the slack in his reins.

Straightening up, the knight unsheathed his sword, held it high. "So come at me, sir!"

His command served only to startle Hubert, who yanked on the reins so hard that his mount stumbled backward. The men making an arc around him laughed, hooted.

I got to my knees and parted the grass to rush out. I had only to get breath enough for it.

But then, digging his spurs deep, Hubert began the charge.

The horse had lifted and planted its hooves only a few times before something moved through the air and pulled Hubert off the saddle, leaving the animal to gallop almost to the place where the knight sat motionless before it swerved off, trotted riderless a short distance, and then stopped.

At first I couldn't understand what had happened. Stretched out near the riverbank, Hubert wore a steel hoop around his helmeted head, and the steel hoop was attached to a long pike held by one of the men-at-arms.

The knight, smiling, switched his mount forward until coming up to the fallen boy.

I saw then that the terrible hoop had two steel points lodged firmly against the lower part of Hubert's helmet. Opened frontally, the hoop had been shoved from the rear at his neck. Then the points within the hoop, attached to the open ends, had moved back on springs to let Hubert's helmet in—the thought of it made me tremble violently—and had sprung forward again to entrap and yank him off the horse. I could not take my eyes from the horror of the hoop.

Hubert had not been knocked unconscious. He moved his metal-heavy arms and legs like a giant bug, which made the men kneeling around him chuckle. If he moved too much, the man wielding the hoop gave it a jerk, so the steel points were forced harder against the throat of the helmet, holding him to the ground, biting into him. *God in heaven, I beg, I beg of You, almighty—*

"Well, sir," said the knight. Smiling down on Hubert, the knight said calmly, "Did you really think I'd fight a peasant? Accept a challenge from you?"

Dismounting, his sword still in hand, the knight stood over Hubert. "Now," he said. "Are you content?"

I thought, He is going to kill my boy.

Instead, shaking his head, the knight sheathed the sword and remounted his horse. With a shrug he said, "Let the fool live."

*Thank You, almighty God, I swear from this day forth I will—*I was saying to myself when the knight, having trotted away, suddenly reined in. He yanked his horse around and returned to Hubert. For a while he gazed down at the poor boy stretched out, still held by the hook.

Stroking his stubbled chin, the knight looked at Hubert, at his men, at Hubert.

"This is not right," he said. "I'm out a good squire. I won't have it.

"You," he said to one of his men, "give him the pike."

When the man stepped forward, lowering the pike at Hubert, the knight added, still rubbing his chin, "But not too much. I want the bastard to feel it awhile."

When the man walked up to Hubert, who was motionless,

controlled by the terrible points of the hoop, I said to Niklas, "Pray, Brother, pray—"

I tried to pray, too, but words wouldn't come to mind. I said, "God," I said, "God—"

And at the same moment the metal cone of the pike sank into Hubert below the breastplate, with a slow gingerly motion, as if the man-at-arms was afraid of putting it in too deeply.

Indeed, the knight warned him of that. "No farther. Pull it out. I want him to know what knights can really do."

When the man pulled back so that the metal end of the pike appeared again, Hubert grunted.

I crossed myself.

Grunted, moaned, but didn't cry out. Hubert's courage with the pain did not please the knight, who moodily stroked his chin. "Do you think you're noble, you peasant son of a bitch? A man of mark? Do you want to know what I think? I think you're womanish." Leaning over the thick neck of his horse, the knight peered down at Hubert, whose hands were planted on the bubbly red hole below his breastplate. "Remove the *désarçonneur*," the knight said.

Instantly the man-at-arms with the piked hoop shoved it forward until the steel points sprung together and released Hubert from their grip.

"Remove the helmet."

A man stepped forward and roughly pulled it off.

"Dear boy, I love you," I muttered aloud when the handsome face appeared—handsome still, though his mouth twisted in pain. "Look this way, look at me," I said under my breath.

His eyes, wide and fearful, stared only at the mounted knight.

"That's right, you're a womanish thing. You're a whore. So we'll have you." The knight glanced at his men. "Remove his hose and spread him out. Be quick. He's dying."

I felt Niklas's hand rummage in mine to find comfort, and our fingers entwined as we watched them pull off Hubert's leg armor and hose, leaving him naked from the waist down. They threw him on his stomach. Instantly the ground on either side of him grew dark from blood.

I said to my brother, "Don't look." I turned him around so our backs faced the men.

Now at last Hubert screamed.

The scream echoed in the trees until a dark cloud of birds scattered from them, cawing above us, and the queer idea came to me that they were actually God Himself flying away from my boy in his anguish. *Almightly God, don't abandon him at the end, I beg You be merciful, God—*

"Who wants him next?" I heard the knight say.

"Sir, he's dead."

"Well. Throw him in the river. I won't let a squire of mine go quarterstaves with a peasant again."

There was silence. Then the sound of something thudding against the ground. Hubert's breastplate? Stamped by a hammerman with Uncle's seal.

Next I heard a splash. It was like a bell ringing, sounding to the depths of my heart. The splash did not go away, but rang in my ears a long time. Without realizing it, I had put both arms around Niklas and held him thus tightly. I became aware of my right arm being soiled by his vomit. Rocking Niklas in my arms, I said, "It's all right, Brother. He's with God now."

But it was not all right.

From the moment of hearing the splash I was determined to bury Hubert decently, for though God had turned His back on his suffering, I could not.

Crouching below the marsh grass, I led Niklas down to the riverbank, where I hoped to find Hubert soon washed ashore. Instead I saw something white caught in midcurrent by a half-submerged sapling. In the rapid water Hubert's arms and legs, held in the branches, seemed to have a life of their own, flopping this way and that as if attempting to get free. His naked body was very white in the water that parted in blue ropes around him.

As Hubert was trapped and buffeted by the current, so was I trapped and buffeted by the sight of him in the black branches. I could not look away, though the pain the sight gave me was unbearable. I wanted to think of something, but it was too far back in the shadows of my mind.

God, I said soundlessly, God, but nothing more.

Unable to move, not one muscle, stunned as if one of those men had hit me with a war hammer, I waited for something to happen—for the men upstream to leave (I could hear their voices, their laughter), allowing me to wade out and pull Hubert to shore.

But when something did happen, I still could do nothing.

The thin sapling, pulled free by Hubert's weight, sailed off downstream, until within seconds it swirled to a bend in the river. At that distance the little tree looked like a spider whose black legs gripped something wrapped in its white web. Then it swung beyond sight.

"Stay here," I told Niklas. "Don't cry," I told him, feeling tears in my own eyes. His were wide but dry. There was vomit on his mouth and chin. "Don't you cry," I told him severely.

Creeping back through the marsh grass, I reached the spot from which we had watched everything.

To my horror they had built a fire near the bloody ground where my poor boy had been degraded and killed. They had butchered the other two geese and on sticks now the three were roasting.

I sat there dumbly and listened to the men talk of the weather, the cooking birds, the dead boy.

I wished with all my might to be a man. I thought of myself armed and strong, leaping from the grass with a battle-ax in one hand, a sword in the other. I saw myself coming down on the surprised men, hacking them to pieces. I heard myself laugh with joy when the knight's head rolled into the river.

Not till that moment had I wanted to be a man. Nothing else but manhood would have satisfied me then, except the return to life of our parents and Hubert. My life was worthless if I couldn't take revenge. Despair and horror gripped me as the sapling had gripped his dead white body.

It was necessary for me to crawl away, far beyond the men's hearing. I felt anger boiling in my throat, coming out in groans and whimpers. I dug my hands into the soft earth, ground my face into it till mud filled my nose and mouth.

But I was not crying. Unable to do a man's work on this riverbank, at least I would not cry.

Minutes later I rejoined Niklas, who had something in his hand. When I sat down in the damp weeds, he gave it to me. It was a cross made of sticks, cut so that one piece slotted into the other.

I nodded. "Yes, Brother." I jammed it solidly into the earth and looked at Niklas. "You haven't cried. Good. We won't give them that."

Without a thought for what I was doing, I opened the door to Rabbit's wooden cage and took him into my arms. Gently I smoothed his fur. His tight crouch eased after a while, and his nostrils twitched in a slow rhythm. I stroked Rabbit and stroked him and stroked him as Niklas and I stared at the river.

21

WE spent the night there in the marsh grass, somehow, and I woke the next morning curled up with arms crossed, knees to my chest. I felt the warmth of sunlight on one cheek, cold earth on the other. One eye looked at bending reeds, the other was shut tight against the swampy ground.

I thought of our mother, and closed both eyes to see her again, with hair fanned out on the bed at morning. I ran to her and snuggled up, smelling the depths of her hair, feeling the warmth of her soft cheek, and I cried without ceasing, and I said, "Hold me, Mother, I'm hurt, I'm afraid, I'm too young for what's happening."

I remained that way a long time, seeing our parents and the mill and the waterwheel until the blades seemed to turn in my mind steadily, like parts of a clock. And then I saw nothing but a great black hole, knowing it was time itself, and I wanted to enter there fully, never to come out again.

No, I thought.

"No," I said aloud. "Get up."

With effort I opened my eyes and sat up to look around. Nearby was Niklas, curled up in a ball too. Scuttling over to him, I looked through tears at my brother. I had never been sure what Niklas felt, aside from the pain of others and his love for me. Sometimes in his long, deep silences there had been the mystery of a world known only to him and God, and it was frightening. At such times I had pushed him away in my mind, poor brother. I had not always been good to him.

While he slept and whimpered in his sleep, I stroked his pure white hair and smoothed it on his forehead. My brother's cheeks were still childishly plump, but soon enough he'd be as tall as a man. What might the world do to him when he reached manhood, Hubert's age? I thought of Hubert, of what the world had done to him, and I vowed never to part from my brother. Niklas would stay with me and I would look after him until we died.

I sat beside him a long time. Finally he opened his clear blue eyes and stared at me.

"Niklas," I said, "we won't cry."

My brother just looked at me.

"Because he was a knight and tears would embarrass him. He'd want courage from us. I loved him, Brother." Taking a breath, I added, "And you did too. We'll pray at the cross you made."

Going down to the riverbank, we found jammed in the earth the cross he had fashioned from twigs. I clasped my hands and Niklas clasped his.

"Divine Lord," I said, "take our dearest friend to Your bosom. Forgive his sins and love him. Amen."

The rest of that day we sat on the riverbank, watching the river. There was nothing to eat, and I remembered that my money pouch had been inside Hubert's saddlebag. So the knight and his men had taken everything: horse, armor, money. Only because I'd been wearing the roll of drawings on my back were they still mine.

At least the knight would never have a clock made from my drawings. That was a comfort.

We hunted for berries along the bank and found some. We washed them down—they were black and bitter—with a cool drink from the river. Then we slept again, and woke the next morning only after the sun was high.

I said, "Niklas, we're going now."

He just looked at me.

"To the city. Get up now, Brother."

He sat with legs crossed on the marshy ground. His tunic was streaked with mud, his face, too, and his bare feet (shoes left in the saddlebag) looked whitish at the toes from being wet so long.

"Get up, Brother. We can't stay here."

He seemed to think deeply before getting up, as if not sure he wanted to go anywhere. Finally—his lips pressed together—Niklas got up and followed me out of the marshes.

I turned for a last look at the river, trying to keep it in mind as something other than a raging thing that had carried my beloved away. I looked until it seemed cool and smooth and blue. Then I set out, beckoning for Niklas to come along.

We walked hard into the afternoon, asking people which way led to the city. Because of rough and rutted paths, Niklas's bare feet became raw, started to bleed, but we couldn't stop, I told him, we had to go on. I tore strips from the sleeves of my bodice, wrapped his feet in them as best I could, and we went on.

From a wagoner with a load of turnips we begged two little ones and ate them on the way.

"You see," I told Niklas, "there are good people in the world." But if he understood my words, perhaps he didn't believe them.

After spending the night in some woods, we rose the next day and filled ourselves with cool water from a stream, but by noon I was dizzy from hunger and surely Niklas was too.

So when I saw in the hazy sunlight ahead, hovering above distant fields, a large forest of bare trees, I thought they were only in my mind. As we trudged on I realized they were real, but not trees. I was looking at a forest of spires.

"Everything will be fine now," I assured Niklas, "we're coming to the city."

And within an hour we were entering its gates. Passing under the stone arch, I looked up and saw guards staring down at us from watchtowers. One of the men, young, winked at me.

There were people and wagons and donkeys everywhere, yet I chose to see none of them. Hunger gave me an aim—to find the clock tower and the goldsmith who was building it.

When someone would stop long enough to answer a question, I asked for the clock tower. No one knew what that was.

To Niklas I said angrily, "They don't know what a clock is, Brother, but they will someday."

We crossed a timber bridge on stone piers that arched over a canal. Shops lined the bridge, selling foodstuffs that made my stomach feel emptier. I saw two pretty women in blue gowns and white wimples selecting pigs' feet from a stall. One of them gave me a disapproving frown as our eyes met, for I suppose in my frayed bodice and muddy skirt I looked like a beggar who might accost her.

Beyond the bridge was a maze of narrow streets and through them drifted the heavy stench of guts from tanneries that came into view. And past the tanning sheds with the carcasses boiling in big vats were the butcher shops, and my empty stomach seemed to roll over as I gawked at dressed pigs and sheep hanging from hooks within touching distance. We passed as quickly as pack mules allowed us; once the side of a mule loaded with baskets knocked me off-balance and I stepped into a gutter. I pulled my feet back streaming with black water and bits of animal parts thrown from the butcher shops.

This made me go faster, and by the time we reached the end of this street, I had us almost running.

Ahead, suddenly, was open space.

In it was the clock tower. Half built, it stood in the middle of what recently must have been a small meadow within the city. Scaffolding had been placed alongside the walls and all around them were sheds for cutting timber beams and housing forges. The meadow was filled with masons chipping stone, plasterers hauling mortar. The ground was littered with picks and wedges and hatchets, buckets and spades and sieves. The air thundered to the sound of hammers biting into granite. Grindstones screeched at the honing of iron points. Facing so much noise and motion, I forgot hunger.

"Niklas," I said, "this must be the center of the world."

When a man came by carrying a mortar sieve and trowel, I

asked him where the goldsmith was—the Officer of the Corporation—but the workman just scowled and went on. Then I asked someone else for Justin and with the same result. This happened each time I asked. The men gave me a glance, then walked off. One of them leered, muttered something. Another warned me to get out of the way.

I saw women lugging beams of timber for use as trusses in the scaffolding. Approaching, I hoped for better from them, but they, too, stared contemptuously. One of them said, to general laughter, that if I wanted to peddle myself, the best place for it was around the tents. She pointed. That's where the masons stayed.

There must have been a hundred people in the meadow, but none to help us.

I looked at Niklas, who grasped Rabbit's cage with both hands tightly. Perhaps the noise frightened him. There was so much shouting everywhere. And a giant saw in front of a nearby carpenter's shack made a terrible racket, ripping timber.

I wanted to reassure my brother, because this place would be our home. Would it? What if I couldn't find the goldsmith in his surcoat of green, as I remembered him, with his one eye closed in a lump of burned flesh? Or what if I found him but my drawings were no longer needed because Justin had brought his in and they were enough? And if my drawings weren't needed, would the Officer of the Corporation wish to help a girl with a brother who had white hair and never spoke?

Wheelbarrows came rattling by, with the mortarers cursing us for being in their way. But I stood in the turmoil of such noisy labor, stood there determined to look.

Stonecutters were pounding wedges into blocks of granite, splitting them down. Others were dressing the stone with picks, leveling each shape into the purity of straight lines. Still other men were hauling the finished blocks toward the tower, which was already far above the ground.

The long arm of a crane dangled a line over the wall. Two men were strapping a web sling to a stone. I heard the crack of a whip from within the tower.

Drawing nearer, with Niklas (clutching his cage) at my heels,

I saw from the doorless entrance that three oxen were being lashed to move around a platform on which the crane sat. As the beasts trudged forward in a circle, they wound a thick rope on a windlass. When the barrel turned, both hemp and wood creaked with a snapping sound, like a great tree falling. As the rope tightened and pulled through the overhead pulley, it picked up the sling from the ground and lifted all that weighty stone high into the air. The stone began swaying above us like a gray cloud buffeted by wind. Workmen up there, balancing on the edge, yelled instructions to the master of the crane. Reaching out, they grasped the stone and maneuvered it into position.

"Let out your line! Let it out!" they shouted down at the master of the crane, who stood on the platform inside the tower. Slowly the block was lowered into place.

I felt sweat dripping into my eyes. It had poured out from anticipation and fear as the stone hung in midair. Plasterers embedded the block in mortar.

When they were finished, I turned to Niklas. "Did you see all that?" I asked. "Did you see it? Did you see it, Brother? Did you? Did you see it?"

I hoped the force of words would help him feel my excitement and create in him some of his own. But he looked grim, pale, small. He looked hungry. With surprise I remembered my own hunger.

"We're going for food now," I told him confidently, as if I knew how to get it. "We'll find the Officer of the Corporation later. Now we'll eat."

And so I led us away from the frantic meadow and the tower ringed by scaffolding.

We crossed into another part of the city. After we'd taken a few steps into an alley, the walls seemed to close in on us, the sun to fade into shadow. Muleteers sat beside a tavern holding bowls of beer and yelled at me to join them. From hunger and thirst I was tempted. Across the way hung banners announcing shops for cloth and jewelry, and when I looked up at them I stared past them at chimneys and timber rooftops and old gray towers and spires that seemed ready to pierce heaven.

We came again to an open space, but this one was cobbled

and lined with three-story houses of brick with red roofs and blue-trimmed windows. In the middle of this square was the bishop's cathedral, immense, rising upward as if thrust from the ground—caught for a moment in flight before continuing toward the home of God.

I halted to look at the buttresses and carvings. "Niklas," I said.

But then I forgot what I was going to say, because ahead of us, seated below triple portals, were two lines of people, more than a dozen on each side, who formed a corridor through which anyone entering or leaving the cathedral had to pass. I watched two men in velvet doublets come out and toss a few coins at the seated beggars. Hands all along the way stretched out eagerly. I heard a loud chorus of "Alms! Alms, sirs! Alms! In the name of Christ Crucified, alms!"

"That's where we go," I told Niklas. "We'll sit with them and when we have money enough, we'll buy food."

Crossing the square, we promptly took up positions at the end of the line. I put Rabbit's cage behind us and smiled at a woman next to me, who didn't smile back. She had a big dirty bandage wound across her head and over one eye.

A man approached, moving beads in his fingers, and when the others shouted, "Alms!" so did I.

"Alms! Alms!" I leaned forward, stretching my arm out and nodding for Niklas to do the same. "Alms!" I yelled at the backs of the passersby, and pulled Niklas's hand out farther into the corridor.

I was still pulling my brother's hand when something struck me hard in the side.

Turning, I looked up at the red face of a small man wearing a sock cap and a fur-trimmed jacket (on a hot summer day) with scalloped sleeves.

"Who do you think you are, you dirty bitch?" he yelled, kicking me again, bending down so near to my face, I could see the veins in his eyes.

"It's all right," I said first to Niklas, whose mouth had dropped open in astonishment. "We're hungry," I then told the small man, meeting his angry look.

"Stupid bitch, we're all hungry."

"We don't know another way to get money for food."

"Neither do we."

The two of us stared at each other.

He straightened up, his face less red. "This is guild work, girl. You have to belong to the guild."

Someone seated across the way began to laugh.

"Don't laugh," the little man said, glaring. "Maybe this isn't a guild, but I'm master here."

Looking my way, he said, "If you don't think so, you'll find out soon enough. If there weren't a master of beggars, who saw to business and controlled it just like a guild, they'd overrun the city, I mean the beggars, and befoul every foot of it until the duke sent in soldiers to slit every beggar's throat they could find. Yours included, bitch."

"Can we sit here today?" I asked. "We're so hungry."

"You can sit here a whole week. But first contribute to the guild."

"We haven't got money. If we did—"

"You wouldn't be here. But you would. Begging's a good living in this city if you contribute."

"Then we'll try somewhere else."

He shook his head with a grim smile. "That won't work, girl. Anywhere you go, you'll find a master like me. And a lot worse than me. In some places if you put your hand out for alms, you lose it and your eyes too."

"Please," I said.

"You have to give to get." Leaning down, he showed me his yellow teeth in a wide grin. "You may be dirty but you're young, aren't you. I tell you what. I'll do you a favor. You can forget about money. Let's go over there in the alley, the two of us. I know a place."

"No," I said.

With a little sigh, he shrugged. "Who wants you anyway, you dirty bag of shit. Get out of here," he told me.

As we got up I remembered something. Aside from the drawings and Rabbit, what we still had, I thought, was one of my brother's carvings.

"Where is it?" I asked my brother, reaching out to feel his breeches.

Sure enough I drew a wooden rabbit out of his pocket and held it toward the man. "Here."

Squinting, he snatched it from me and turned it around in his dark fingers. "What is this thing?"

"A rabbit."

"I know. But what for?" He glanced from me to Niklas, then back to me.

"It's a carving. We sell them all the time," I lied.

Turning it again, the master of beggars pursed his lips. "Well, I knew what it was. He sells them?"

"He makes them, I sell them."

"I know that. He can't sell anything. But he makes them?" He gave Niklas a thoughtful look. "Well," he said, "maybe I could get something for it. There are people in this city will buy anything."

"We can sit here today?"

"If I get money for this, you can sit here a week," he said. "I'm not a hard man. I'm fair." He gave me a sidelong smile I didn't like.

"Rules," he said. "You pay each week. You can't sit, if you can't pay. I'm master here, so I'm judge of what you have to pay. Another thing: Keep to the end of the line. I don't want to see you getting close to the door. The best spot is near the door. People coming from prayer will give when they first step into the air if they give at all. Near the door is for those I've known a long time. It's the rule. You," he said to me, "you don't sit at all. Only him."

"Why?" I asked.

"Because you're not sick, and you're not stupid like him. Maybe if you're nice to me some day"—he smiled—"I'll show you how to fake tremors. Speaking of which, does he have them?"

"No."

"But he's mad, isn't he?"

"No."

"Then give him red berries to chew and have him spit the juice when someone comes along. Get him a head bandage soaked in red dye, something like that. People don't usually give to someone just stupid or mad. But they give for bleeding.

And take that rabbit away from here. Let people see it, they'll wonder why you don't eat it. So get that boy in his place and you wait over there." He pointed to a wall next to the cathedral.

I went over there and sat down. From behind the wall came the sound of voices chanting. They were high-pitched. It was probably a convent. All day I sat against the wall, watching Niklas and the others reach out when worshipers came to and from the cathedral. My brother never got a coin. Only about half the others did.

Beginning to despair, I thought of the carved rabbit. Why hadn't I thought of selling it myself? Perhaps because I had never thought of Niklas's carvings as having worth. Would the master of beggars really sell it? Now and then, as twilight drew near, I thought of Niklas's knife. Maybe we could sell that. Later I'd get Niklas another. But would he understand? He'd think selling his knife was like selling Rabbit.

Such thoughts were plaguing me when I noticed, coming through the light of dusk, some men on horseback. One of them had a strange face, something wrong about it. As they came across the square, and when they drew close enough, I saw that the rider with the strange face was missing his left eye.

Where it should have been was a lump of flesh.

Rising and rushing forward, I said, "Here, sir! Officer of the Corporation!" In despair I saw the men glance my way, then spur their mounts briskly into a trot. Running after them, I yelled breathlessly across the cobbled square, "Albrecht Valens! Albrecht Valens!"

The man with the burned face reined in and turned. Trotting toward me, he leaned into the twilight air and squinted.

"Albrecht Valens!" I shouted again, and reached behind to grip the rolled canvas. "I have his drawings for the clock!" When the scarred face smiled, I swear my stomach smiled back.

Part III

22

FOR whatever reason, Justin had never reached the city. Perhaps he had died at the hands of wandering soldiers or run to a nobleman with his set of drawings or sold it elsewhere. "He is not brave," Uncle had said. In violent times the fate of such a man can be anything.

With Justin's set of drawings unavailable, the city needed mine.

For a while I was not sure I was needed, too, because when Alderman Franklyn, Officer of the City Corporation and head of the inner council of the goldsmiths' guild, had the roll of canvas securely in hand, he seemed to forget me.

"Good," he said from horseback. "Give her a coin," he told one of his companions.

"Sir," I began, not knowing what else to say.

I watched the alderman unroll the canvas for a look at the drawings. Then my stomach gave me words that were bold enough.

Ignoring a coin offered by one of the horsemen, I said to Alderman Franklyn, "I can read these drawings, sir. I know what they mean." He was holding them upside down.

Lowering them, he gave me a long look. "I remember you."

"Niece of Master Valens. Yes, sir. He was very good to me, taught me about clocks. I made these drawings, sir. My uncle taught me how. And I can read them too."

"So can others."

"But, sir, they were drawn by me. I know them as well as anyone can."

He frowned at my impertinence, yanked a bit on the reins. I swear the lump of flesh where an eye had once been was staring at me.

"You know them as well as anyone can," he repeated. It was difficult to say if he was mocking me or considering my claim.

"Yes, sir. Believe me, sir, I know them as well as anyone can."

Rolling up the canvas and sticking it under his arm, the alderman said, "Then you may be useful. Come to the tower tomorrow."

Turning to the man who had offered the coin, I said, "Thank you, sir," and held out my hand until he bent down from his horse. This time I snatched the coin from his fingers and curtsied as our mother had taught me to do.

Next morning I was at the tower early, watching the laborers straggle bleary-eyed into the meadow. In following months, I would always be there, standing beside the wall as they arrived for the day's work. And I would go to my own tasks, for I had been hired to work on the clock.

I often saw Alderman Franklyn when he came for consultation with the works master, a big fleshy ironsmith from the north named Eberhart.

The two would stand in the meadow, studying the progress of work on the tower. I stayed near them in case they wanted one of my drawings explained, although in those days they attended mostly to the tower. I think Alderman Franklyn asked me questions now and then to satisfy himself that he really did need me.

He was chiefly concerned with the speed of construction. He wanted the tower built and the clock installed before other cities in the region did the same.

I heard him say in cold anger to Master Eberhart one morning, "You are going too slowly. We're paying to get this done and done right and done soon. Mark this, sir: No excuses acceptable. This is a city of righteous men. We mean to receive what we pay for." His one-eyed face was terrible to behold.

I think the alderman disliked his works master for having served noblemen most of his life: working the forges to shoe their horses, fashioning their chain mail, shaping their weapons, and, for their estates, making plowshares and nails and wheel rims.

When they stood together watching the tower go up, Alderman Franklyn would remind the works master of the taxes good burghers were paying for the privilege of having a city clock.

And when he felt the work was slowing down, the alderman reminded his works master of what Eberhart would never be given the leisure to forget: the trials and tribulations of a free city. Good burghers had already paid dearly for the charter—won from the duke in exchange for money to pay debts incurred during his grand adventures on a Crusade. Good burghers had earned their freedom from military service by submitting to property tax and sales tax. They had denied themselves the profit of collecting taxes during fairs—giving such forfeits to the duke so he would not forget one day and for his amusement turn troops on such benefactors. And these God-fearing burghers had stood unmoved by the bishop's threat of excommunication when he disputed their right to trial outside of ecclesiastical courts. Such good men, these burghers, had stood up to nobles and clergy for their freedom. And now that they had it, they must defend it, not only against old enemies but against new rivals as well—other cities whose welfare depended on the ruin of their neighbors.

"Mark me well," the alderman often warned his works master. "Men of this nature will not tolerate bad service. The tower and clock stand for them, for their pride, Master Eberhart. Unlike your noblemen, they understand the value of things."

I knew little about the other burghers, but I knew that Alderman Franklyn in his velvet jerkin and with the left side of his face puckered in burned flesh did indeed know the value of things. If other merchants were like him, I pitied the bishop and the duke, dangerous though they were, and felt sorry for the burghers of other cities who stood in the way of this city's success.

In truth I was on the alderman's side, for we had something in common: We both believed in the clock.

What he said about cities had little interest for me. I cared not if it was true as he claimed: that one city's gain is always another city's loss. But I admired Alderman Franklyn when he made his other claim: that the clock would bring good fortune. That it was a way of telling merchants from afar how great this city had become. That they would hear of the clock and route their caravans through these streets.

Even if raising the tower and installing the clock meant greater taxes, as well as a larger grant of aid to church and duchy, Alderman Franklyn believed that the result would be worth the cost. Such a sign of civic pride stood for progress and progress meant an increase in business and business was the lifeblood of mankind.

I liked what he said about the importance of the clock, even though admittedly I hated to look at his terrible scar, turned like an open eye to his listeners.

The works master from the north seemed equally uncomfortable in the alderman's presence. Eberhart was an ironsmith who understood masonry as well. I discovered that he had been hired for those twin skills, yet knew little of clocks. He could fashion the rods and wheels all right, but without truly understanding their operation.

So I was there to teach him the ways of a clock.

He was shy and hesitant, in spite of his brawn. Master Eberhart sidled up to me and asked questions as if I were a man who could look him in the eye. It was very strange. I could have been proud, yet something withholding in his manner encouraged me to regard him with suspicion rather than liking, and I took no pleasure in his little flatteries as we studied the drawings together.

When not at Eberhart's side, I wandered through the meadow where stonecutters were working. I watched them fit wooden molds over the cut blocks to ensure uniformity of size.

Wearing a sock cap and bulky clothes, even though the weather was still warm, I tried to hide my womanliness. A few men continued to wink or call out something foul when I passed, but because of my standing with the works master I came to be acceptable to most men at the site.

The women carters, however, often shouted obscenities at me, unwilling to believe I could be favored without surrendering my body. But then they lived terrible lives. More than one died from exhaustion in that meadow. They had no room in their hearts for more than their own pain.

Time passed quickly that autumn and winter. I spent it watching the tower rise. In my dreams at night I saw what I had seen by day: hickory mallets and pitching tools and shorted-headed hammers with broad striking faces and points and chisels and gouges. I even dreamed of the banker-marks carved on stone blocks by masons—a double *O* or triple *X* or some other number by which each craftsman collected his pay: the signatures flew like birds through my dreams.

During long winter months, while work continued in the icy air, I huddled at fires with the masons and with them ate onions and barley bread and cheese, all of us squinting up through falling snow at the tower. The outer wall needed only a few more courses of stone for completion. The inner wall was half done, and already a few steps of granite had been laid between the walls. Soon there would be a staircase to climb.

A crew of carpenters, recently arrived, sat apart at their own fires, sullenly watching us. They were here to work not on the clock tower but on buildings to stand near it: warehouse sheds and stalls and even a meeting place for the weavers' guild. Construction spanned a long arc nearly halfway around the tower, midway between it and the meadow's edge. Soon there would be as many people working on these buildings as on the tower itself. Looking at the heavily trussed walls going up in the meadow, I thought of the clock at their center as a kind of heart, a pulse around which the life of this city might grow and thrive.

Each day we saw merchants in velvet doublets come strolling into the meadow. They came, like Alderman Franklyn, to over-see construction. We heard that the alderman had purchased a large portion of the meadow on which these new buildings would stand. And there were also rumors of complicated agreements not only between the alderman and other guild merchants, but between rich traders and churchmen and royal agents of the king as well. They were carving up the meadow in front of the clock tower. These rumors put me in mind of candles in a large, cold room and men seated at tables piled high with gold.

Because iron smelting for the clockwork had also begun, I stayed close to the works master, answering his questions. Mas-

171

ter Eberhart was uncertain about the sizes of wheels and rods, having neither skill at numbers nor experience with the motion of iron shapes. During those days, I thought frequently of Uncle, who had taught me so much.

The foundry shed had been expanded and lay alongside a goldsmith's shop (we learned it was being built for Alderman Franklyn). Crunching each dawn through the snow, I looked first at the tower, but then my heart quickened when next I saw the low-slung foundry and the charcoal shed behind it. Within the clay and timber walls of that foundry each part of the clock was going to be fired, hammered, chased—and someday assembled up there in the tall tower. A clock above the city. Uncle's clock as well as the city's clock. And my clock too.

23

DURING this time Niklas and I lived in a house owned by Master Dollmayr. I was taken there by a servant of the alderman after I had been hired to work on the clock. The alderman would pay our room and board and give me two coins each month besides.

That first day, as we walked to Master Dollmayr's house, the servant told me how an old carpenter, a boarder there, had died last week.

"That's why you'll get the room," explained the servant. "The old man did carpentry for Alderman Franklyn." The servant was an old man himself. "And from his grumbling, I'd say you won't like this place. It's cheap enough. That's what the alderman considers. Rich men like him aren't going to spend money on white-haired boys and girls like you, even if you do know clocks. And you won't like Master Dollmayr either."

Master Dollmayr was head of the artists' guild. All the members of it, painters and wood-carvers, worked at his house, boarded elsewhere.

His house was a narrow three-storied building of squared

oaken timbers stiffened by corner braces of lead and joined by wooden pegs. Such details of carpentry were known to me from days of trailing behind Father at millhouse chores. Each time I saw a well-built house like this one, I thought of the mill, of Father's big hands gripping hammer or saw.

Upper stories of the house projected into the street, so that the windows (shuttered on the third floor where Mistress spent her time) could nearly be touched from windows across the way. Behind the main house was a workshop for the wood-carvers and behind that a vegetable garden that led to other buildings: kitchen, storeroom, woodshed, latrine. Still farther within the compound was a small yard with chicken coop and pigsty, and behind it a two-horse stable.

Although the house looked sturdy from the lane, each room within it was grim, bare, and dark. Master Dollmayr's office on the first floor contained nothing except a small table, a chair, a bench.

In the dining room were another bench, a trestle table, a padlocked cabinet.

I thought of our uncle's grand style of living—the goblets, the candlesticks, the roaring fire, the long table loaded with dishes fit for a king.

There was never good cheer at Master Dollmayr's table. Portions of food were never generous, not for him or anyone. Terrified of Clotilda the Housekeeper, the serving girls never set tidbits aside, as the girls in Uncle's household used to do. Nor did they put away uneaten scraps, not even for themselves. By Housekeeper's orders, such scraps—I must say they were rare in that house—went into the next day's meal. Everyone, including Master, lived much of the time on porridge.

Upstairs was one long room, a studio used by two painters and their half-dozen apprentices.

Three small bedrooms occupied the third floor. Mistress stayed in one of them the day long. Master slept in another at night. The third bedroom, between the other two, belonged to Clotilda the Housekeeper. Hers was the same size as the others, but cozier, because she kept a colorful quilt on her bed.

Clotilda was a big, rawboned young woman with a long face

and black hair pulled back in a bun. From our first day there she was unhappy.

Standing outside Master's office, I heard her say about our arrival, "Children bring trouble into a house."

Master didn't answer right away—he must have been thinking.

"Yes, well," he finally said. "I can understand that. But the girl's not really a child."

"So much the worse."

There was a long silence.

"Satan's work," she said finally.

"Well."

"Satan's work. Think of the men in this house. She could tempt and corrupt them and you would lose by it."

Again there was a long silence.

"You are right, Clotilda. But it was Alderman Franklyn who sent them, so we must have them. And they are paid for."

"I can't like it. Why does the alderman favor them—a whorish girl like that and a boy who can't talk?"

"The girl knows something about clocks, they tell me."

"Does that bring favor? I can't like it."

"Keep an eye on her."

"I can't like it."

"Well, perhaps she is innocent after all."

Clotilda snorted.

"We have no choice," Master said more firmly. "It is God's will." And the matter was left at that.

Master was a middle-sized man with a soft round face. His eyes bulged, his lips parted in a smile that never faded. Never once that I knew of. He had lank brown hair that lay close to his skull. Even in hot weather he wore a fur-trimmed jacket. It closed in the new fashion, not with ties but with buttons, and he kept it buttoned to his chin. Bundled up that way, he looked smaller than he was.

Agents for the guild and art buyers came to the house every day, so that I was reminded of the bustle of Uncle's establishment. But little else was similar. The artists' studio, for example. The men in there moved so quietly! Mixing colors, cleaning brushes, they were quiet as cats.

On the day of our arrival I remember standing in the studio doorway with Niklas. We watched an artist applying dabs of paint to the shoulder of Christ Crucified.

"That is our Lord," I told Niklas.

He was staring at Jesus nailed to a cross of wood upon a panel of wood.

"We are His children and He died for us." Of course, this was not the first time I had explained our Lord's crucifixion to my brother, but never before had he seemed so interested. I had to yank him away. "It's quiet in there," I said uneasily.

Even in the guild's wood-carving shop it was quiet. Chisels sliced almost silently through pine, and mallets of hickory thudded dully against oak. Even the rasp of files seemed muted, as if such noise was smothered in sawdust like the air itself.

A childhood spent close to creaking waterwheels and pounding mill hammers must have prepared me for wilder sound—I yearned for the loud meadow around the tower.

But when Niklas stood at the workshop door, listening to the faint scraping of a riffler, I wondered if he liked this place better than a foundry because its work went more quietly. I knew that sometimes he would clap both hands to his ears when the banging of metal against metal grew too loud. Standing outside the wood-carving shop, Niklas looked as if he'd feel at home in there, among the muffled sounds of wood. But I pulled him away, fearing those workers might mistreat a boy who couldn't talk. We didn't have our uncle for protection.

"Brother," I said, "that place is not for you."

When my eyes opened each morning, I thought of the masons and the carpenters who would be that day at the tower, yelling for tools and help. I thought of the noise, the motion. It spurred me to rise in our tiny room below the gabled roof. There was space in it for us, two blankets, and Rabbit's cage.

"Well, it's ours," I had told Niklas when first we saw our room. "A scullion told me in many houses the servants sleep where they can, in this or that corner, curled up on a cold hearth without blankets. But we have blankets and a place of our own to put them down on. And without windows the wind can't blow in, so we'll keep warm."

But it was cold anyway. That winter the entire house was cold. Master never spent money on logs. The downstairs fireplace was used only a few times each month. And yet, swathed in furs, Master never looked cold. As for Clotilda, she believed that people standing near a fire used up its heat. So it was forbidden to slip into the kitchen and stand near the stove while something was cooking. Throughout the winter I never once felt warm.

At night Niklas and I snuggled closely in the thin blankets. Often I was kept awake (my brother never had trouble sleeping) by sounds from below us. From beneath our heads came the creaking of boards as someone paced, often until dawn. This was Mistress.

During the day I rarely saw Mistress, a skinny woman hardly taller than my brother. Her gray hair and drawn face made her look older than her husband. Sometimes she sat alone at the dining table and ate a little soup, her rosary beside the bowl. When the beads were not on the dining table, they were turning in her thin, nervous hands. As she climbed the stairway the beads traveled through her fingers and her mouth moved, but without forming words that other people could hear. When she did speak, her voice was small, far away, the sound of pent-up sobbing. She looked worried, often frightened.

When I asked a serving girl why, I was told that Mistress feared the coming of Antichrist, the end of the world. So every night she paced, creaking the boards with the steady motion of clockwork.

Less often, from below our feet, came other sounds in the night.

They came from Clotilda's bedroom.

One morning, restless, I got up earlier than usual and went down the loft ladder, hoping to wheedle out of Cook a piece of bread for breakfast.

As one foot touched the third-story floor, I glanced down the narrow hallway and saw Master standing there, wrapped in a thick robe, reaching out to open his bedroom door. And from her own bedroom, wearing a nightdress but no nightcap, Clotilda was leaning into the hallway. She was smiling at him, but the smile vanished when our eyes met. As I scooted down the staircase beyond their sight, I felt upon my back the force of Master and Clotilda glaring at me.

That very same day, while returning from the latrine, I noticed the door to the storeroom ajar. I heard crying within. Pushing the door slightly, I eased it back upon a strange sight: the Housekeeper was standing over a girl unknown to me.

Crumpled at Clotilda's feet, the girl was whimpering. There was blood on her lips, a welt on her cheek. Her braided hair, which must have been yanked violently free, fell about her shoulders—it heaved up and down with her sobbing.

The Housekeeper loomed over her like a mountain, hands on hips. Seeing me in the doorway, Clotilda grinned.

"Well, there. Another favored girl," she said. "Do you see something interesting?"

I backed off a step.

"No, no, no. Come in. Curiosity must be satisfied. We must favor a favored girl. Especially one who works with men and keeps rabbits in her room. Come in, come in. Come see the way fortune can deal with a favored girl. This favored one"—Clotilda looked down at the girl between her feet—"had a blacksmith for a lover. Such a splendid bold fellow. Am I right, dear?" she asked the girl in mock friendliness. "So expert with steel. So generous. The money he got from swordmaking didn't stay in his pocket. Did it, dear. Oh, no, not at all. It went to buy you clothes. To buy you sweets."

Clotilda glanced at me. "She'd come from him like a lady in her wimple and pointed shoes. What a beauty this favored girl was. What a fine lady. And when I warned her not to run away with him, she wouldn't listen. What, to me? I'm just a housekeeper. Much too rough for a great lady like herself. Stay exactly where you are, you bitch," Clotilda said to the girl, who was getting to her knees.

The girl slumped down again, cowering like a dog.

"Someone so favored wouldn't listen to a housekeeper," Clotilda went on. "She was too fine and too pretty and too favored. But this is the interesting part. When this handsome bladesmith had used his own blade long enough on her, why what did he do? Say what he did, dear," Clotilda cooed, bending over her.

With a glance at me, Clotilda said, "He sent her back. Had his fill of fine ladies. He sent her right back here. And so here she is. Our favored girl come home. Crying and sniveling and begging for work," Clotilda said, swiping at the girl with her big hand. "Pleading for work, are you? Get up," she yelled. "Get out!"

The girl was still whimpering at Clotilda's feet when I rushed away.

At my back the Housekeeper called, "Don't forget!" Her bellowing voice followed me. "You saw what happens to favored girls!"

"Niklas," I said that day. "Stay clear of the Housekeeper. She's a bad woman."

Did he understand me? All he seemed to think about was the wood-carving shop. When we came home from the tower, he would rush to it and watch the carvers at their work until they packed up their tools to leave.

One of the carvers, an old man who smoked a clay pipe, stopped me one morning on my way to the tower.

"Let the boy come with me today," he said.

I looked at Niklas, who was gripping his knife with one hand, holding my hand with the other. "He should be with his sister," I said.

"We'll look after him," the carver assured me. When I studied his old eyes, there seemed to be truth in them.

But I said, "Niklas should be with me."

"I've seen him carve. I can make a wood-carver of him."

We looked at each other hard, then I turned to Niklas. Did he understand what was happening? Nothing was in his eyes. Yet when I said, "Go with this man," he dropped my hand instantly and gripped that of the old carver.

I watched them turn and walk together toward the house.

Feeling tears in my eyes, I set out for the tower. In Uncle's house we had often gone our own way, yet in a few steps I could always reach my brother. We had always been together at the mill. We had never been separated, not in our lives. The knowledge of being apart for the first time burned in my heart like a coal.

Yet the old carver was right. Niklas should learn something.

Because someday he would reach manhood and face the same world that Hubert had faced. What if I failed then to protect him? A strange and terrible idea formed in my mind: Niklas might have to protect himself.

24

I WORKED often with Barnabas that winter.

He was foundry master, having also come from the north, where he'd made fire cradles for castle hearths. Accustomed to working with big pieces of iron, Barnabas was a good man for this job, though at first he didn't believe in the clock.

He would flex his powerful arms and glower from eyes ridged by thick black brows. "The Church tells us when to pray. That is enough. The bell over there gives us what hours we need."

And it was true that the seven canonical hours thundered each day from the cathedral, as if defiant of what we were doing but a short walk from its carved doors.

I explained to Barnabas that when we had our clock, it might toll hourly but the distance between each hour would stay the same all year.

He shook his head. Barnabas disliked the thought of winter and summer being equal, because everyone knew they weren't, he declared: winter days were shorter. To think otherwise was against nature—and maybe even against God. He also kept wondering if a clock would affect pay. Men got more in summer when they worked longer. What would happen when the clock came in?

Even so, with time he came to know the clock. I explained the machinery from my drawings. I could see his big heavy face awaken to the thought of a foliot, a striking train, a driving weight. In turn, he taught me to use the grinding wheel (in Uncle's smithy I had never touched the tools) with its treadle drive and foot pedal. Even though I was a girl, Barnabas let me

179

sharpen cutters and drills. He showed me the right amount of emery and tallow to smear on the thick leather of the walnut wheel. He guided my hands to set the tool edge at the right angle. Barnabas laughed when I did it well.

I told him about the coiled spring our uncle had worked on so that someday we could make smaller clocks—small enough to hold in the hand. That was too much for Barnabas. He laughed scornfully.

I liked him in his slow, ponderous way, and he treated me with respect. Perhaps he was nice because the works master asked me questions in his presence. Barnabas made a practice of yelling at other women in the meadow—at the timber and stone carters.

One day I caught Barnabas rubbing his jaw, staring at me thoughtfully.

When our eyes met, he said, "How old are you, Anne?"

"Eighteen." I was almost that old.

"You learned how to draw the clock from your uncle?"

"From him and another man, Justin."

"Still," he said. "You're young to know so much."

It would do no good to tell him how old I felt.

"What I think you do to make yourself older," he said earnestly, "is look at things. You look closely. As closely as I've seen anyone look. I think that's why you seem older."

Because he meant well, I couldn't tell him what looking closely had done to me: that by looking closely I sometimes saw what wasn't good to see. Not a day passed but I lived in my mind the massacre at the mill and the murder of Hubert. I saw everything, each part slowly and separately, until I shook. There were times when I wished never to look closely at the world again. And so have less to remember.

At such times I remained all day in the foundry shed, swallowing the hot breath of a bellows. Memory rarely followed me among the throw wheels, the pulleys, the tongs, the drilling tools, the wire gauges, the files and pins and cutters and hooks and vises and chucks and fluxes and chains, and singing anvils, and lengths of heated iron as liquid as water. I felt free of the past near the forge.

With my sock cap on and in baggy clothing I did the work of a man. In the company of smiths I rarely spoke, but Uncle had prepared me to stand up to them if the need came. I felt confident around iron that would make a clock. Perhaps I felt as confident as any smith there. I felt blessed. Carefully I hid this feeling from my companions, but it was there. Within the foundry walls something took me over. When molten hunks of the earth turned into wheels and rods, I was no longer a girl of seventeen but someone of vague features who stood beside men like Uncle and watched a clock growing out of noise and fire. In this hot, loud world my heart glowed with pride, like a bloom of iron heating in the forge.

The clock did this to me. Building the clock made me prideful, and I believe now that God must have looked down at my arrogance and judged me for it.

When snow began melting in the meadow, the tower was completed.

I watched carpenters erecting a timber roof over the last course of stone. The roof would rest on thick beams at the four corners. The carpenters clung to stone and wood up there like cats, and for people on the ground they seemed to defy air in the carefree manner of demons as they went about cutting and hammering their timber.

Each morning they climbed the stone staircase and each evening came down it, which gave purpose to the tower within. What I saw from outside was more than a tall thing of shaped rock: The tower was useful at last.

When Barnabas had finished casting the iron bar from which to hang the bell, a half-dozen men carried it to the tower. The bar was hoisted by pulley alongside the stone walls. Taut lines kept it from swinging on its way up. Everyone in the meadow stopped work to squint at the six men appearing at the top of the tower. No one stirred below as they reached out and pulled the bar in under the timber roof.

I remember exactly how it was: the men balancing on the rim of the stones, maneuvering the thick bar in their dozen hands, raising and fitting it into brackets athwart the underside of the roof. And I remember the next thing as clearly: When the left end of the bar slid into place, one of the men, giving it a final push, lost his balance and toppled from the tower. He turned slowly, it seemed, and around at least twice before hitting the ground.

We all ran toward him. I could see his upright face, young, with open troubled eyes at one end of a body strangely angled. I turned, walked away, feeling an old horror that the dead young face had forced me to remember. My beloved Hubert.

I heard someone say behind my shoulder, "Well, she's only a girl. Never seen much death."

"Nobody can live five years in this shithole of a world without seeing plenty of death."

"I mean death like that."

"Did you know him?"

"He was a mason who worked with Tobias. Do you know Tobias?"

"Big fellow from the south?"

I realized then that I was sobbing. Ashamed, I rushed away.

But the next morning, as usual, I got to the meadow early. No one reminded me of yesterday, and I thanked my companions silently for that.

The forge grew hot, the wild music of a hammer on metal pulsed in my head. I checked against my drawings the dimensions of a wheel that belonged to the going train. It might be too small, but we wouldn't know until the whole train was assembled.

From the foundry shed I watched some men digging a deep pit. A brass founder came that afternoon to take charge of casting the great tower bell inside that pit. First he constructed a brick sheath—something like a dagger's scabbard—to hold the clay mold for the bell.

I strolled out to watch him make a wax model of the bell itself. It stood as tall as I was. This mold of wax was placed in another clay frame and lowered into the sheath.

Every day, when there was time, I sat on the edge of the pit to watch. The brass founder, ruddy and small, was nice to me. He would look up from his work and explain each step of the casting.

One day a great fire was built in the pit, and the next day, smothered in a bed of fiery charcoal, the mold of wax heated until it bled away, drained from within the sheath like the blood of a man. When the wax had all run out and the fire had died away, the brass founder and his helpers turned the brick sheath over, using long-handled tongs. They grunted, sweated, their faces crimson.

I crouched near the pit while two of the men poured a red-hot liquid into the sheath.

"What is that?" I asked.

"Copper and tin," said the brass founder, and added with a wink, "the blood of my life."

Out of its iron crucible the sputtering mixture flowed into spaces left empty by the melted wax. It flowed sluggishly, like a stream heavy with ice.

"See that, girl?" said the founder. "What do you think?"

"It's beautiful."

He laughed and turned to his helpers. "She says it's beautiful. Beautiful." And they laughed too.

When they axed off the casting jacket after cooling, what emerged from the cracked pieces of clay was an ash-colored metal bell. It was like a chick hatching from its egg.

"Is that beautiful?" the founder asked me.

I nodded.

Next morning he chiseled something on the finished bell, then beckoned me over from the shed. I climbed into the pit where the bell was sitting on a platform of timber. Near the brass rim he had carved a shield with three bells, his founding mark, and some words.

"Can you read?" he asked.

I nodded proudly and bent to see what he had scratched onto the bell.

I SCATTER THE CLOUDS FROM HEAVEN

Below those words he had chiseled his name.

Then with a hammer he banged on the bell. The tone of it billowed into the air with a deep, dark sound, as if it had been struck beneath water.

"Hear that? Now that's what I call beautiful," the founder said. He had a sweaty red face with a large nose. His head seemed too big for his small wiry body.

Again he struck the bell and glanced at men standing near the pit. With a sigh he said, "Good, isn't it?"

They nodded in agreement.

Winking at me, he said, "That's a virgin tone. That's what we call it. Do you know why it's called a virgin tone, girl? Girls should know why." He winked past me at the men. "Because no one has got inside it. Understand? It's still intact. There's no need to get inside a bell of mine and chip it out for a better sound. My bells are always virgins. They don't need tuning. The sound in my bells is cast right into them. God gave me this gift. Here." He handed me a chisel.

"If you can read what I put on the bell, you can make letters of your own," he said. "Is that true?"

"Yes."

"Go on, then. Write your name."

So I sat beside the long-waisted bell of the tower and scratched ANNE upon its chased brown side. The brass felt cold to my touch, but when I finished and laid my hand across the chiseled name, the metal felt like something alive in a river, something moving ever so slightly in the cool depths.

During my carving I had forgotten the onlookers, but putting the chisel down, I heard a cheer go up around the pit, and I stared into the smiling faces of masons, founders, smiths. Even a few women carters stood there, smiling.

So the bell bore my name. I would never forget that. Throwing my arms around the brass founder, I thanked him thanked him, feeling the tears blinding me.

A few days later the bell was installed.

But before it was hoisted through the center of the tower, a priest blessed it. In Latin he said, *"Custos campanilis et pulsator horarum noctibus et diebus."* He was a very young priest, tall and handsome. Though he was dark-haired, he reminded me of Hubert. It was in the nobility of his face.

While workmen were hitching a team of oxen to the sled that would haul the bell to the tower, I went up to the priest and said, "May I ask a question, Father?"

For a moment he just looked at me. I knew he was studying the yellow hair that had slipped out of the sock cap. His eyes widened slightly, when he was sure I was a girl. "Of course, child."

"Where do those Latin words come from?"

"They mean—"

"Oh, I know their meaning. Or most of it. 'Guarding the belfry—' "

" 'Guardian of the belfry,' " he corrected, staring at me in surprise.

" 'Guardian of the belfry and striker of the hours in the nights and in the days.' "

"Very good." He said, "Very very good, child," with an enthusiasm that didn't match his solemn face.

"They are fine words."

"My own," he said with a shrug of humility, a shy turning-away.

"Then you must like the clock to make up such fine words about it."

"I like bells, not clocks. Bells call us to prayer."

"This bell will ring every hour as well as those for prayer," I reminded him.

"So, unfortunately, I have heard."

"Why unfortunately? A clock should do what it does."

He frowned, showing me I had been too bold. This boldness came from my spending so much time with men. I bit my lip in shame.

We turned our attention to the oxen, who were straining to pull the brass bell out of the pit. Creaking heavily, the sled eased up a wooden ramp.

"Child," the priest said, turning to me. "What are you doing in this place?"

I explained to him my work on the clock.

He listened solemnly, pressing his lips together, giving me sidelong glances from eyes as big as a girl's.

After the oxen had pulled the bell to the tower, a large group of workmen took over. They shoved it through a large hole left open in the inner wall. Back at the mill I had seen ants like that —shoving a huge piece of something to their nest. The bell edged forward inch by inch, as exhausted men fell by the way and others took their place.

Inside the inner wall, the bell was secured to a great hawser. Then this ox-drawn rope, running through an overhead pulley, lifted the bell toward the roof. The only noise in the meadow was that of the oxen driver lashing his team with a whip.

As the bell completed its journey inside the tower and its brown shape appeared at the top, I turned to say, "Look," to the priest. But he was gone.

For a long time I stood with others and watched the men balancing on the stone rim of the tower, attempting to shackle the bell on the bar that would hold it. I thought of the man turning in air and lying then on his back, his open eyes troubled, his face pale and unlined and so young, and once again the horror of Hubert's death seized and shook me till I felt weak.

Why, I don't know, but I began thinking of my brother in the wood-carving shed. I couldn't ask him if he liked the workers, if he liked what he was doing. What might the world have in store for my brother when he reached Hubert's age? My mind snagged on that question the way Hubert had snagged on the half-submerged tree.

Men around me were cheering. The bell was secure. Yanking off my sock cap, I waved it in the crisp air of early spring and yelled along with my companions.

That evening, when I left the meadow, someone came toward me through the dusk.

"Ah" was the only sound that came from the priest as he smiled hesitantly.

We walked together, side by side. He made clear that he hadn't meant to speak against clocks. This was why he had returned to the meadow—to explain his opinion to me.

I looked at him in the dim light. He might have been as tall as Hubert, but much thinner. I could see his thinness despite the flowing robe.

As if he had waited a long time for the chance, he talked without stopping. In his opinion a clock would be good for the Church. It would help to improve the accuracy of services. The bishop had recently said so too, which is why the cathedral might someday get one.

I told him the bishop wanted a clock as an alarm for the bell warden. That meant more accurate ringing of the canonical services, but the clock wouldn't be used to let people know where they were in time every hour of the day.

He seemed less interested in the bishop's aims than in my knowledge of them. I could feel him brooding about that as we walked along in silence.

Suddenly I was near the house.

I feared being seen by Clotilda in the company of this handsome young priest, so I halted before getting there. It was nearly dark, and what I saw of his face was its long, thin outline.

We stood there awkwardly. I told him about Niklas, what a fine boy he was although he couldn't talk.

The priest was silent. I felt his eyes through the twilight as if they were a tool boring in, cutting through the dark air, getting to me with a cold, hard touch.

I told him how Niklas was learning to carve, so he might have employment. I paused. There was more silence.

Finally the priest said, "God takes special care of little children like your brother."

There was another silence. People were passing on either side, hunched into a crisp little wind.

"I must say good night, Father."

"Child," he began, lurching toward me. To my astonishment I felt his hand on mine, his fingers pressing mine with a furious strength that made me wince.

"Child," he said. "Young woman," he said. "This is the first time I have talked to someone, to a woman, in such—as if . . . but that is not so, not at all. It has been, I have enjoyed what we said. I have felt—"

Then he fled, vanishing quickly into the darkness, and I stood there perplexed within a surge of people heading home. Such feeling had there been in the pressure of his hand! But what feeling? Loneliness? Despair? Even love? Impossible. Not love. But the lust of a man? No, impossible. Not that.

Shaking off such odd thoughts, I went home.

Even so, I knew for certain that he would never come to the meadow again.

187

After we had eaten some porridge that evening, I brought Niklas and Rabbit (in his cage) back to the meadow. We let Rabbit out to nibble at tiny shoots of grass where workmen had not trampled them. I stood in the moonlight with Niklas, his hand in mine. We stared at the bulky wooden shapes in a ring around the tower.

The tower itself seemed enormous against the stars. A giant hand might have thrust it out of the earth and sent it flying toward heaven. We were watching it in midflight.

I couldn't see the bell below the timber roofing, but it was there, and it had my name on it. A miracle had happened to me.

Looking into the star-filled sky, I wondered where God was. Had He done this for me? Had I deserved such good fortune? Must I now pay for it?

Such questions faded into a moonlight that flowed across the meadow like white water.

"What a beautiful moon," I said to Niklas.

We watched it move across the sky and come to the tower. It vanished, then split in two, an arc on each side of the dark stone column. We looked until the moon emerged whole.

Glancing around to make sure of Rabbit's whereabouts, I squeezed the hand of my brother.

"Niklas," I said, "we have a tower now and a bell. Next we shall give them a clock."

25

"MASTER always says, 'We must let God decide.' What he means is let Master decide. He always knows what is good for him, what is good for him and for him alone."

I was sitting in the wood-carving shed, listening to some of the workers discussing Master Dollmayr while they wielded their chisels and gouges.

One of the carvers pulled a small ivory statue from his apron. "They are doing these things up north nowadays. I got this in the market." A few men gathered around and examined the little piece. "We could make things like it out of wood, but he says no. He says people want saints and nothing else. I say a knight or lovely lady will sell too."

"Let God decide," someone said.

They chuckled, one of them turning slightly to wink at me. I was accepted in their midst because of Niklas.

The old carver told me about my brother one day as we watched him bend over a jig-held block of wood with a gouge and hickory mallet.

"He can't talk and he's got white hair," said the old man with a smile, "but he can carve. Master says we can keep him only because the plague took off half the guild and we're short of workers. But that's not why. Master just wants an excuse not to pay him apprentice wages. The boy would belong here plague or no plague. He'll become a great carver."

"Then he really can learn?"

"I show him something and he just looks at me. Can't ask questions, can't say he understands or doesn't. I've learned, though, to trust him. Because I tell him and soon I see him driving a tool like I say—not against the grain, not with big cuts, not overworking a surface. I show him how to drive the gouge into wood about the length of his little fingernail, and when he drives it, I look and that's what he's done: the length of his little fingernail, no more, no less. He does what I show him."

We watched Niklas rough out the main shape of his carving. Quickly, easily, the chips fell away, revealing a saint in the attitude of prayer.

"See?" the old man said with satisfaction. "He handles a parting tool, a skew chisel, a riffler, like he'd had them in his hand a lifetime."

But Clotilda was not convinced of my brother's worth. I found her standing at the top of the third-floor stairs one day, studying me hard. There was something in her look that made me stop and wait.

"The boy," she said thoughtfully. "He's not right."

"He can carve."

The tall rawboned woman waved off my remark. "I don't

care about that. He can't speak, he's got white hair. He comes from another world. You've heard of the basilisk?''

"Yes, in sermons."

"Holy Writ says, 'Tread upon the adder and the basilisk.' One glance from a basilisk turns you to stone."

"Then my brother isn't one. He's turned nobody to stone in this house," I said.

"Maybe because he chooses not to. Maybe he's waiting for something first."

"For what?"

"For the end of the world. Mistress tells me it's coming. You're a bold thing, aren't you."

"Why?"

"Telling me he's turned no one to stone in this house. That's bold. But the wheel of fortune turns, even for a favored girl like you. One moment up, one moment down. One moment good fortune, bad the next," Clotilda said with a smile that chilled me. "Anyway, the boy isn't right."

Then another person judged my brother. This was a seller of art named Werimbold.

From things the carvers said about him I put together this picture of the man: He had lived on his peasant father's holding until old enough to fend for himself. Then he became a vagabond, taking his share of alms from abbeys, hiring out at harvest, enlisting at times of war. He joined caravans, sailed on cargo ships, became a beachcomber who looked for shipwrecks and from one of them accumulated goods enough to set up as a merchant. He made profit in coastal trade, then lost it all, and eventually turned to the sale of artworks. Werimbold bought loads of wood carving from the guild, which he sold at festivals.

The wood-carvers liked him because he was rough-and-tumble and did not pretend, when he sold the saints and Virgin, that he was performing acts of piety.

"He harvests on earth," someone said of Werimbold, "as if this place is where he'll be forever."

One day as I was returning from the tower, I met him coming from the house.

"Wait," he said. Werimbold was a short, thick man in leather breeches and a sleeveless jacket with fringed shoulders. But what marked him was a coiled turban of silk. What could such a man want of me? Yet he said, "Wait, Anne Valens."

"Sir."

"You have a brother?"

"I have."

"Look at this."

I studied at the statue he gave me from out of a bag. It was the Madonna and Child.

"Did my brother do this?" I asked.

"He's very good. He has feeling." Werimbold clapped one hand enthusiastically to his chest. "When he's older, I'll recommend him to the studio of a great sculptor." Bending toward me, the art merchant said in a low voice, "He belongs with better than these. They carve the same thing day after day. They're not chosen by God the way he is. Don't worry. I'll see to his future."

That night, when we lay on the blanket in darkness, I said to my brother, "Niklas, I talked to a man of importance today. He believes in you as I do. But he knows more about carving than I do, so what he thinks is more important. Someday he wants you to work with a great carver. I'm proud of you, Brother."

Two days later I again met Werimbold, but it seemed as if this time our meeting was by design. I had no sooner turned the corner into our street than he appeared at the stoop, sweeping his turban off and greeting me as a nobleman greets a lady.

I laughed uncomfortably.

Again he swept it through the air. "Lady, permit me a word with you." He behaved with such gravity that I laughed again, this time more freely.

"Beautiful sister of a great artist," he said with the measured intonation of a priest, "do me the honor of a glass of wine at the tavern. Do me that honor and I am content to die."

When I laughed again, so did he. Without more thought I went with him, for Werimbold was a man who had made me laugh.

When we reached the place, he called for a private room. I made no protest, for he had overwhelmed me with his manner.

Soon we were seated behind a closed door at a table with large cups of wine before us.

Werimbold removed the turban; he was almost bald. I saw that he was older than I had thought earlier.

He began to talk of the artists' guild. There was grumbling among the workers, and in his opinion some of them would leave to start their own business.

"Can that be done?"

"Oh, it can be. The duke and the Church don't own the city anymore. The bishop no longer excommunicates workers who ask for higher wages. The duke gets his tax money without threatening the guilds. There's freedom now. Even for women," he said. "Even for beautiful women like you."

The way he looked at me I understood that leaving this room without his permission would not be easy.

He said, "I hear you work on the clock. But it's hard to believe of such a pretty thing. How can that be?"

I told him about our uncle and my apprenticeship in the foundry, but Werimbold's eyes were telling me something as well: The look of me had distracted him from anything I might be saying. And indeed, he suddenly interrupted my talk of clocks.

"Please, dear lady, remove that cap."

I did so without hesitation, feeling my hair tumble about my shoulders.

Without more overture than a gasp of approval, Werimbold leaned forward to seize me. His lips burned on mine; then roughly he thrust his hand into my bodice.

When I pulled back, he frowned and sat back too.

"What's wrong, girl? Don't I please you?" His voice had a new rough sound.

"Sir," I began, and said no more.

"Come, silly. You work with men, don't you?"

"Yes, sir."

"Then tell the truth. Be honest, girl. Don't some of them have you?" he asked, leaning close again, leering.

In moments I was out of the tavern, rushing down the street. He did not try following. After a brisk walk I understood how disappointing to me that was. Had he kept after me, I would have gone back with him, surely. I could feel the decision in my loins. He was not handsome or pleasant and in his opinion I was loose enough, yet nature being what it is, I would have overlooked these flaws in him had he come after me with flattery again, with the promise of passion.

Did I have the look of looseness? This question, not Werimbold, followed me down the street.

I remembered the young priest who had walked with me from the tower. How he had gripped my hand with the sudden desperation of a lover. Would he have done so had I not encouraged him? Had I encouraged him? How? Was there something in my manner or eye that had set Werimbold on me? Gloomily, I glanced at men along the lane, wondering if they saw walking past them a creature of unbridled lust, as I had heard women described in sermons.

So I felt like a sinner without having sinned.

Within a few days the encounter with Werimbold gave me something besides sin to think about. I feared again for the future of my brother, realizing lust alone had brought on Werimbold's championing of him.

Every night, as I listened through the darkness to Niklas's breathing, I wondered if anyone aside from the old carver would ever help my brother.

26

THERE was trouble in the city and trouble for me.

It all began during the time we were assembling cogwheels and rods within the foundry shed, testing weights and balances, recasting when the parts didn't fit. The walls echoed from the filing of clockwork teeth and the drilling of holes to make lantern pinions.

Works Master Eberhart came daily to judge our progress. I could always tell from his lips if he had been scolded for imagined delays in the work. If Alderman Franklyn had berated him for something, his lips were small and tight and thin in his heavy face.

Workmen said he drank too much in the taverns and fondled boys there. For all his physical size, Eberhart was timid, gossipy, unsure of his power. I would have disliked him had he not liked the clock. But his enthusiasm, as the machine took shape in the foundry, seemed to match mine, and in this mood of shared appreciation for Uncle's clock I agreed to make the works master a set of drawings of his own.

"But don't tell the alderman," he said. "He would not want me to have them. Nothing pleases him."

Eberhart talked from the side of his mouth like a conspirator. "Nothing he does pleases others. Have you heard?" He was confiding in me as if I were a man. "The Corporation of the City has raised taxes again. This is to pay for the tower bell and the great door that's coming and the cobbling of the square. Merchants hate him for it. He's one of them, yet taxes them more than the duke ever did. That's the talk in the taverns. They paid less to the duke when the city was under his control by royal grant." Eberhart was smiling at the same time as he shook his head in disapproval.

"Everyone," he continued, "speaks against Alderman Franklyn. But after all, the clock was his idea, wasn't it? That's what everyone says. That's what you hear in the taverns. And the bishop's angry at him, too, because the Church doesn't have its own mechanical clock." Eberhart's face lit up at the thought of an angry prince of the Church. "The bishop might even excommunicate the alderman. Yes, that's the rumor. After all, it's sinful for the city to have a clock before the Church does. That's how the bishop reasons and many agree. So what about us? That's the question, isn't it? We're going to build another foundry and cast another clock for the cathedral—that's not a rumor, that's already been decided. Didn't you hear? After all, you work hard and understand the drawings, don't you? I think they should let you know these things. What was I saying? Not a big one, but a clock of any size costs money, and the cost will come out of the alderman's pocket."

Eberhart was chuckling and bobbing his head. "Yes, *out of his own pocket*. The Corporation won't pay for a clock that doesn't belong to the city. Why should they? So the alderman is responsible. He's going to give it to the Church out of piety. That's what he says. I've heard him, they've all heard him. Truth is, if the bishop isn't satisfied, he'll bring the king and nobility into a council and maybe call the city into ecclesiastical court—don't think I am just talking—and keep us from installing the clock, or at least that's what I hear in the taverns and what you hear there is generally true. So the alderman is forced to build another clock that no one will hear strike except the belfry guard in the cathedral." Eberhart guffawed. He enjoyed the trouble of others immensely.

"That's right. Only the bell ringer will hear this new clock. According to the bishop a clock should be used as alarm and alarm only. It should be guarded like a relic deep in the womb of the Church." Liking that idea, Eberhart chortled loudly and smacked his thigh.

"So the bishop's clock won't help the city, it won't draw caravans this way. The alderman is beside himself with fury."

I had never seen Eberhart look happier. "And then there's the problem of the city clock sounding the hours—how many times a day ought it to strike? Just during daylight hours or all twenty-four? Every guild seems to have a different opinion. I've heard them arguing in the taverns. Then there's the larger problem—wages."

Eberhart moved his head from side to side and rolled his great eyes in the big face. "Wages, girl. Wages, wages, wages. For the merchants, believe me, it's a worse problem than ever. Plague has taken off half the workers, yet those left are refused more pay. Why? they ask. Isn't that a proper question? You should hear them grumbling in the taverns." Eberhart was smiling at the doorway of the foundry, as if Alderman Franklyn might stagger through it with the whole city at his heels.

"I tell you, Anne, the alderman is not happy these days." Eberhart was beaming. "I wouldn't want to be the fellow, believe me. When he told me to build the bishop's clock, I said to him boldly, for you know how I am, I said, 'Alderman Franklyn, I will build it, but who will pay for it?' You should have seen his face—red as a forge—when he said it was going to be his gift to God. Furious, he was utterly furious. But doesn't he know, to have power you must pay for it? Every day he comes around yelling orders and talking about the pride of the city and displaying himself. Well, for the privilege he must pay." Eberhart pursed his lips in satisfaction.

"I hear he's fortified his house. A nasty bunch of mercenaries are camping in his yard, befouling it with cooking fires and threatening his servants. People call him a coward. Yet I don't blame him. In his shoes I would worry about defending myself. No doubt about that," Eberhart declared with a triumphant sigh. "He's made the Church furious and his merchant friends too. Yet in his shoes I'd rather face all of them than step unprotected into the square among grumbling workers. I'd fear the square if I were him."

People had begun calling the meadow a square. The meadow had changed beyond recognition since I had first seen the tower standing alone in the middle of it. The meadow seemed to have shrunk in size. Behind the front row of buildings that encircled the tower, another row had been built and yet another. Buildings sprang up all along the lanes that converged at the tower. It loomed over guildhall, tavern, and stall as if a great stone net had drawn into its presence more than half the city. Shops of tailors and chandlers and saddlemakers and coopers and cloth merchants clustered around it the way pious men gather around a saint.

For months—ever since the citizenry understood what the tall stone building would contain—workmen from many trades had gathered in the meadow to squint up at the round sides of the tower. They all asked the same question: Would the clock bring prosperity?

The guildsmen had no idea how that might happen, but the size of the tower and the mystery of a thing striking inside it suggested to them that something strange and perhaps wonderful or possibly terrible was going to happen to the city, and whatever happened would somehow empty or fill their pockets. Then in the midst of gentle spring the question grew so loud, so urgent, that something did happen.

We were in the square, Niklas and Rabbit in his cage and me. It was a Sabbath afternoon and seemed as though the whole countryside as well as the townspeople had come here for a stroll. The cobbling had been completed, so we all walked on stone, and I watched people staring at the rough hard surfaces their sandaled feet moved across.

It was a hot day, so I stopped a wine crier and bought a cup for myself and Niklas. My brother smiled as the crier pulled a stopper of hemp on the leather flagon and poured the rich red liquid.

I said as we drank, "Ah, Niklas, we are home at last."

Handing the cup back with my coin, I said to the crier, "Thank you," but he didn't hear me. His voice was already raised to the crowd again, telling them how tasty the Narbonne was. And it was.

We strolled on, attracted by a crowd gathering near the west side of the tower. Over their heads we could see a man waving his arms and talking. Coming nearer, we saw him standing on a hooped barrel.

The man was small and weathered, with hands too big for the rest of him. As he swung them through the air, I watched their broad palms and knobby joints.

"See there? See there?" he was saying when we joined the crowd.

Both huge hands were flexing toward the west. "That's where I give my heart's blood every day. I'm a fuller of wool, I full it the whole day long—beating and pressing and beating and pressing. A lot of us do business not a hundred feet from where I'm standing."

I knew that all right. The woolmaking guilds had moved their sheds and equipment into the neighborhood, overrunning the west side of the square.

"I'm here to talk about that clock," he shouted at the crowd, and someone shouted back, "We don't need it! Take it away!"

The man on the barrel squinted narrowly. "Who said that?"

"I did," said a man. "Who wants to think of time? God takes us soon enough."

People tittered.

"Is that what you think the clock is for? To remind you of death?" asked the fuller grimly.

"Well, I do my work, I eat, I sleep. Why tell me all day long I'm getting closer to the grave?"

The fuller smiled. "You're a fool. You are all fools, if you don't see the truth," he said, looking over the crowd. "Because that thing striking the hours up there can help you—help all of us."

His gaze kept sweeping the crowd as he told them that if time is known, they could be paid by time. Instead of getting paid by the number of pieces done, like the carders and weavers of the wool trade, they could get paid by how long they worked. "That means the masters can't force you to work harder than you want. Your master is the clock."

"Who understands what you're saying?" someone called out. "How do we get better pay out of rich merchants?"

There was a swell of approval in the crowd. I noticed a man grinning at me, winking before I could turn away.

The fuller kept trying to explain. He said a merchant can hire you to work the day, but if it's a summer day, you work a long, long time—look at the dyers and fullers of the wool trade. But what if you hire out for exactly ten hours, for ten strikes of the bell in the tower and only ten? Think of it. That way you get the same pay summer and winter.

So he understands the clock, I thought.

But someone yanked him off the barrel and took his place. This was a big man who held a long-handled scythe with lateral grips. He must have come from the countryside.

"Listen to me!" His voice boomed through the square. "The poor alone are righteous and at Judgment Day they will stand before the rich and judge them for their sins on earth. 'Why did you take bread from our mouths? So you could live in fine houses? Why did you steal from hay merchants, from chandlers? Why did you steal from masons? Why did you make us so poor in the countryside that our daughters came here to sell themselves in taverns?' And the rich at their judgment will cry out, 'Ah, these people who were nothing now sit at the feet of the Lord!' "

"Get down, get down!" people were shouting impatiently. In spite of his size and the scythe, he was pulled down and someone else mounted the barrel.

A kind of snaky motion rippled through the crowd, and I felt for a moment a terrible fear, as if the force of a flooded river were surging into the square. But the feeling passed. I edged Niklas away.

"Come, let's look at the doors. You haven't seen them yet."

We circled the tower until reaching its entrance. The doors of paneled wood had come from afar. In each panel had been carved a scene describing Good Government under God. There were prelates and aldermen on their knees before the Eternal Throne. Poor men received alms. Oxen pulled wagons filled with produce along streets lined with churches and guild-halls. Men carried spades. Angels gazed down approvingly.

While I looked at the wrought-iron hinged plates that had been hammered into scrollwork, Niklas went up close to study each carved figure on the panels.

"Someday," I said, "you'll do such carving. Not just small pieces of wood as you do for Master Dollmayr, but great planks like these. Men will come to you from afar, just as men of this city went far away to find the man who carved this door. And such men, Niklas, will ask you to carve for them. You already carve as good a linen fold as I see here." I pointed to the design that ran along one side of a panel. "Someday you will carve a great likeness of Jesus Crucified."

Late into the afternoon we strolled through the city, coming at sunset to the river. In our nostrils was a pungent stench from tanneries we had passed: burning oak and fermented bran and the pigeon dung used for softening hides. At the waterfront we looked at boats tied alongside docks.

"Some of them have come from the East," I told Niklas. "Smell that? It's spice from the East. Someday the two of us will go there and see the men with three heads and the lions that fly. I'll build a clock and you can carve them statues for their churches, because it's said even the heathens pray."

Coming back from the piers in the misty dusk, I noticed above the rooftops a spurt of flame. We had not walked ten steps farther before I heard a shriek in the air that made me halt and grip my brother's hand.

Then I yanked him with me against a store wall, because

lurching around the corner and rushing down the street came a great mob of men and boys, waving staves and knives and axes and pitchforks and billhooks. They were stumbling and wobbling and screaming "Death to them! Death to them!"

As they passed, I spread my body as flat as possible against the wall, holding Niklas tightly by the hand. I could feel the air of their violent passage on my back, and their cries of "Death to them!" rang in my ears.

A boy smaller than Niklas, holding a rusty old dagger, came by. Reaching out, I grabbed his arm.

"What is happening?" I demanded.

His large frightened eyes stared at me without seeing. "Death to them," he said.

"Death to them? Who?"

Pulling free he yelled, "Merchants!"

Slowly, with Niklas's hand in mine, I edged up the street and turned the corner. What I saw again brought me to a halt. A three-story house was on fire. From the ground floor came a series of rapid screams, a deeper shout, another shout. I knew what was happening in there from the sounds even before she leaned out of the window, retching blood, her naked breasts on the sill. The next moment a man had dumped her out on the street, naked, dying, and I said, "Mother."

A group of men were holding someone spread-eagled on the ground. As we edged past them, I glimpsed the fallen man gripping a billhook handle while one of his tormenters was twisting it deeper into his stomach.

"Who are you?" one of the onlookers said, catching my eye. He had a gold cup in his hand and lifted it to drink.

In that moment I ran, holding on to Niklas.

Farther along the way were other men carrying bits of furniture, tapestries draped on their shoulders. A few of them wore elegant gloves over their rough hands and fancy hoods and winter robes of camel hair and long loops of pearls over their sweaty jerkins. They were laughing, drinking from gold decanters, chalices of silver. One man held in his big hand a mass of linen wimples of various colors, as if he were a maid bringing her mistress a selection to choose from.

"Come here!" someone yelled at me. My heart stopped

when I saw him and two companions start across the street, axes in hand, a spillage of wine trailing their heavy steps.

There was a lane nearby and I turned blindly into it, with Niklas holding my outstretched hand. We rushed into the gathering darkness, knocked once into someone, and raced from lane to lane until a tug at my hand brought me finally to a halt.

Niklas was gasping, unable to go on.

I noticed a narrow alley. We crept into it, and with just enough light left for looking, I found some hooped barrels stacked at the far end. We got behind them, squatted down. The oily smell of pickled fish surrounded us as evening closed in. We stayed within the circle of this smell, hearing that whole night long such cries of terror and pain that the hair of my neck stood on end, and countless shouts of fury and the crackling of fires and the heavy swishing sound of houses falling, until I told Niklas, "It is the end of the world."

At dawn I looked at Niklas, who had never let go of Rabbit's cage one moment of the night.

"So it is not the end," I said to him. "We'll try to get home now." Rising slowly, we moved around the barrels into the alley. A light rain was falling, so the way was muddy.

I think I was looking down at my sandals, splattered by mud, before they turned the corner at us.

And there they were, two men.

One of them, the shorter, was wearing a sallet, cocked jauntily to one side. From the looks of them, they were workers, so they must have got the helmet by looting or worse. The taller man held a flagon and kept sweeping it through the air so the wine erupted out of it in tiny spurts. I remember well.

"Who are you?" the taller one asked drunkenly as they approached.

There was no way around them.

"I work on the tower."

"On the what?" asked the helmeted man.

"Where they are putting the clock."

"You haul stone?"

"Yes," I told him.

201

"You don't look that strong." He grinned first at me, then at his companion.

I looked at Niklas, who must have understood the danger, for he had encircled the cage with both arms.

"Where are you going?" asked the helmeted man.

"Home." I could smell the strong smell of leather.

"No, you're not."

And they were on me. In an instant, I saw the tall one hit Niklas, who had lunged between us, still clutching the cage. As I went down, I saw my brother go down, and I screamed.

I don't know how many times I screamed, until one of them stunned me with a blow. Then I lay there, saying something. I believe I said, "Don't hurt us, don't hurt us," even while one of them, pulling my skirt up, began hurting me.

I was silent then, perhaps even patient. I was waiting patiently for time to get me beyond these moments. And yet a voice inside my head kept yelling, "Thief! Thief!" as if someone were stealing my drawings of the clock, for they were all I had, all save the body these men were taking from my governance. The voice inside was yelling, though I was not.

Then the other took his turn.

Seeing I was calm, the helmeted man did not bother to pin my arms, but sat moodily apart, looking above us at the wall, while I stared at him without ever getting his attention. I smelled leather. The smell of it was overpowering.

When the tall man was done, they left. They staggered into the early light of day without a word. Rolling over, I searched for Niklas and saw him where he had fallen.

His eyes were open. He was looking at me. I sat up, embarrassed by his gaze. They had not torn my bodice in their eagerness. Pulling the rumpled skirt down, I got to my feet and went to Niklas.

Then I saw why he hadn't straightened himself. When they had knocked him down, the cage had gone down, too, and broken. Rabbit had got out and gone to Niklas. Hunched up, breathing hard, Rabbit shivered against my brother's chest.

When I asked Niklas if he was all right, he looked at me.

"It's all right," I told him, hearing the smallness of my voice.

"God has taken care of us. Look—Rabbit is all right. We must leave this place. We must get out of it."

I took them through the smoky streets and lanes, past torn bodies and smoldering fires and men staggering into daylight.

At the river I told Niklas to wait. I walked to the edge—the river had the look of metal in gray morning—and lifting my skirt I stepped into the icy water, going into it to my waist. Then I washed vigorously, glad to be alive, to feel the sting of coldness against my legs, between them.

Getting out and drying myself with the hem of my skirt, I went to my brother, who stood on the bank, holding the cage.

Trying to stay calm, I said, "Now we go home. It's all right. God has saved us. The three of us are together."

27

THE next day was the Feast of Saint Martin, but the city did not seem to know it. I lay on the blanket in our dark attic room and heard distant human cries instead of cathedral bells ringing out a joyous time. With eyes closed, I felt now and then the soft padded paws of Rabbit touching my side, my arm, my forehead, as he hopped around to avoid raindrops falling through cracks in the roofing.

Niklas left us early, going as he should go into the wood-carving shop for his daily work, though none of the guild carvers had come today. Surely all of them were tucked away somewhere safe, out of the turmoil promised by distant voices of horror and fury.

For myself, I heard little of it. The telltale sounds of fighting rarely got past the memory of yesterday. Since returning home, I had curled up, knees to belly. I tried to forget and in so trying, failed to let go of the slightest detail. Often I dozed, but that was worse, because in dreams both known and unknown demons sought me. The known demons came out of the past: the soldier with sheepskin mittens who butchered our mother; the bearded knight on horseback; the two men barring my way in the alley at dawn. And though by scrubbing my legs in the icy current I had cleansed my body of those men, my nose was still clogged with the earthy smell of leather. I remembered everything, awake or dreaming.

How would I look at the world tomorrow?

Twice in my life I had crouched beyond the border of violence and watched. Yesterday I had been within that border, feeling on my own body the heat of violence. How could the world go on as it had done? Not only for me but for everyone? God Himself must have witnessed what happened, and if He loved me as a suffering child, would He not, today, bring the whole world within my circle of pain? Would He not say, "One of my children, however humble, has suffered"? "You cannot go on as before," He would say to the world. "Because one child has suffered, every life will be changed forever."

But if that were so, then long before my own misfortune, we would have all known and suffered the misfortunes of others. Such ideas rushed through my head like mice scrambling between roofing boards.

Such ideas at last roused me from the blanket. I stood up to shake them away, and in so doing discovered with surprise that I was hungry. So I knew my life would go on.

Going downstairs and slipping into the kitchen, I faced Clotilda, who eyed me curiously and asked why I was not at work.

Cook, standing there, turned and raised her eyebrows. "What decent person is going outside today? Who wants to die?"

Clotilda pinched her lips, studying me. "What's wrong?" she asked.

"Wrong?" I said.

"You heard me. Something's wrong. What's happened?"

"Nothing."

"Something's wrong."

Cook said, "The girl's frightened. Leave her alone." And turning to me the stout woman said gently, "Master has stationed a gang of toughs outside with swords and war hammers. They look as fierce as soldiers. We are safe."

"Something's wrong," Clotilda repeated, staring at me.

"And the duke has sent men to town," Cook said, brandishing a ladle. "There will be a lot more butchery before this day's done."

"Are you sick?" Clotilda asked sharply.

"No," I said.

"Is it fright, then? You look awful."

"Leave the girl alone. It's a terrible time."

"What happened yesterday?" I asked Cook.

She began stirring a huge black pot with the ladle. "There were speeches in the square about justice and money. Then the talk continued in taverns. Men grew bold enough to go looking for merchants. One thing led to another, I suppose. Anyone who looked like a merchant was killed. Houses were fired even if merchants didn't live in them. Some guildsmen fired that magistrate's house up the street. And women, well, you can imagine what happened to anyone getting caught. But now the duke's men have come. Don't you worry, girl."

During this explanation Clotilda had left the room. And as Cook fed me—more generously than usual—I wondered if Clotilda herself wasn't afraid.

Next day I went to work, learning from smiths at the foundry that there had been a pitched battle on the city bridge. The duke's mounted men in full armor had rushed a group of rioting workmen, who panicked and fled, only to be cut down by the men-at-arms swinging axes and swords from their horses. It was slaughter. I heard that hundreds died, but did I care? What had happened to my body had numbed me to the misfortunes of others.

Walking to the square next day, I noticed on gibbets erected near the cathedral a line of six hanging men. One of them I recognized from his big hands, which swelling had made even bigger.

I stared at his bloated head, at his tongue lolling from an open twisted mouth, at his huge hands, which in life had moved gallantly through the air while he spoke of what the clock could mean to workingmen.

And at that moment I understood something about my life. From the fate of most other raped women—talk of them was everywhere—I should have been murdered in the alley. But my attackers had walked away when they were done. They had not killed me by plan—not their plan but His plan. God may have been indifferent to my suffering, but had kept me alive for a purpose.

He had spared me because of the clock.

Then it seemed as if I understood something about God Himself: He was not so much indifferent as bent upon the achievement of a plan. Like workers who hated merchants for being rich and like merchants who despised workers for being powerless—each intent upon his own interest—God turned neither right nor left as He studied His own interest in the world.

It was a strange and terrifying idea that stayed with me each moment of coming days that I spend measuring and judging the clockwork.

A new idea took shape in my mind: God was like a clock. Each moment of time was planned by God, who cared only that it clicked past the crown wheel of His mind.

So I came to think in those days. If the world was a clock, so was God.

Such thoughts were the kind my uncle might have had in the sanctity of his workshop, and I welcomed the way they could protect me from memory. But sometimes the thoughts didn't come and I was prey to memory, as I had been to the two men. At these times I often cried, the tears sudden and torrential, like a summer storm. And sometimes memory wasn't needed for them to begin. In our room I would hear the heavy tread of my brother's footsteps on the ladder and a downpour would start from my swollen eyes that nothing could stop. I bent double, holding my sides, as if this action might bottle up the tears, but the tears came anyway. At such times I turned my back on Niklas and faced the wall, with eyes fixed on the floorboards. I felt him watching me from his own tear-filled eyes, and I wanted more than anything to flee from his watching. He had seen my shame in the alley. My only consolation was that he had not been full-grown, like Hubert, and so had not tried to stop those men, or they would have killed him.

One afternoon as I sat hunched in the corner, feeling the

tears well up from the dark spring of memory, I heard him behind me and the next thing, I felt his hand in mine. Turning, I saw in the dim light that he was looking at me and I fought to avoid his eyes. But his held mine. He would not let me look away. Gripping his hand hard, I let him look into my eyes and see my shame and what he gave back to me was his own love. I felt that. And afterward, in the passing days, I cried less often.

Some weeks after the riot, I saw one of my attackers on the street. It was the shorter man who had worn an iron helmet cocked to one side.

The jaunty helmet was gone now. He was lugging a saddle. Grasping the pommel and the cantle with both hands, he shuffled forward with the leather skirt and hanging flaps knocking against his legs.

I was standing across the muddy lane and could smell the leather. It was a powerful odor coming from his skin as well as the saddle and it put me horribly in mind of the alley. He came along heavily, struggling with the weight in his hands. There was a stubble of beard on his square face. His eyes were red and veined. In memory I had made of him a man of more terrible aspect, but he looked almost helpless behind the big saddle.

Yet I wanted a sword—to rush with it into his path.

"You!" I would shout. "Why did you hurt me?" And then with arms as powerful as Hubert's I would swing the sword and kill him.

But that would be too easy. He would be gone in an instant with no understanding of how he had hurt me.

"Why did you hurt me?" I would shout and lop off one of his hands. But they had done that to my father. I could never do such a thing, never.

I tried to think of other bloody revenge, but the struggling saddlemaker was nearly past me.

So without thinking, I bent and shoved my hand between my feet, scooping up a mound of black stinking mud.

When I hastily threw it, some of the mud splattered across the saddle, a few gouts against his face. He turned to face me a dozen feet away. His mouth dropped open in recognition.

I opened mine to say something, but not a word came out. I wanted to hurt him as he had hurt me, to kill him forever in my

207

mind. But we just looked at each other, while bits of mud slid down his stubbled face. He stared in bewilderment, then, I really believe, in reproach, as if I had truly injured him. He stepped out slowly, one foot in front of the other, bearing the saddle fixed with plates of iron and hammered metal. I watched the tired little journeyman turn the corner.

I should have killed him.

Looking down at my muddy hands, I felt ashamed. There is no worse torment in the world than helplessness. All the way home I held an imaginary conversation with my brother.

I met him, Niklas—the shorter one with the helmet. If I had been a man, I would have killed him with one sword stroke. I smelled the leather and the smell maddened me and I wanted blood. As it was, I hit him with a clod of mud and he walked on. So there is my revenge. And I still have my shame. And this strange thought: God is a clock and His world is a clock, but we in it do not always work as clocks. We are sometimes broken things, with no sense of what to do. Yet we live in His clockwork. We live in the fixed machine but are blown around like dust. That's a mystery our uncle might not solve.

I understood, on the way home, I would never speak such despairing words to Niklas. I would learn to live with shame until it went away. As for revenge, I had taken as much of it as the world might offer to a girl.

Once home, mounting the ladder slowly, I peered through the gloom to see Niklas crouched in the corner, holding something. Going closer, I saw that he was holding Rabbit, whose legs were stretched out stiffly.

Rabbit was dead.

I sat beside my brother and touched the cold brown furry body that he held.

"Niklas," I said, "dear Brother."

We sat awhile in silence before I said, "Maybe he was cooped up too long. Rabbits need room. Or maybe he got fever. They get fever. But he had a good life with us. He was happy. Always remember that—how happy he was. Niklas, you must understand: Rabbits don't live as long as we do."

He wouldn't understand, of course, so we sat together in the growing darkness, our only light a glow from the roofing cracks. We sat through the tolling of vespers from the cathedral. He held Rabbit, while I laid my hand on his arm.

Next morning, at dawn, we left the city through the east gate and buried Rabbit in a copse of greenery not far from the road. He would not let me dig. I waited until the hole was big enough, then together we lowered Rabbit in his cage into the grave.

"Holy Lord," I said when we had covered it and knelt with steepled hands beside the newly turned earth. "Please take to Your bosom our friend Rabbit, who never harmed anything on earth. We loved him and we hope You love him too."

I did not tell Niklas the dark secret that made such hopeful words of mine a lie in my mouth. With whatever understanding my brother had, surely he believed that God loves. Or so I hoped for his sake.

After retracing our steps from the woodland and leaving Niklas at the house, I went to work at the foundry. On this day we decided that the parts were ready for installation in the tower. I felt myself trembling. We had to test the clock in place. We had to measure the length of rope needed for the stone weight that by rising and falling would give the clock its power. Any mistakes from this moment on would mean disassembly within the tower, would mean delays, would mean threats from Alderman Franklyn, and perhaps would mean more trouble from workmen uncertain that clocks bring prosperity.

Carpenters had put a floor beneath the bell, so I could go to the top of the tower and stand at the parapet, only a few feet from the cool, silent bell that bore my name. The Corporation, so Eberhart had told me, was still debating whether the clock must sound every hour of the day. I hoped all twenty-four would be struck, for though I disliked Alderman Franklyn, I shared his ambition. If the clock struck every hour of sunless time, our city would be conquering darkness. And conquering darkness was surely desired by the Almighty, for every creature comes from His divine illumination and every agent of Satan stems from darkness. The clock stood for God Himself.

So I felt in those days.

From the tower I looked down at the jumble of red roofs,

forgetting awhile the pain and horror that could so easily take place beneath them. Standing above the city, buffeted by swift currents of air, I knew that God had willed what was happening. When the first pure note of the struck bell was heard across rooftops, we could be sure that God had spoken.

28

PIECE by piece the clockwork was lifted to the top of the tower. The burnished metal swung on a rope toward a pulley attached to the parapet. I watched each rod and cogwheel go up, like living things, like rabbits or fish or boys or birds, up up up in the sky.

Then we assembled the clock, putting the going and striking trains side by side, with their weights dropped through holes in the flooring. Assembled, it would stand higher than my hands stretched over my head, and its width would measure three times the length of my body. As we bolted the frame to the thick planking of the floor and fit gear to rod, the clock began to resemble a shiny black creature of some sort, maybe a crouching basilisk or monstrous leviathan, as I imagined them from sermons delivered on Holy Writ.

Except the clock was on the side of the angels. Of that I was certain, even if clerics regarded it as a machine of Satan (they climbed the stairway to stare at it with narrow suspicious eyes) and merchants feared the change it might bring to their profit, and workmen, to their pay.

A dozen of us kept at the assembly a fortnight. But when all the wheels were fastened to their seatings and the lantern pinions fitted and the rods inserted and the ropes wound on the two drums and the stone weights dropped below to swing a bit before settling, when everything had been done and we sighed and smiled at one another, the clock failed to work.

Two months passed before it did.

Wheels had to be taken off. Steel jigs and files came into play again, as new wheels were cast and punch-marked and drilled and their teeth shaped. We changed stone weights on both trains, first lengthened and then shortened the ropes attaching them to their barrels.

Alderman Franklyn was there to watch everything, his lump of left eye an angry red. Fiercely he would slew his head around to face people from the left, as if he could see through the puckered flesh.

The daily abuse that Works Master Eberhart took from the alderman was then bequeathed to me. Unable to shout back at his employer, Eberhart looked around and singled out the girl among men. Following his example, workmen began grumbling about me too. By overhearing snatches of their conversation, I understood they were blaming the strange unnatural girl for trouble with the clock. Her drawings had been wrong. She was too young. She was a woman. She might well be an agent of Satan. At any rate, she lacked sense and courage and everything else, I suppose, they might think of.

I turned away from them and thought of the clock.

At twilight, when the others had left, I would climb the stairway to the top of the tower and lean over the parapet, where the air was pure and swift and I could clear my head of doubts. There was nothing wrong with the drawings. We just didn't know how to measure things properly. If Uncle were alive, he might find a way, but no one here understood the numbers well enough to solve every problem of installing a large clock. I would come down the steps of the tower comforted by that truth.

In fact, I grew bolder, as if to prove my value. I went to Eberhart with a plan to put in a jack. Before the clock had struck a single hour with a simple hammer, I wanted a man-sized wooden jack sculptured and rigged and run along an iron track. I told Eberhart we could fix a war mace to the jack's hand, so a soldier of the city, instead of a plain hammer, might strike the hours. It would only require a bit more mechanism. We could run it on a track attached to the vertical shaft of the striking train. The shaft was already placed, coming into the bell chamber through the flooring from the clockwork below. It would be simple to gear. The jack's war hammer would swing by using a horizontal wheel meshed to a gear on the track.

Eberhart looked at me as if I had lost my mind, then walked away.

As work neared completion, I grew even bolder and went to him with the idea of attaching an outside dial to the face of the tower. I tried to recall Uncle's explanation for such a possibility, when I told Eberhart we could drill through the tower, insert a rod-and-gear system, and by this method operate the pointer. We could have a six- or twelve-numbered dial.

It would be simple, I argued.

This time he pushed past me like a plow horse.

Then the day came that we let the clock strike: The weights with their length of rope were correct for providing the right amount of power; the rhythm of the foliot was set after days of trial and error; each gear and rod functioned with the precision of the sun.

When the hammer struck the bell, we all cheered, even Alderman Franklyn.

Yet that night I felt let down. Now that the divine plan had been achieved, would God have any more use for me?

Each day after the first striking, I climbed to the clockwork chamber and watched the metal at its complicated whirring. Time, I began to see, did not follow a slow seamless path, like the sun across the heavens. Time was chopped up. It was the one-and-two and the one-and-two of someone walking. Of a falling leaf, falling not in one smooth motion but in countless jerks, at each stop remaining motionless for an instant, then dropping into another stop. Ticktock through the autumn air so quickly that the falling leaf seemed to go down in one smooth continuous line.

If what I thought was true, the world was not what it seemed. God had other plans than we knew.

Could this be what Uncle had discovered? That God saw the world in a way we did not? I was sure now that the world moved in little pieces, sliced from the motion of wheels and rods. I wondered if what God gave us to see was never what He Himself saw or perhaps even what He meant by creation.

The thought of peeking into a secret of the Almighty gave me forbidden pleasure—like sin. Like rolling on the warm earth with Hubert and receiving him without proper marriage into my body.

Once the bell had been struck, everything changed in the square. Masons and plasterers and carpenters and other workmen pulled down their tents, packed their tools, and left. It was as if they had never been there and the tower had raised itself. I was relieved that the founders remained. There was plenty of work for them in the city.

As for the merchants, they listened to the clock, and I heard them say among the crowded lanes, "Time is money."

It was a strange thing to say, but as the clock tolled every hour, the words caught on. Shopowners opened and closed their shutters according to the struck bell. Rain or shine, they conducted their business according to sounds coming from the tower. So time had indeed become money.

I began to understand another thing about time. Instead of its being linked to the events of the city, time led a separate life. But the city changed according to time, its life controlled by what happened in the tower. So in a way the clock didn't exist for the city as much as the city existed for the clock.

As I strolled through the lanes, hearing the bell toll, I felt how securely, in spite of itself, the city was caught in the ironworks of the clock like an insect in a spiderweb.

Was it good that the clock had so much power?

It was a question I couldn't answer. Already the clock had caused a riot. There was continued grumbling among workers who no longer wished to be paid by what they produced but by how long they labored.

Others, like master masons, were against payment by time. Time, they argued, was a leveler. Any fool could breathe through the same number of hours as a man of skill. Clocks were on the side of the lazy, the unfit.

Guild councilmen agreed. Paying by time would lead to sloppy work in trades producing a great quantity of goods. Spinners and weavers already failed to make cloth that met guild standards. What might they do when the quality of their work was less important than the time they spent on it?

Yet other guild merchants saw value in the idea of payment by time. In winter they would get as much work from their men as they did in summer—and winter was longer.

In every street of our city such ideas were debated. It was a world my parents would not have understood. What they had known of time was the change of seasons that affected the mill.

Each day I looked up at the bell that bore my name and wondered what we had done.

At least this was sure: We had done what someone else would have surely done. There was no holding the clock back. We had acted the way rivers do when they flow as they must.

And we had conquered darkness, as God must have wanted us to do in the struggle of Good against Evil. To conquer darkness: surely that was the Divine reason for our clock. Its working was a way to bring us out of night. Because of the steady tolling, we knew where we were in time, though around us the air might be as black as pitch, as filled with demons as hell.

There was mankind's reason for the clock too. Out of civic pride the Corporation had decided to sound each hour of day and night. Our ramparts were fixed like a rock in the stream of eternity. Our clock went back and forth like a cradle, for we lived now in a world that had a future.

And from the cathedral, at the time of canonical hours, came the deep-throated tolling of a bell matched to our own. The alarm clock obtained by the bishop enabled the belfry guardian to strike his bell with ours, and the competing sound vibrated through the streets: it was like the glad noise of God's trumpets.

Such a steady and joyous ringing of time told me I was not done with clocks. I wanted to help with the making of better ones.

So I was happy to hear that Eberhart had been asked to build another clock in a far-off city. He would take me, of course, and I would bring Niklas and the world would move along.

But when I went to see Eberhart, the world seemed to stop. The works master was going alone. He told me that, curtly. "You cannot go with me, Anne. I am going alone."

"But I can help."

"I am going alone."

"Haven't I done my work?"

He didn't answer.

I was accustomed to his gossip and love of rumor and also to his bluster and shouting. This new manner seemed to match his great bulk of body. Overnight he had become slow, heavy—not the man to fondle boys and drink in the taverns.

When I claimed that he needed both me and my drawings, Eberhart shook his head.

"I have the drawings you made for me. And I can read them now."

At that moment I saw him at his next job: bragging in a tavern how he had made his own drawings for the last clock.

Two canvas bags were sitting beside an anvil. I saw my drawings wrapped with hide into a long tube.

"Uncle taught me things," I said. "You wouldn't be sorry if I went along."

Bold as I was, I couldn't find words to say that the house of my uncle had been a place of magic and in its workshops I had learned not only about clocks but about things I didn't yet know I knew, so powerful had the mind of my uncle been in teaching me.

"We have been friends," I simply added.

Eberhart shrugged, as if that was not important.

"Even when you shouted at me, I knew it was only to get the work done. It was because of the alderman."

"You're saying I feared him?"

"We all feared him."

"I have never feared anyone save God," Eberhart boasted.

My drawings were within reach. I might snatch them up and run and what then? In thinking of them I forgot Eberhart until his big frame passed in front of my eyes from tool rack, where he had been standing, to anvil.

Reaching down, he took up the rolled drawings. So he had them for sure now.

"What you do is not right," he said.

"What have I done wrong?"

"My friends used to talk about you—"

"In the taverns?"

"They said what I say: Women should cook, clean—"

"And carry stones," I said.

"Women do not build clocks."

"They do if they were taught by a man like my uncle. Can I help it if he changed my life?"

But Eberhart had turned away.

Walking into the square, I looked up at the tower, amazed by what was happening to me: All of a sudden I had nothing to do. I could not even wind the clock. That was done by ironsmith Barnabas, who had been put in charge of it. The clock had nothing more to do with me. I was now a stranger to it.

But I was no stranger to metals, I thought.

Going to the foundry, I spoke to the new master in charge there. He was a short broad-shouldered fellow who looked me up and down boldly with a smile.

"So you know foundrywork, pretty girl?"

"Ask anyone. I know metals."

"Put on twice your weight. Build your arms up twice their size. Then come back and I'll try you at the anvil and if that doesn't work, I've got something else in mind I'll try you at."

The foundrymen laughed along with him, though most of them knew me. I had bent with them over my drawings, our sweat mingling on the paper. I had spent hours with them in the glow of the forge, yet now they laughed at me.

The alderman's goldsmith shop was nearby. I stood awhile at the open shutters and looked inside. One smith was hammering a plaque, another incising a cross, and behind them stood a smith at an anvil. A boy was lifting a bellows from a hook. A counter that ran the length of the shop was scattered with calipers, hammers, drills.

Then I saw Alderman Franklyn emerging from a back room. Seeing me, he scowled yet came forward.

I kept my gaze steady on the red lump of flesh and told him my desire to work as a goldsmith apprentice.

When I had finished, the alderman nodded. For a moment my hopes rose.

Then he said, "What insolence. I always thought you were an

insolent girl," he said quietly. "What makes you think I would apprentice you? The guild would never hear of it. And, of course, I wouldn't want you. The idea is absurd."

"But, sir—"

"You brought your uncle's drawings here. You helped a bit— for which you were paid. Now it is over. If you need work, look to service in a home as any decent girl your age would do."

The rest of that day I went from merchant to merchant in the square. I went aimlessly, searching as much for a purpose in life as for work. Most of the merchants had known me a long time, had questioned me about the clock, had seen me at the side of Alderman Franklyn and the works master. Yet in each frowning face I read the same message: My acceptance among men had been the result of need; without that need I must do the work of women.

And so I did.

Returning to the house, I went to Master Dollmayr and asked for service.

To my surprise Clotilda spoke in my behalf, and of course that settled it. I was hired to do chores.

Although only a miller's daughter, I knew how to read and write. Our uncle had favored me and because of him so had the builders of the clock. All this time I had looked at servants from afar. Now I was one of them.

First I took off my sock cap and undid my hair to look like a woman. Clotilda approved of that when I went to her for instruction in my duties.

Soon I was on a daily routine: dusting, cleaning, washing, mending—tasks I had learned to do from our mother. In addition I was responsible for bringing in logs for the fire when Master reluctantly decided to have one. I worked in the vegetable garden, beat and shook woolens, emptied chamber pots, filled the water vat in the kitchen, put down fresh rushes on the floors, and generally worked through the striking of every hour save five.

After I had been at work but a single week, Clotilda let a chambermaid go. I was to do her work too. It was then clear why the Housekeeper had recommended me. I was now in her clutches.

But I was also close to Niklas again. Knowing he was nearby in the wood-carving shed gave me strength during the long days.

I liked Cook, too, and often worked for her in the kitchen. She did not like Clotilda either, which gave us a common bond. Listening to her ceaseless chatter made the time pass quickly when I cleaned the pots and kettles.

"My last mistress was a good one," Cook would often say with a sigh.

"She was always on the lookout for trickery in the market-place. When she caught someone cheating, what a noise she made. Crowds gathered to listen. Shopkeepers cringed when they saw her coming. They called her the Scourge of God. And she was. What an eye and nose she had! She was strict with me, too, but I didn't mind. How we ate in that household! What menus! None of this barley bread and pease pudding and bowls of curd. In that house I made dishes of mutton boiled in white broth, roasted goose, tarts of prune. None of this boiled udder that Master likes because it's cheap. We had dried cod and brewet and venison frumenty. Not a couple of chickens a month as in this starving house. I used to do plovers with meat jelly. I cooked meat tile with a spiced sauce of pounded crayfish tails and almonds." Cook, sighing, placed both hands on her ample belly. "It's a pity. Master and Mistress were taken off together."

"Plague?"

"Of course plague." Shaking her head in memory, Cook added, "You should have seen the food those two could pile on their trenchers."

I managed to survive in that household because of dear Cook. She saw to it that my belly was full after each day of work. She'd slip me pieces of dried fish with mustard, more beans than Clotilda would want me to have, and a slice of boiled tongue, if Clotilda left any on her plate—Cook having boiled some for her on the sly (Master was no spendthrift even with his lover).

One day I was cleaning the third-floor chambers on hands and knees. I came to Mistress's room and knocked.

She said, "Come in."

Taking my bucket and soap into the room, I dropped down quickly to begin work. A glance told me that the tiny woman was standing at a window facing the neighbor's wall.

When I had scrubbed about half the floor—the room contained nothing but a chair, a bed, a small chest—I felt her eyes on me.

When I glanced up, our eyes met.

"Today," Mistress said in her far-off voice, "I am thinking of seven."

After a long silence, she added, "Listen to me."

"Yes, ma'am."

"There are seven days in Creation, seven in a week, seven parts to the Lord's Prayer, seven churches of Asia, seven trumpets, seven plagues, a seven-headed monster, and the Lamb had seven eyes. There were also seven seals."

She stared at me, waiting.

"Yes, ma'am," I said.

"Heaven is above us, hell below. There are spheres of air and fire around the earth, the flaming walls of the world."

When she paused again, I said, "Yes, ma'am."

"Do you wear a clavette?"

"Ma'am?"

"A chastity belt."

"No, ma'am."

"There are boys who would have your treasure. Locked up, it's safe."

When she stared at me, I said, "Yes, ma'am."

"For the end is at hand."

I agreed. "Yes, ma'am."

"There will be earthquake and the sun black as sackcloth and the moon like blood. And the stars will tumble down and every mountain move from its place. Sinners will hide from Him who sits on the throne. They will hide from the wrath of the Lamb. For the great day of His wrath is coming. Who shall be able to stand?"

This time I said nothing, but our eyes met for a long time.

She was pale, thin-lipped, mournful. After a raw cough, she turned back to the window. All she could see from it was the blank wall next door.

I went on with the cleaning—working around her feet that seemed rooted to the floor.

Done, I left the room, but at my back I heard, "Wear a clavette."

Going downstairs, I nearly ran into Clotilda. Our faces were close, mine lower than hers.

She stared a long time before saying with a grin, "You ate the white bread first, girl. Now you will eat the brown."

29

COOK conspired with me so I could leave the house now and then for a breath of fresh air. Heretofore, a fat girl younger than I did some of the shopping. Cook complained to the Housekeeper that the girl often strayed or bought the wrong things (which was in fact true), so it would be better to send me. After considerable thought, Clotilda agreed.

Three times a week this got me out of the household routine for a while, a needed respite from drudgery. I would stroll into the narrow streets of the market and buy eggs, salt, onions, and sometimes vinegar, which Cook had daily need of. I'd buy loaves of bread, for according to guild contract Master Dollmayr had to give his painters and carvers a daily meal. Waiting leisurely at the bread stall, I watched the baker take his loaves from the oven with a long-handled spoon and stamp them with his seal. Then I might go to the herb shop for basil, rue, savory, or some other spice that would add flavor to the watery pea soup our household consumed.

One day I was turning a corner into the market, when to my surprise I saw Niklas hurrying down a narrow lane, carrying something.

What was my brother doing in the streets? Did he know how

to get home? But he was lost in the marketing crowd by the time I decided to follow him.

Back at the house, I went to the old carver.

"Where is my brother?" I asked fearfully.

"Out, as usual."

"As usual? He goes out often?"

"Every day for a few hours. If he was getting wages, it would be different. But we let him come and go as he pleases. Not, of course, that Master knows. Why?"

"Then he finds his way home?"

"Of course."

"Where does he go?"

The old man smiled and patted my back. "Do you think he tells me? Give him some freedom, girl. Don't worry."

But I did. When I questioned Niklas, what I got for a response was what I always got: a cool, steady look from his blue eyes, a mouth set in a way that told nothing. I nearly forbade him to leave the house, yet on second thought the old man's request did seem reasonable. If my brother could go and return, perhaps he should have the chance.

Even so, whenever I went on errands I kept an eye out for him. And sure enough, one day I saw him hurrying in the direction of the east gate.

He was carrying something.

Trailing far behind, I had trouble making out what he carried —a black stiff thing.

Covered with fur?

A cat.

A dead cat.

He was carrying a dead cat out of the city.

Though there wasn't much time for me to waste outside of the house, I had to see what this was all about.

Niklas trudged with head down, gripping the dead animal under his arm. Out of the city, he marched along the road with the determination of a soldier until coming to a rutted path that led into a small forest.

At last I knew where he was going. My brother was headed for Rabbit's grave.

Letting him get far ahead so as not to hear my step in the

undergrowth, I followed him to the copse where we had buried Rabbit.

What I saw then took my breath away.

Where there had been one small mound for Rabbit there were at least a dozen now, and above each was a cross, about as tall as my forearm.

From behind a tree I watched Niklas dig into the muddy summer earth with a tree limb he must have shaped with a tool into a shovel. When he had dug a hole large enough, he put in the dead cat and covered it.

I remembered with wrenching pain the day we had buried our parents.

I was trying to get loose from the memory when Niklas did something else I had not expected. He went beyond the little cemetery—I followed at a distance—past some bushes to a tree stump that stood waist-high to him. The trunk might have been sheared off by the sort of thunderbolt that had crippled my brother.

The smooth flatness of the stump puzzled me until I realized that Niklas must have leveled it. Around the edges he had nailed some boards, forming an enclosure. It was the jig of a wood-carver.

Then Niklas rummaged in a pile of leaves and pulled out a large goatskin bag. Soon he had a small mallet and a few chisels lying on the ground next to the stump. Also from the bag he took a block of wood. Swiftly he wedged it against the jig and without any wasted motion began swinging mallet against chisel, roughing out the form of a cross.

The work did not go on long.

Then everything returned to the bag, which was slipped again under the leaves. All save the chisel he'd been using. He shoved it under the rope belt of his tunic.

I watched him trudge away into the wood. He was going back to the city. Why had he taken the chisel along? Was he going to hone its edge on a slipstone and bring it back another day?

That would mean my brother planned ahead when it came to his tools.

Walking back to the graveyard, I knelt down for a closer look at the crosses. The upright and crossbars of each was minutely carved with tracery, foliage, writhing dragons. On each was the raised carving of our Lord Crucified. Each loin-clothed body was twisted in its own special attitude of agony. How well he understood the look of suffering. The Crown of Thorns, the nails through feet and hands, the bloody wound: Niklas had managed to suggest all of them with low relief here, with a gash there. My brother had labored long and hard on the cross of each animal. I had never seen anything like them.

And there was more.

I peered closely at each tiny face of Christ Crucified: the open mouth, the shut eyes, the tilted head. None of them had the face of Jesus as I had seen Him in churches. But every face was the same face. And it was familiar.

My brother had given each martyred Son of God the face of Hubert.

Back at the house, I was met by Cook, who frowned gloomily.

"Now you've done it," she said. "You've been gone too long. Clotilda's been looking for you. She told me it's the last time you'll run errands. What happened?"

"What?"

"You're smiling. Or crying? Did you hear what I said about Clotilda? Anne?"

I heard her puzzled voice follow me from the kitchen. "Anne? What ever happened?"

So I no longer had relief from the daily routine.

Day ran smoothly into day, as if time really was a long continuous arc unbroken by events. Summer moved into autumn, autumn into winter. I no longer used the distant striking of the bell to count time by—I used the number of stairs climbed as I hauled buckets, carried laundry. If there was extra work to do, I did it, and the fat maid got fatter.

Then one day Master Dollmayr was appointed to the Corporation of the City. It was, according to him, an event worthy of extraordinary celebration. With uncommon generosity he instructed the Housekeeper to let each maid have an afternoon off. Until the last moment I was sure that Clotilda would find a reason for denying me this privilege, but perhaps she was too caught up in Master's excitement to think about servants that day.

So I was free.

"Come, Niklas," I said, leaning into the wood-carving shed. "Come with me, come!"

He turned from the bench, solemnly put down a rasp, and came along.

We went down to the river where people were skating on the ice. From an old vendor there we rented skates.

"Do you remember skating at the mill?" I asked Niklas, while strapping leather thongs to his foot and ankle so the wooden plate would stay on.

"Do you remember? It was when the waterwheel stuck fast in the ice. Then Father would get out our skates and we would all go, even Mother, almost to town on the frozen river, and the wind would shake snow out of trees along the bank as we skated, and then Mother used the staff to push herself forward, but Father went far ahead until he was just a tiny spot on the blue ice. Remember, Niklas?"

When the thongs were secure, we stepped upon the river. The footplates shod with iron curled over our toes as we moved over the ice, hesitantly at first, then remembering how. A crisp wind blew into our eyes, stinging tears into them. Soon my brother's face was apple red. He smiled—what a fine, rare thing was his smile—as we put distance between us and the wharves.

From the closer bank some boys tossed snowballs at us. I waved. So did Niklas, and smiled again. The boys didn't see his white hair beneath a woolen cap. They thought he was like them and shouted good-hearted challenges at us as we sped along.

It was all right, I kept thinking. Everything was for the best. God had remembered us after all.

Part IV

Part IV

30

SO life in Master Dollmayr's house resumed its daily routine. Master slipped in and out of the Housekeeper's bedroom; Clotilda prowled everywhere looking for work for me; Mistress come downstairs now and then mumbling about the Day of Wrath; merchants came to buy the guild's art; the guild painters stayed to themselves on the second floor, where they turned out dozens of small Madonnas; and in the shed behind the house one wooden saint after another was fashioned by the carvers.

The fat girl, having learned that she could please the Housekeeper by accusing me of laziness, did so every day. This added but slightly to my burden. I had come to accept my life in this household, especially because of Niklas's rapid development as a carver. But I started to wonder if he was working too hard. He looked pale, wan, and a few weeks after our skating holiday he slept late, holding his hand to his forehead.

"Are you sick, Brother?"

He just looked at me, and later went to the shed to work.

But next morning he slept late again. I noticed him itching, and when I withdrew his hand and parted his hair shirt for a look at his chest, I discovered a large shiny red bump. He was hot too.

This time I didn't bother to ask him if he was sick. I went downstairs to the old carver and told him.

"Wait till tomorrow," he said. "Then we'll see."

But the next morning Niklas felt even hotter; his arms seemed to cramp up, and a spasm of pain ran across his lips.

The old carver came to our room and looked at Niklas.

"I don't like it," he said. "You better have a doctor come."

"But I haven't money for such a thing."

227

"Never mind. Come down in a while."

When I went down to the wood-carving shed, all the men turned to stare at me. The old carver poured coins into my hand.

"Where has all this money come from?" I said, looking around the dust-laden room. No one said anything.

With coins wrapped in a rag, I rushed to the house of a doctor who lived nearby.

His servant glanced up and down at me. I untied the rag, took out a coin, and gave it to her.

"He will want his fee now," she said, pocketing the coin in her apron.

"I have money," I told her proudly.

She opened a door to a back room and disappeared. Soon the door opened again and a man peered out curiously.

"You have money?" he asked. He wore a purple gown, a furred hood, leather gloves.

"I have, sir."

"Tell me what's wrong."

During my explanation of Niklas's illness, he nodded solemnly. He was a tall man, skinny but for a paunch that curved out unnaturally over a wide belt made of silver threads.

After he named a price for his visit and had the money in hand, we went to Master Dollmayr's house.

The doctor had a bag and from it took a sandglass. He counted the beat of my brother's heart until the sand had trickled from top to bottom.

He said to me with a sigh, "Food is cooked in the oven of the stomach. If the stomach's too full, it boils over like a kettle."

"But sir, he hasn't eaten in two days."

The physician nodded. "Yes, of course he hasn't. Bring me his urine tomorrow." Rising, he put the sandglass back into the bag. "You will give him a mixture of honey, water, small beer, along with ginger, pepper, and cloves. And make for him a second drink of sugared milk and boiled almonds. If he feels like it later, give him boiled capon. Add ground almonds and white ginger to it and pomegranate seeds if you can find them."

I listened carefully, committing the items to memory. They would cost a fortune.

"What is wrong with him, sir?"

The doctor pursed his lips. "An imbalance of the humors. I'd say too much black bile, not enough phlegm. The moon has been waxing crescent the last few days. That should help put him in order. Bring the urine tomorrow and bring my fee."

When I had seen the doctor out and closed the door, Clotilda was standing behind me. She demanded to know who that was.

When I told her, she smiled. "Illness is the punishment of God. Come along."

She took me to Master, who seemed truly worried about my brother, until I realized that his concern was for the statues Niklas was not carving.

He said, "I've had good work from the boy lately. I want him back on the job."

"He will be soon," I promised.

"But he's sick now," said Clotilda.

We were standing in front of Master Dollmayr's desk, where he hunched over some parchments, holding a quill.

"Sick," Master repeated. Wrapped in fur that was buttoned to his chin, he looked small and uncomfortable, though smiling as always.

"The boy's getting bigger," he said thoughtfully. "You can't deny that," he said to me. "We can't have people living here who don't earn their bread."

"No," said Clotilda. "And if buyers know someone in the house is sick, they might go away."

"Please," I said, looking through tears at Master's soft round face. "I promise to work hard."

"Well. A promise," he said with a larger smile.

"Harder than ever. I'll work for two."

"Good," Clotilda said. "In that case, Master Dollmayr, we can get rid of the other one, the fat one. She displeases me anyway. If this girl works for two at the wages of one, I think you can be generous."

"Indeed," he said. "Let the boy stay."

Master leaned back for a better look at me. "Mind you do as promised. We aren't wasteful here. Fill the hours properly. Time is money."

Outside the office, Clotilda stepped in my path so I couldn't get around her.

"God has put every creature in its rightful place," Clotilda said in a low voice I had come to fear, for often it preceded a kick, a push, a slap. "Yours is a mean, low place. You should never think of leaving it. You have sinned enough. You have been favored enough. You are where you belong."

And to my surprise, Clotilda stepped aside, allowing me to pass.

For the next week my brother either improved or stayed the same. It was hard for me to tell, and though the doctor came each day, he never told me which.

He talked of the stars that influence bodily humors, of Galen's three spirits that control all living things, of the difference between tertian, quartan, and hectic fevers. For these daily lectures that left me bewildered, I paid him.

By the end of that week my money ran out. I couldn't ask the carvers for more—they had families of their own to feed. Girding my courage, I went to Clotilda and begged for an advance on wages.

She regarded me carefully before saying, "If God wanted you helped and favored, Master would help and favor you." Which was her way of saying no.

About that time a new buyer of carvings came to the house. When we approached each other in a hallway, our eyes met in slow recognition.

I first recognized the ugly-looking wen, bigger now, on his left cheek. He had a dirty rag twisted around his neck—perhaps the same rag he wore in the inn that other time we met. He was the statue merchant who had slipped under the stairway next to me.

"I know," he said with a grin. "You were looking for your uncle. Knights were fighting over something."

"One said the other rode a mare into battle."

"And one of them got killed?"

"I heard the winner toasted."

"You had an older brother," the man said with a chuckle. "But I didn't believe you. You were frightened."

"No, sir."

"You were frightened, though of what I'm sure I don't know. I was only there to give you advice."

I was watching him grip the dirty rag at his neck with both hands. It was as if he were holding on to a log in a flood.

"You're older and prettier though. You were fat then, as I remember. But what is this—you're a scullion? What happened to your uncle?"

"Dead, sir."

"Call me Gian."

When I brushed past him, he caught my arm. "Still the great lady?"

"Sir?"

"I remember trying to be nice to you and you acting the great lady."

Pulling free, I went down the hall and rushed upstairs.

Niklas was coughing terribly when I got to him. I held his head while he vomited.

God, I beg of you, help us in our need, I asked silently.

Taking my brother's hand, I gripped his fingers hard, but he didn't seem to feel the pressure. Leaning toward him, I smelled the flesh of his fingers—they had a strange odor, like rot.

I remembered the old man in the monastery shed where we slept one night during our journey northward. He had stood with me over the twisted corpse of a woman.

The old man described the terrible illness that must have killed her: the itching, the shiny red bumps, the fingers turned numb and foul, the vomiting, the thrashing and burning— Saint Anthony's fire, which had killed the old man's son as well.

When the doctor came next morning, I asked him if this could be Saint Anthony's fire.

"Nonsense," he said, looking down at me from his great height. Putting out one gloved hand, he said, "My fee."

"I'll have it tomorrow. Are you sure this is not the fire?"

He picked up his bag with one hand and held his furred hood close to his throat with the other.

"If you have my fee tomorrow, bring it, and I will come."

"You must help him now! Please!"

He gave me a stern look. "I have been licensed in the Pope's name. You are impudent, you are rude." He ducked low and started down the ladder.

I called at his back, "Is it not the fire? Are you sure?"

But he was gone.

That day I kept an eye on Master's office door. Sure enough, out came Gian with his wen and the dirty rag about his throat and his clay pipe.

Seeing me, he started to grin. "That man-of-arms who is your older brother is also a carver, I understand. I bought five of his Saint Agnes and three of his Virgin and two Christ Crucified. What kind of smile is that you're giving me? Is that the smile of a pious lady?"

I kept smiling as boldly as I could recall the girls smiling in dark doorways near the riverfront.

Gian invited me for a cup of wine.

When I accepted, he grinned broadly.

"To tell the truth, girl, I was expecting a change in you. Come along and have some wine and you can tell me about your poor brother."

I will make short work of what happened.

At the tavern I declared my need for money and he, his need for me. We went behind a screen and with few words exchanged between us, he had me. Coldly I watched the wen move on his cheek, his cloudy eye fix me in a slit of concentration when the moment was on him.

"A cup of wine?" Gian asked when we were sitting again at the table.

Smoothing my skirt over bruised thighs, I was thinking of the money he had given me.

"I asked you, will you have a cup of wine?"

There was enough money to pay the doctor for a week.

"You refuse to talk to me? Am I unworthy? Do you still fancy yourself a duchess? After what has just happened? Am I still dirt under your feet?"

I turned to Gian, who was moodily stroking his stubbled chin.

"Yes," I said.

"God punishes whores like you."

"Then I pity Him."

"That's sacrilege!" he yelled at my back as I got up and moved toward the screen.

Turning, I had a final glimpse of Gian, who gripped the rag around his neck with both hands, as if holding on. I saw the wen, too, and his cloudy eye giving me a sideways injured look.

"You'll go to hell," he muttered.

"What I'll regret most is meeting you there."

It was the grandest thing I ever said.

Night had fallen when I got back to the house.

My brother's coughing grew worse, and indeed he began thrashing violently. I tried to muffle the sound of his retching, but in the middle of the night a voice called up from the ladder: "Keep him quiet or get him out of here!"

It was Clotilda.

I nearly suffocated Niklas at each new seizure. If I had put my hand on a hot bloom of iron, it might not have felt hotter than the head and limbs of this suffering boy. He opened his mouth like a bird drinking. His lips clacked up and down, but nothing emerged from them, not the slightest vomit or spit. It was as if his insides, once emptied, had dried out. He shivered and jerked, grew rigid and limp in my arms by turns, as I wept over him and stuffed a rag into his mouth to muffle his retching.

Toward morning he grew calmer, and I took his hot hand in mine. Leaning close to him, I whispered, "Remember in spring how we used to sit by the river and watch the ice break up and the wheel start turning?" Our eyes met. I smiled. "No sister was ever more blessed with a brother than I've been with you."

I could say no more, for words clogged in my throat like ice in the river I spoke of. I squeezed his hand, and his own fingers squeezed back with a surge of strength that made me hope. But then he had another coughing spell. Early light slipped through the ceiling cracks, so that I could see his pale, drawn face, the blue eyes wide open as if looking for something.

I said, "Brother, you'll see our parents soon." Again I pressed his hand, this time receiving no reply.

Leaning forward, I peered in the first dim light at his blue eyes. Did he see me? It was hard to tell. Suddenly I felt as though my whole body was falling away like loose earth on a hillside. Gritting my teeth, I fought the panic.

I held on and held on and held on until a dagger of sunlight crossed his face and reached our clasped hands. Aware then of how rigid his fingers had become, gently I withdrew mine and laid his hands together on his chest. For a while I kept both of my hands against his. "Niklas, have you left me?" My words floated through the silence like ice in a river. I sat there until Clotilda yelled up from the stairway.

I remember now that the old carver located a mason who had worked on the tower and had known me. This mason donated a gravestone for my brother. I think I thanked him at the gravesite.

I turned and looked at all the carvers and thanked them, too, for coming. What money I had left after paying the priest who came with us I gave to the gravediggers—two Jews with yellow circles sewn on their jackets. It was a cold day and they cursed the hard ground.

The old carver held my hand while the priest said words over the grave. Then my brother, wrapped in a white shroud, was taken by the Jews from a hardwood coffin I had rented (not letting the carvers pay again) and was slipped out of it into the hole.

After the grave was covered, everyone walked away.

I stayed to watch the two Jews fix the gravestone in place. I watched their yellow circles ripple as they struggled with the heavy stone.

Where had Jacob the copier gone?

When I had known him at Uncle's house, Niklas had just started to carve things with a little knife.

I looked at the motion of their yellow circles as the two Jews patted the earth, smoothing it over the grave. Was Jacob dead too? Mother, Father, Uncle, Hubert, Niklas—and Jacob?

Niklas would have carved a lovely cross for the grave. It would have made him seem like soaring out of the ground, upward into the air, soaring into the light.

But he was under a flat gray stone that weighed him down. I didn't feel he was there when I looked at the grave. I gave it a final look and went home.

31

"YOUR brother has just been buried, but you won't cry," Clotilda said. She waited as if expecting my tears to come. When I stood there like a rock, she told me to go back to work.

I swept, dusted, shook out the bench cushions, and removed grease spots from clothes. As I was throwing slop water into the backyard, three words came suddenly from my mouth, as clear as tolling from the clock. I had said the words, yet they seemed to have come from someone else, from another head.

Shaken by them, I began to pluck a partridge for dinner— Master was having a rare guest. The feathers, well joined to the flesh, were hard to pull out because the bird had been freshly killed. I tried to think only of those things: Master's guest, the partridge feathers.

I worked fiercely, trying to forget the terrible words that had somehow come from my mouth.

And all of a sudden, looking down at the carcass, I said them clearly again: "I hate God."

I said them again, "I hate God," firmly, without hesitation. They thundered like a struck bell.

I glanced around to see if someone heard. In the backyard, fortunately, there were only the pigs, some chickens, the half-plucked partridge in my hands.

"I hate God" came again. The words flowed like a river from my mouth, "I hate God I hate God I hate God," without ceasing. Sweat poured from my brow. What if someone heard? Yet through rigid lips I said the words anyway.

Work continued on the partridge. Its feathers flew into the air as I tried to forget three words that could send me to hell.

And so it began: the time of the three words.

At first I said them aloud, but soon I was able to mutter them in a whisper, so that within a few days I no longer feared people overhearing them. And within a week I no longer whispered them—they were said only in my mind.

Though this was bad enough, at least I had gained mastery over my voice.

Of course, the worst was to come.

As time passed I became aware that the words were spoken to someone. To whom was not clear at first. Then one day I realized with horror that I was saying these terrible words to God Himself. They were not the idle words of an impudent girl, said to the air. They were a defiance flung at the Holy Throne.

So this, finally, was the worst of it. Each time "I hate God, hate God, hate God" went through my head, God was listening.

It was almost unbearable on Sabbath days, for when the cathedral bell summoned the city to Mass, I lay on the blanket in a pretense of illness, hands jammed against ears to keep out both the call to worship and the sound of my secret defiance.

Knees drawn chestward, I lay sweating in the corruption of my thoughts. Within a dark world of my own making, I told our Maker how much I hated Him for taking Niklas away. The horror of pure hatred shook my body. And after a while things grew even worse, for in the blackness of terror I began to sense the closeness of God. I stopped imagining myself before His throne. Indeed, I realized that He was not only close but actually inside my head, squatting in a corner of it like a vengeful demon, listening to the earsplitting clang of those ironlike words of mine as they sounded in my head much like the thunder of struck hours in the turret.

Clotilda, of course, was soon aware of something wrong with me.

I'd be listening to words I could no more stop than men can stop a flooded river from overflowing its banks—so intent on the constant noise of confession that I failed to hear her giving orders to do this or do that. If she shouted in my ear not a foot away, I scarcely heard it.

"What is wrong with you, girl!"

I'd mumble an apology or make an excuse.

"Has some boy got you with child? Are you stealing? What wickedness has put such a look on your face? Has the devil got you? Has the devil got our favored girl?"

She was perhaps closer to the truth than she might know.

One morning after chores I decided to tell someone what was happening. Someone had to help me with the horror of my defiance.

That, of course, could only be Niklas.

So I threw on a cape against the chill and left the house. Outside the main gate at a fork in the road, I turned down a rutted lane to the little wood where Niklas had buried Rabbit and the other animals.

It was a grim, foggy day. Soon I was up to my ankles in cold mud. Reaching the tiny cemetery beneath leafless trees, I sat on a boulder for a long time before saying, "Niklas."

I said, "Surely you're here with Rabbit and the others, not in the city graveyard."

After a pause I said, "Yes." I said, "You are here."

A slight breeze rattled the bare branches overhead. "I am sinning, Brother. I say terrible defiant words and can't help myself." Looking from cross to carved cross above the little mounds, I said, "But you can't help me either, can you. If only you could pray for me, if you could help me . . ."

But I asked in vain. Though certain my brother had listened, I knew that Death wouldn't let him help me, even if he could find the power to speak and pray and plead. Looking at the crosses he had carved and the graves he had dug, I was glad then just to be near my Niklas. After a while, when the wind grew colder, I went home.

Entering the house, I realized something strange had happened. Since going to visit Niklas, I hadn't once said the bad words. This gave me hope.

But that night, as I moved to the verge of sleep, the words boomed suddenly through my head like great cracks of thunder: "I hate God, I hate God, I hate God!"

Once again, until dawn, I lay in a river of sweat, fighting the terror.

Those days I often wandered through the streets of the city, trying to shake the words loose from my mind.

One day I found myself staring at something without recognizing it—so loud were the words, so merciless for attention. I was standing in front of a small church.

Upon reflection I wonder if the words themselves hadn't drawn me forward then, because I entered the church without thinking, as if without choice. People were taking the sacrament of penance. Another group were awaiting confession.

Still without thinking, I joined those in front of the confessional box. Dully I watched the curtain open, someone step out, another step in, the curtain close. Dully I waited, hearing the tower clock strike two, then three. At last I came to the head of the line.

Pushing the curtain aside, I entered and knelt in darkness when the curtain fell.

I began at once—a flood of words rushing from my lips. Not since the death of my parents, I told the confessor, had I taken the sacrament of penance.

"Father, I have sinned. I have lied to people."

"Be sincere in your repentance, child, and beg God's mercy."

The words kept coming. I told the confessor I had not always treated my brother kindly. I was sometimes lazy. I was jealous of people who had better food and a better room than mine.

To each confession the priest said, "Be sincere in your repentance, child, and beg God's mercy."

When I told him of my hatred for the housekeeper where I lived, he said, "You must not hate people. Hating is sinful because we are all God's children. Be sincere in your contrition. Beg God's mercy for what you have done." After this, he cleared his throat, as if signaling that he was ready to assign penance.

"Father," I said. "There is more. I have sinned with a man without the sacrament of marriage."

The confessor then told me what I already knew: that I had committed a sin of special gravity for women, whose purity should be their key to heaven.

As he spoke from behind the wooden grill, I heard something familiar in his voice. From his first words I had wondered and then I was sure: One day in the past I had heard the soft, hesitant speech of this man as he groped for the right word.

My confessor was the priest who had blessed the bell, who had waited at the edge of the meadow, who had squeezed my hand before rushing away.

Knowing my confessor, I might then have been more guarded, yet in his sympathetic presence I wanted to confess the worst sin of all.

"Father, I have sinned even more."

"Yes, child?"

"I hate God."

"Child, watch what you say. This is His house."

"The words go through my head. Three words: 'I hate God.' Again again again again. Since my brother died, they've been with me: I hate God hate God. But I can't mean them, can I? I believe in heaven and hell. I don't mean them, Father."

"But you say them."

"I say them."

There was a long silence. "This is a grievous sin, child. What happened to your brother that led you to such transgression?"

"He died of fever. He is dead."

"We all die, child. Death is the return of light to its origin. Light in the soul flies back to the bosom of God from whence it came."

"Yes yes. My brother couldn't talk. He had pure white hair. He was innocent and good and died horribly."

"Ah," breathed the priest, and in this sound there was recognition. From my description of Niklas he knew me at last.

Facing the grill on my knees, I listened then to his soft voice explaining the seriousness of my sin. Careful or you will be apostate, he warned. He spoke of eternal damnation, but with such gentle sympathy that I heard only a sweet human voice giving comfort to my troubled soul.

In reply to him, when he paused, I said words that astonished me even as I spoke them. "Repenting what happens in my head won't save me, Father—not if it keeps happening. Isn't that true? If God is indifferent, I'm doomed."

"Indifferent?"

"I beg God's mercy, but the words still come. If He won't help me, isn't He indifferent? If He alone can stop the words but won't?"

"It is not for us to tell our Lord what to do."

Again there was a long silence.

Then a thought came to me. I said, "Or if He won't stop the words, can you stop them, Father? Do you have the power? Has God left it to you?"

Again there was silence. Someone coughed in the waiting line. How long had I been in the box?

"Tell me about the man," he said.

"The man?"

"The man you sinned with."

"The man I sinned with?" For the moment I had forgotten that sin.

"He was young," I said. "He meant no harm. He brought me here from a town."

"As his mistress?"

"He was paid by my uncle to bring me here."

"So you were not his mistress?"

"I was not."

"But you sinned with him."

"I did, Father."

"Where did you commit this sin?"

I hesitated. "In the woods."

"Once?"

Again I hesitated. "No."

"More?"

"Yes, Father."

"How many times?"

"I can't be sure."

"Then the man didn't force you?"

"No, Father. He did not."

I looked in vain at the dark grill for a glimpse of the priest's face. With each question he was pushing me away. He was fixed on Hubert, not on my soul.

"So you consented to the sin?"

"Yes, Father. I consented."

"Without coercion?"

"Yes."

"You are sure? Without coercion?"

"Yes, Father."

"He promised you nothing?"

"No."

"Did he make promises to marry you or give you things?"

"No promises, Father."

"Then are you telling me you consented from desire?"

I said nothing, so he repeated the question. "You consented from desire? You wanted to commit this sin?"

"Yes, Father, I did."

From the anguish in his voice I could tell I was wounding him. Was each answer of mine driving a nail into his heart? Into his *heart*?

"Do you regret having committed this sin?"

"I am sorry I committed it. I have suffered for it."

"I understand the hindsight that gives you judgment over desires of the past. But if you could do it again, without the suffering you speak of, would you? Would you do it again? And with that same man?"

I didn't reply.

"Would you?" he insisted.

"Father," I began. If only I could see him, was what I was thinking.

Then I said, "Love is powerful. It comes from God. Doesn't love come from God?"

When he made no reply, I said again, "Doesn't love come from God?"

Behind the grill there might have been no one, except through the silence I could hear him breathing.

Leaning forward, I asked softly, "Is it love?"

The silence was complete then. He must have been holding his breath.

Finally, with the boldness of desperation I said, "Father," I said, "your love comes from God."

Could love save us both?

I let that sudden thought make its way through my mind to find words for saying it. "Talk to me. Let me listen to you,

Father," I whispered. "Not here but out of here. Anywhere," I said—no more able to stop these words than stop the three bad ones from coming.

"Tell me what to do," I said. "Let me hear your voice because I believe in it. Because you alone can save me. I see that now: It is God's will. Go with me somewhere and let me hear your voice and lie in your arms because your love comes from God."

Suddenly the words stopped, as if I had crashed into a wall. My breath was gusting through the silence. And I heard my heart hammering. Out of the darkness *I hate God* came at me then like a thunderclap. In my throat there was sobbing—if it got past my lips, it would be a howl of anguish. Swallowing hard, I fought it down.

"Please," I began, not knowing what I meant.

He said nothing.

"Forgive me," I said.

Behind the grill he remained silent. He was not going to speak, no matter what I said. It seemed as if my last chance in life had come.

Rising, I put my lips against the grating that separated us. "I am going to wait for you." Taking a deep breath, I said, "I am going to wait outside the church until sunset. If you come, it is God's will. I'll go anywhere with you. I see it clearly now. We must help each other. I'll be outside until sunset. I'll be waiting."

Brushing the curtain aside, I hurried past people who stood in line. They must have been looking at me. Had they heard my heart pounding in the box?

Huddling near the church wall, I watched the sun edge lower and lower, its shadows lengthen till they started merging into a sea of darkness. It was silent. Even my head was silent, because the three words had gone away awhile, letting me live in the blessed emptiness of silence. I thought of nothing but the silence, watching the light change within it.

A brisk wind came up. Shivering, I braced against it and waited, but he never came.

When it was too dark to see the mortared lines of cobblestone, I glanced at the church door and walked away.

By the time I reached my room, one thing was clear: God had not been indifferent this day. Lying inside the blast of bad words, I drew my knees up, shut my eyes, and thanked the Lord. While the bad words thundered in my head, I said aloud, "Thank you, almighty God, thank you thank you thank you."

I said those words of gratitude against the battering of three terrible words. I shouted into their storm, "Thank you thank you thank you, Lord!" I shook with relief, for God had saved me from sending a good man to hell.

32

A SABBATH morning after Mass, while lying curled on one side with hands cupped against my ears, I felt a sudden thudding pain between my shoulders.

Opening my eyes, I looked up at Clotilda, whose fist was still clenched as if to hit me again.

"Master wants you out of the house. Today. Now."

I sat up slowly, trying to appear calm; a look of confusion might encourage her to hit me again.

"Master wants me to leave? Why does he want me to leave?" Although the words were said as calmly as possible, I heard trembling in my voice.

"Something's wrong with you. I know it and so does Master. He wants you out." Both large hands were ready for more work if I argued. "So get out. Today. Now."

There was, of course, no hope of changing Master's mind—not after Clotilda had wormed out of him a promise to send me away. He would think he had to be strong, though in truth he merely did what Clotilda told him to do.

As for Mistress, she was probably in her room, passing beads through her smooth fingers, this world forgotten.

So I shrugged and got up, thinking everything was finished for me in this house.

But in the next moment I understood that finishing with this house was not so easy, because Clotilda, waiting till I bent down to put on my shoes, hit me again hard, squarely between the shoulders. And in the next moment, head pressed against the floor, I was looking at her shoes set big and black not a handsbreadth from my nose. She was going to give me a terrible beating.

She began laughing, but I didn't look up.

Then she stopped laughing, and in the awful silence I heard her breathing heavily.

"That rabbit," she said finally. "I killed the animal. I smothered it."

Then my arms, possessed terribly of a will of their own, shot out and grabbed for the stout calves above her shoes. I felt the warm flesh held in my fingers when they jerked backward, as if the touch of Clotilda was like touching live coals. And as they pulled back, my fingers brought with them her feet. I was yanking her legs out from under her! She fell like a tree, crashed against the wall.

In the utter silence I asked myself what had happened.

It took a while before I could believe that somehow I had knocked Clotilda flat. Rabbit had given me the strength and quickness. Scrambling up, I looked at the powerful woman slumped against the wall, her head lolling to one side, a muscled arm thrown across her paunch, her heavily muscled legs ending in enormous shoes that pointed upward, as still as death.

Was she dead?

Bending down, I peered closely at the big breasts; they were rising and falling. She breathed. And suddenly from her half-parted lips came a little groan.

Quickly I threw on a skirt and bodice, gathered my things, what there was of them, and ran out of the house.

Where was I going? I had no idea.

But hurrying down the lane past laborers and carters, I felt myself smiling. The priests tell us to turn the other cheek, but truthfully I sensed in my body a fresh lightness that came from revenge.

Yet not far from the house I heard them drumming in my head again: three words of doom, *I hate God I hate God I hate God!*

So powerful were the words, I failed to realize where my feet had been taking me.

A few paces ahead was the Good Government door of the clock turret.

It was padlocked. Going round the tower into a courtyard littered with firewood and old mortarboards and broken stones, I came to a low-slung building of the same kind of stones. They had been building it when I last ventured into the tower square—months ago.

Knocking, I waited a long time and was about to leave when suddenly the door opened.

Barnabas, a full growth of gray beard on his square chin, stood there smiling. He could not have looked better to me than an angel clothed in gold.

"There she is," he said. "My little clockmaker. Come in, come in. Welcome to the house of the Governor of the Public Clock," he said with pride, and ushered me into a cramped, smoky room.

I remembered our last conversation. He hadn't been sure of this new job, entailing so many responsibilities. The city expected him to wind the machine twice a day, check the loss or gain against a sundial, reset the foliot, grease the moving parts, examine the pulley ropes for abrasion.

"Do it," I had advised him.

Now, as governor, he had lodgings in this house behind the tower and a stipend that kept his family of five in food.

When I appeared that day, trembling and confused, this good man did not hesitate but took me in. He and his young wife fed me, put me to bed in the next room.

In the morning, refreshed by sleep, I went up to the trestle table where they sat. Barnabas smoked a clay pipe. His pale little wife fed an infant boy from a bowl of gruel.

"You've treated me with kindness," I said. I think their generosity had renewed in me the desire to live.

"And now I'm hoping for still more kindness," I told them. "You know me well, Barnabas. How I brought plans from my uncle."

He nodded.

"How I worked on the clock as long and hard as any man."

I could tell my bold words astonished his young wife—no older than I was. As I spoke her eyes grew round and fearful.

"What you say is true," Barnabas declared. His face was lined in such a way that he seemed to smile, though he was always a sober, cautious man.

"I have nowhere to go now," I continued. "They turned me out of my place through no fault of my own. And I have no money. But if you let me have a corner of the turret to sleep in and a little gruel daily, I'll pay you back in time. And I'll do no wrong here to anyone," I said, turning to the young woman who fed her baby.

Barnabas cleared his throat. "What you say is well said and seems honest. You brought the plans. You worked as long and hard as any man. I'd be false to the memory of your uncle if I didn't offer food and shelter. You are welcome here and we ask nothing of you."

Thus did I come to live in the heart of the clock.

I slept in the tower above the machinery next to the bell. I had a wool blanket and a bowl for the gruel that was brought to me twice a day by one of the children, usually by the older girl, who solemnly watched me wipe the bowl clean with a trencher of bread. Of course, such charity would have to end soon—the Governor of the Public Clock was not a rich man; his wife being pregnant, he would soon have another mouth to feed.

Yet for a fortnight I remained there like a wounded animal, never leaving the turret except for a quick walk to a nearby latrine. All day I huddled next to the bell that rang on the hour, and at night, curled in the blanket, I heard it pealing through my troubled sleep.

The tolling of the clock competed with the tolling of words in my head. The striking of the bell was so loud that I could not hear my own defiance. After an hour had been struck, I sat stunned in the aftermath of such tumultuous sound, head abruptly cleared of hatred. The sound was like a great flood washing through a village, shoving debris out of it.

The longer I stayed in the turret, the less frequent came the words. At last I rarely heard them.

But I wasn't sure that beyond the sanctity of the turret I'd be rid of them. Without the bell ringing in my ears would the three words return in all their pounding horror? The only way to find out was for me to leave the clock.

So one morning I went down the stairway and stood squinting in the light. Barnabas's wife and children watched curiously from the yard. I smiled at them and stepped into the passing stream of townspeople on their way to market.

That day I found work in a wheat field belonging to the bishopric.

Lying just outside the city gate, the field was being planted by a score of people who had come from the countryside in search of fortune. Now their need for work of any kind had brought them back to the work they had left home to be rid of. It was hard work, but each morning the spring air did for me what the clock bell had also done: cleared my head of defiance and terror.

Each dawn we trudged out from the city together to plant the seedlings, following the progress of a plowman with his big swing plow equipped with a hitch and a long beam and a thick wooden plow share that cut the slices of furrow. We walked behind him, even as he walked behind a team of four oxen harnessed in tandem, while the bishopric's cleric-in-charge whipped them forward with a leather lash attached to a pole.

Bending down in the warm sunlight, I heard the voices of my companions raised in complaint and good cheer—sometimes, it seemed, both at once. The human sound blew through my head like a cleansing breeze.

When I heard from beyond a neighboring wood the tolling of hours from the city tower, I thought of time. I thought of it while moving my hands over the newly furrowed earth, plunging seeds into it a distance the length of my fingernail.

Of time. Now, at the age of eighteen, I was rushing through time so fast that soon I'd be old. Glancing around the field, I saw people not much older than I was who were already bent by hard work, haggard from illness. The way time had drawn them into its whirlwind made me love them. We were all hurtling through time together without a foothold. We were spun into the whirling hours that finally would come to a point some distance away, where God, reaching out, would gently take up each speck of dust and return it to His horde of them.

We bent to plant seeds together and hurried through time together and I welcomed each day that it happened.

Once, near the market, I saw Clotilda approaching down the street. Naturally my first thought was to run. But I had seen dogs become snarling killers when one of them showed weakness, so I forced myself to keep walking.

When we were nearly abreast, our eyes met. To my astonishment I saw in the big woman's eyes the look of fear that I was trying to keep from my own.

She feared me!

In fact, Clotilda stepped to the side, as if dodging a hell-born creature only she could see. That Sabbath morning when she had ordered me out of the house, she must have been as bewildered by my surprise attack as I had been. Since then she must have convinced herself that by satanic magic or mysterious skill I had overcome her. Not to revenge a rabbit's death.

Indeed, her fear of me was better than revenge of a physical kind. I strode briskly past Clotilda and at the last moment gave her a quick smile of triumph. Our eyes met again, this time in understanding: Never again would she bully me. We were quits forever.

Life improved at the clock turret. When I handed over my first pay to Barnabas in front of his wife, they smiled with such joy and surprise that I understood they had truly expected nothing from the strange girl in the tower.

Now that I could pay for lodging and food, Barnabas's wife was quick to offer me a bit of space in their quarters. I was brought down from the tower to share a bed with the younger girl. At mealtimes I helped the women serve Barnabas and the boys, then ate with Clare, for that was the wife's name, and the two girls.

Sometimes the older girl came with me to the tower and we sat together, watching the going train and the striking train their series of wheels moved like plodding iron-gray oxen through the dusty air of the turret. We watched the stone weight on its rope descend by slow inches toward the ground, and the crown wheel turn one tooth at a time, the pallet that governed it rocking back and forth like a cradle.

I said to her, her name was Clare, too, "Clare, you can learn how the clock works."

"Not me."

"Why not you?"

"I know nothing."

Clare had big solemn eyes, the sweet expression in them reminding me of her gentle father, who was often watched by us as he slowly wound the capstan to bring the stone weight up through the turret again.

"Clare," I said, looking at her sad white face, "people know nothing when they start. But they learn."

"No one will teach me."

"Someone taught me, so I can teach you." And thereafter I took the rolled charts to the tower with us and pointed out on them each part of the clockwork. Clare learned quickly. Her long white finger traced my explanations against the chart, and when she understood how the chart matched the iron pieces moving slowly in front of our eyes, the girl smiled with pleasure, and so did I.

This is how my days were spent, while spring moved into summer.

33

IN the fields where I labored at weeding the ripening grain, the three terrible words rarely got through the sunlight anymore. The sun's heat seemed to dry and blow them away, like the weeds I pulled up and threw aside. Perhaps someday I would learn to pray again. I had given up prayer for it seemed a double sin to blaspheme against God in my mind, then praise Him. I had no wish to add deceit to blasphemy. Yet when I heard from the distance the hours strike in the city tower, I felt the need to blaspheme lose its power until it began vanishing like the sound of a struck bell.

But even the sunlit field and the voices of my companions humming within it could not bring me happiness. Sometimes the thought of my brother's death came from the neighboring wood and across the field like a stormy wind, blinding my eyes, tightening my chest with grief.

Knowing he was close by in the small graveyard with Rabbit and the others, I felt I could speak to him and he would listen. Each time the thought of his death rushed at me, I would say, "Niklas," under my breath so people couldn't hear. I would say, "The sun goes over the edge soon." And I would say, "But it comes back over the other edge tomorrow." The idea of that happening day after day was something I knew he would like. That was how I handled my brother's death when the thought of it swept over the field like a storm.

Each day the wheat was growing taller. The heads of it emerging from the last growth of leaves were bearded like boys coming to manhood. I loved the smell of the grain, hot and earthy in the sunlight, and I felt that if yellow smelled, it would smell like wheat.

Usually I hoed with two other girls about my age. One girl was Mary. Broad-shouldered and thick-armed, she wore her hair under a liripipe for work, but at day's end, when she pulled off the long hood, a great amount of soft dark hair tumbled to her waist, like a flow of black water. Men were after her, but Mary was waiting for a village boy to come get her someday and take her back home.

The other girl, Catherine, was carrying a child, and people said that someday we'd leave the field with one soul more than we came with. She didn't know who the father was. She'd say, to the cruel jokes of field-workers, "I don't care who he was. I just want my boy to be strong." She never got angry except if someone said she would have a girl. And then, "No!" she'd yell. "I can feel his little thing tickling me."

We were at the western edge of the field one afternoon, near the wood that bordered it. The wheat was shoulder tall, breathing out waves of earthy yellow heat as our hoes went up and down between the furrows, cutting away weed. A strong wind came up as we worked, so loud in our ears, we could scarcely make ourselves heard though we worked within hoe-length distance of one another. The wheat flowed goldenly beneath the battering of the wind.

As I was lifting my hoe I caught from the corner of my eye something within the wheat.

"Is someone there?" I called out.

Something was coming through the stalks of wheat, mowing them down like a boat churning through water. Then two men stood before us, wearing torn jackets and torn breeches. One of them had leggings of mail, the other a rusty-looking hauberk over his chest and an iron skullcap on his head. For an instant I was sure that both men had the same face, one familiar to me, that of the man who had speared my mother.

"Girls," one yelled into the wind, grinning.

I saw a dagger scabbard shoved inside his belt of rope.

The other, taller man wore a sword on a broad leather belt. He was not grinning, but looked from Mary to me and back to Mary, ignoring Catherine.

I leaned forward—they were within reach of a sweep of my hoe—so they could hear.

"We don't have anything," I said. "We're just working in the field."

"Oh, you have *something*!" the stouter one bellowed into the wind.

"Be good girls," said the other, "and we won't hurt you. Take off your clothes."

"We'll yell for help."

"In this wind you can yell all day and nobody'll hear you. Take off your clothes."

"We won't," I said, raising the hoe chest-high.

The taller one snorted and slowly drew his sword. "A hoe can't deal with me."

"We have three hoes. There are two of you," I said. "Mary," I said. "Catherine." I could feel them on either side of me, not giving way.

"Don't think three girls can deal with two like us." The tall

251

man took a step forward. "We'll have you and then cut your throats if you don't put down the hoes. Put them down!"

"No!" I yelled back at him. "We sharpened these hoes at a grindstone this morning. They'll cut through bone and gristle."

Standing in a yellow spout of parted wheat, the two men looked at us without expression for some time. Wind was hurtling against the tassels, rattling them like slivers of iron. Then a cloud, trapped in the sun's path, sent a shadow down on us across the field. The dark blue shadow was so big and fast that even the men turned to look in awe as it skimmed the waving grain and hurtled toward us like something solid.

I remember crying out, "The hand of God! The hand of God!" as it swept over.

The words rushed through me like winds through fields—just appeared, were there.

Hardly was the shadow gone before the men were gone too. Gone, vanished as if they had never been here at all. Gone, lost in the stormy wheat.

Suddenly there was a loud noise—thunder cracking over the treetops of the neighboring wood. And then I was laughing and so was Mary. We turned to each other and embraced, laughing and crying and trembling.

She yelled against my ear, "But the hoes aren't sharp! They won't cut butter!"

"Mine's loose on the shaft! If I swung it hard, the hoe would come off!"

"You said, 'The hand of God!' " Mary shouted. "And it was! The hand of God!"

A mass of clouds was traveling over us, and in its rumbling black-blue wake came a fierce shower. The two of us stood within the cool veil of rain, still clinging to each other, sobbing and giggling. Then there was another sound—a long anguished groan followed by a sharp cry.

Turning around, we saw Catherine lying between furrows of hoed-up earth that was rapidly becoming mud.

"It's happening," Mary said. "The men made it happen."

We rushed to Catherine, who had instinctively parted her legs. They gleamed from rainwater and looked sticklike compared to her swollen belly, which seemed now, as she lay there, like a great mound of earth. Her hands had reached into the mud, digging into it. I had seen our livestock give birth at the mill and many horses foal, but this was the first time I had seen a human birth.

Minutes later, while Mary held her shoulders, bracing her for the pain, Catherine grunted and shook and grunted some more and from between her spread legs appeared a small wet head, the blood on it washing off in the rain, and then with more grunts, as if the sound itself did the work, Catherine slowly pushed the whole body into the world. I took up the infant, slick in the pelting shower.

"Cut the cord!" Mary yelled.

With the edge of the hoe I sawed back and forth, severing the cord binding Catherine to her baby. The head seemed so large for the body that I laughed and held the child up into the rain to cleanse it of mud and blood.

I scarcely heard Mary shouting at me: "Spank it! Spank life into it!"

And so I did. With a sharp crack of my hand against its tiny buttocks I struck life into its lungs. The baby cried lustily. I had struck the bell of its life.

"What is it?" Catherine asked, raising her head for a better look through the rain.

"A girl," I said in a soft voice, knowing it was not what she wanted to hear.

"What? Show me!"

"A girl," I said, holding the baby toward her.

"Is everything all right? Is she strong?"

"Everything's all right. And listen to her cry."

Throwing her head back, Catherine started to laugh with more power than I thought she could have in herself then. Breathlessly she kept yelling, "Strong! She's strong! Praise God!"

Catherine was still saying it when some men carried her from the field, with Mary holding the baby wrapped in a gunnysack. The summer storm had passed, leaving a clear lake of blue over the field.

"You're smiling," a field-worker said to me as I stared after Catherine.

Turning, I said, "Why, yes."

"It's the first time I ever saw you smile."

"Today I saw the hand of God."

"Where?"

"Here," I said happily, throwing my arms out at the field.

One day perhaps a week later, as I sank the iron edge of my hoe into hot soil, I thought of the three terrible words, and it occurred to me with a touch of wonder that I couldn't remember the last time I had said them. They no longer belonged to me. I thought of them as words that had come from another life. And I never said them again.

34

IN midsummer Barnabas took sick. We thought for a while he might die, but slowly his wife nursed him back to health.

Meanwhile, because work was slow in the fields until harvest, I had time for the clock. In fact, with young Clare's help I took over its operation. Barnabas gave his consent, because if the Corporation of the City knew of his illness, they might throw him out and bring in another governor.

Clare and I wound the clock together twice a day. First we disengaged the barrel from the clockwork. Then we set the rachet and click on the winding barrel so the stone weight wouldn't fall. Twice a day we worked the three-spoked windlass, hauling the stone up through the turret shaft turn by turn. We moved one spoke upright, then clasped the next and with great difficulty pulled it around to the upright position, and so on, spoke after spoke, around and around the barrel. This was hard enough, but then the rachet failed to hold and we had to keep tension constantly on the rope or the weight would fall. Our hands burned on the wood of the spokes. Our eyes met in fear that the windlass might get away from us, the rope spin loose, and the stone go crashing to the bottom of the turret. That was how we wound the going train.

We then had to wind the striking train, which was easier because the rachet and pawl worked properly on that barrel. So twice a day we somehow managed, while Barnabas's older boy of eight years pestered us to help.

Clare and the boy followed behind me while I oiled the clockwork. They squatted nearby when I checked the shadow thrown by a sundial to see how much the clock had gained or lost in a day. And they stood at my shoulder when I moved little weights on the foliot to bring the clock back to correct time.

I explained how certain things worked as we went along. Soon even the boy understood what a crown wheel, lantern pinion, and arbor were. In her nightly dreams Clare began to see an escapement rocking to and fro and iron wheels turning like stars across the sky. The boy claimed to hear the click of machinery whenever he closed his eyes. We lived, the three of us, within the life of the clock, our clock.

I told them that our clock ought to have jacks. "Jacks are wooden soldiers that strike the bell with hammers."

"Has a clock ever had jacks?" Clare asked.

"In a few great cities. Maybe someday even this Corporation will pay for jacks. And for a dial too," I added boldly.

"A dial?"

"A circle with numbers on it. Clocks don't have dials yet, but my uncle Albrecht knew how to make them. Pointers on the dial show you the time."

"Without the bell tolling?"

"You just look up at the face of the tower. You tell time from pointers moving around the dial. Not just the hour. The time between hours too."

Their white faces looked at me in disbelief and awe.

"Yes," I told them. "Someday."

When the leaves were turning, Barnabas got out of bed and walked around. Soon he claimed to feel well enough to work the capstan himself. But I stood nearby, fearful he couldn't do it: his big strong frame had been terribly weakened by illness. Even so, he managed to turn the capstan and haul the weight up. As each spoke came to the upright position, he gave me a proud if painful smile.

"Anne," he said one day, while together we watched the crown wheel click along its route, "without you I wouldn't be Governor of the Clock today. But you ran the clock. You saved my family."

"Clare helped."

He moved his big hands through the air. "Well, but she's a girl."

I could see that Barnabas did not think of me as a girl too, although I had but two years on his daughter. Because I understood the clock, I had entered his world or at least stood on its threshold, whereas other women could never get close to it. His acceptance did not make me happy. Why couldn't he let his daughter stand beside us?

So I repeated, "Clare helped." Said it again, which made Barnabas stare hard at me, his head cocked in puzzlement.

"Yes," I said, "without Clare working, too, you wouldn't be Governor of the Clock today."

We never talked about Clare after that. For one thing, I was too weary from working in the harvest fields to talk about anything at the end of a day. And then whenever I came along, Barnabas would look somewhere else, as if unsure what to say to me. Clare stopped going to the tower, and so did the boy. And then, finally, so did I.

Barnabas alone watched the pinions and wheels turn up there through the daily hours.

I knew that when the harvest ended—and it would end soon —I'd have to leave his family, because once again I'd have no money. Where would I go? I had lived in the town long enough to grow accustomed to its ways, so going elsewhere seemed difficult. And, of course, I wanted to stay as close as possible to the graveyard where Niklas, Rabbit, and the others were. And I'd miss Clare, Barnabas, the rest of the family. I'd miss the clock.

The harvest had finished, yet the family let me stay on though I had no money for lodging and food.

Their kindness gave me time to find a way: I got work in a

butcher shop. The two brothers who owned it took me on because their third brother had owned the field I'd helped harvest, and he recommended me as a hard worker.

Slaughtering was done in the back of the shop. The butchers flung the offal onto a dirt floor muddy from blood. It was my job to clean up and also to lead the goats and pigs from outside pens to their deaths. The shop smelled heavily of guts steaming in the chill air. No matter how hard I scrubbed my hands and arms to the elbow each night, the stench of death lingered on my body. Even though I took pieces of meat home to the grateful family, my smell was so strong that even Clare hung back from me and I was given a pallet to sleep on alone.

There were many shops on the street where I worked. I saw many things. I saw the fishmonger redden his stale fish with pig's blood to make it seem fresh. I saw the cheesemonger give his bland cheese a richer odor by soaking it in broth. I saw the baker use a rigged scale to weigh his loaves of bread. The trickery of life bore down on me, yet I never said the three defiant words, not even when the animals I led to the slaughter room squealed piteously and reminded me of the graveyard where Niklas had buried Rabbit and the others. I could no longer hate God, even when the world around me wallowed in deceit and smelled of death. I was thankful for money enough to pay for my pallet and for the pieces of meat I could take home each night to Barnabas's family.

I was carrying home a ragful of meat one evening, when someone from behind me called out, "Anne! Anne!"

Turning, I saw through the mist a very short but powerfully built man. When he came toward me smiling, I recognized one of the carvers from the artists' guild.

"Are you well, girl?" he asked, looking me over.

"Well enough. Yes, I'm content. And you?"

"Everything has happened. Come along for a cup of beer," he offered. So I went with him to a tavern, where we sat in a far corner. He told me that most of the carvers had left Master Dollmayr. They had set up a shop on the outskirts of the city.

"I'm warden," he said proudly. "The guild—"

"You have a guild?"

"We are now the woodcarving guild. As distinct from the

painters' guild. You see, they split away from him too. I'm warden," he repeated. "The guild elected me. We don't have anyone over us now, we elect our own. I supervise the quality of goods we produce. I regulate hours. At six strokes of the clock each evening I tell everyone, 'Time's up!' I prepare the examination for apprentices—we have four now. I see that payments to the guild fund are made by members. And I'll see to it we're honorably represented at the next festival. I'm warden," he said.

I remembered the stout little man favorably. He was no troublemaker. But a rather poor carver, as I recalled.

"What does Master Dollmayr say?" I asked.

"What can he say? We are free men. We're making carvings of knights and ladies along with saints and they all sell." He paused thoughtfully. "Your brother would have been an apprentice with us. Though he wouldn't understand the examination, he would have passed it."

"And Werimbold," I said, "does he do business with you too?"

"He does. All the merchants do. Have another beer."

I did, but declined a third and got up to leave. Through the smoky candlelit room, his eyes met mine.

"Anne," he said, and stopped.

When we got into the night air, he said it again, "Anne," and stopped again.

I bade him good night.

"Anne," he said. "I'm a widower. I'm doing well now as warden of the guild. And you look as though you need a better life. Am I right?"

"I'm content."

"But with me you'd do better. I'm no great man, but I'm strong and true. Come along with me home. I'll see to it in church tomorrow. I'll post bans. We'll exchange vows."

Touching his arm, I said, "Thank you, my friend. But I'm content as I am."

"What are you looking for? What can you have better in life than what I offer?"

"I don't know."

"You see? Here's a chance for us both. God has put it in our way."

"Perhaps," I said. "But for now I'm content as I am."

35

RETURNING from the butcher shop one evening, I met Clare sitting in the yard. She told me that her father, who was up in the clock, wanted to see me. Clare gave me a strange look when she said that.

Climbing the stairway to the clockwork room, I found Barnabas with two strangers. The younger man, tall and wearing a stocking cap, lowered his dark eyes when I came in. The older, bearded man had on a leather mantle fastened with a gold chain at the shoulder. His boots of soft leather had high tops, and a large purse swung from his belt. He looked like a rich merchant and yet, from the breadth of his shoulders, like a workman.

He nodded solemnly when Barnabas said, "Here she is— Anne, the clock girl."

Without another word, Barnabas left us. In the silence we could hear his heavy step on the staircase.

By torchlight the two men studied me, the older one circling as if to judge the strength of a draft animal.

"I am going to make a clock," he said finally, halting in front of me.

He stood so close, I could see little veins in his cheeks. Looking beyond him, I saw the younger man glowering, which made an otherwise pleasant face seem ugly.

"I am going to make a clock like this one in a city up north," the older man said. "I want Barnabas to help me. What do you think of that?"

This man was asking a girl her opinion? His directness surprised me. "Barnabas knows about this clock, sir. Yes, he can help you."

"Can he draw the parts of a clock?"

"No, but he understands their working."

"Do you know how to draw the parts of a clock?"

"Yes, sir, I do."

"Did you make these drawings?" He turned to the young man, who produced from a burlap bag my folded drawings.

Mine! Barnabas must have given them to these men.

"Well?" the older man demanded.

"They are mine," I said, holding out my hand.

The young man, scowling, put them back in the bag.

"How did you, a girl, learn to do such a thing?" the older man asked.

"My uncle taught me."

"Who was your uncle?"

"A master armorer."

The man nodded. Because I'd learned from a relative of skill, he seemed satisfied that I had not learned wrongfully.

"Barnabas," said the older man, "has been very sick." The bearded man in his leather mantle stood near the clockwork, watching the foliot swing. "Barnabas doesn't want to go north. He has a good life here."

When I failed to comment, the man turned to look at me.

"Yes," I said, "he has a good life here."

The two stared at me, as if struggling with an idea they didn't like.

"Barnabas thinks you should come along with us," the older man said after a long silence.

"Barnabas said that?"

"He thinks you could help because you know more about clocks than he does."

Barnabas said that? Dear Barnabas.

The two men again exchanged glances. From his look I knew the younger one disliked the idea of a girl helping.

Then the older man said, "You'd have food and a place to stay."

"Money too?"

The older man worked his mouth soundlessly. I think he was amazed at my boldness. Then he said, "Food and lodging aren't enough? You'd have to work hard for money too."

260

"I know how to work hard, sir."

"How old are you?"

"Nineteen."

"And not married?" The man looked down at the floor. Finally he sighed and looked up. "Very well. Money too."

"You are asking me, sir, to work on your clock?"

"I am asking you. I am Conrad, goldsmith, soon to be clockmaker."

"Will you have a jack, sir, to strike the hours?"

"Why do you ask?"

"Because this clock doesn't have one."

"Do you know how to rig a jack?"

"My uncle knew," I said evasively. For an instant I saw a wooden man-at-arms pivoting at a bell: Jack the Smiter with goggling eyes and a red nose.

"Do you know dials?" the man asked.

"My uncle did. Or I mean he could have put one on a clock if asked."

"You tell me about your uncle. What about you? Can you do the same?"

"I know how to measure gear sizes. Given enough trials I could do it."

"Trials cost money."

"I know."

The man pulled his beard thoughtfully. "If we let a jack strike the hours, could you provide the gearing to strike halves and quarters too?"

"You would do that, Master Conrad?"

"The expense would be in the jack. With it in place, might as well strike hours and the in-between too."

Excitement rose in me. I looked upon the man in a different light. "It's a matter of notching the wheel," I told him eagerly. "If a smith made some trials at cutting the edge and if he got it right, you could have the jack strike as often as you wished."

"You sound confident."

From the pinched look of his face, I didn't think he liked the sound of my confidence. It must have sounded like insolence. But looking steadily at him, I said, "Yes, I'm confident."

"I have decided," Master Conrad said. "You'll come with us. You won't be abused. And you'll do your proper work."

Turning to the younger man, he said, "Come along, Martin," and turning again to me, he added with a smile, "Day after tomorrow we leave."

"If I'm going with you, sir, I'll know by then."

Anger passed swiftly across his face. "*If* you're going? You don't know now?"

"I must think about leaving here." And I added with more boldness than I could have shown had I thought before speaking, "Right now I want my drawings back."

There was another silence. Then the younger man, without a glance at his older companion, shuffled toward me. He offered the bag, which I swept out of his hand.

Master Conrad said, "This is my son, Martin."

After a curt nod at Martin, I turned to the father. "If I work on your clock, you'll know everything I know and if you build another clock, you can then leave me out."

"Ah, you've been hurt here," Master Conrad said gently. "If you help with this one, you have the right to work on another."

I felt my lips trembling, yet asked anyway, "And if you change your mind?"

"I won't," he said.

"I believe you," I said. And I did.

Later, when the family Barnabas and I had finished eating, I walked into the night air with Clare. The wind came in briskly, promising snow.

"He likes you," Clare said of a sudden.

"Who?"

"The young one."

"Not him. Every time he looks at me he frowns."

"He came to me after meeting you and asked all kinds of questions."

"What did he ask?"

"Everything about you. He asked why you weren't married."

"He asked that?" I snorted at the question. "He's a fool."

"No, he's a man and he likes you."

"You're too young to know about men, Clare."

"I am, true, but I know."

"And what did you tell him, Clare?"

"I told him God had not yet put the right man in your way."

Laughing, I said, "You really told him that?"

"I did. And then he said, 'Maybe so. But I think her boldness would put some men off.' "

"He said that?"

"And then he said, 'But not me, it wouldn't mean anything to me.' "

After a few moments, I said, "If he had questions, why didn't he ask them of me since they were about me?"

Clare was silent awhile. Then she said, as we looked up at the moonlit tower, "Sometimes words don't say what we want them to. Maybe he thought you wouldn't take his words in the right spirit. Sometimes it's better to say nothing."

In my own silence I thought of Niklas looking at me with his solemn blue eyes. Sometimes only through them had he let me know he loved me. "You are right about that," I told Clare.

36

"YOU must accept the offer," Barnabas told me the next morning as we stood together near the clockwork in the chill of dawn. "Conrad is a good man, a rich man, a well-known goldsmith. I'm sure his city has faith in him to build that clock. And he won't abuse you."

"I don't want to leave. Besides, his son doesn't want me to go with them."

Barnabas cocked his head, a smile on his weathered face. "I don't think his son makes the decisions. The boy is not much older than you are."

Perhaps that was true, I thought. Yesterday I had seen him as someone older, more important. "There's wear on the weight rope of the going train," I suddenly told Barnabas.

"Yes, I need to replace it soon."

"Are the rachet and click repaired on the barrel?"

"Yes, Anne."

"Leaving you and the family would be hard."

"We'll miss you."

I held back the tears with difficulty, wanting to cry because I wouldn't be around when he replaced the weight rope.

"I don't want to leave, Barnabas."

"But it's your chance. We'll miss you, Anne."

The way he said it this time, I understood that Barnabas and the family had already given me up.

Later that day I was turning into the yard to find the children and say good-bye, when I heard someone whistling. Peeking around the wall, I saw the boy Martin kneeling and coaxing a neighborhood dog to come near. I drew back in the shadows to watch. Without so much frowning, Martin was a nice-looking fellow, I had to admit, with unruly black hair and dark eyes. Not handsome like Hubert but not ugly either. He was patient with the dog, and when finally it came to him wagging its tail, Martin petted it softly. Although his hands were big with thick, brutal-looking fingers, he smoothed the fur gently with a fine motion that reminded me of Niklas with Rabbit.

Finally I cleared my throat and walked briskly into the court-yard. Seeing me, he stopped petting the dog, one hand held in midair. I expected him to frown, but he didn't. His face was set into a look of stone, neither angry nor glad, and yet one glance at his eyes told me that there wasn't hate in him. To this boy Martin I was like a creature he might encounter in a forest, something he must stand back from awhile to see if it was friend or foe.

Beyond the courtyard I found Clare making a rag doll for her little sister. We huddled together near a stream that cut through town. It was cold enough for the edges to ice up, and Clare's eight-year-old brother was skimming pebbles across the sluggish surface. "Clare," I said, "I'm going to miss you."

"Now I won't learn any more about the clock."

I couldn't reassure her. We both knew that her father didn't want her to become a "clock girl" too.

"Whatever you can learn, learn," I told her. But it wasn't

much comfort for someone who loved to watch a going train click through the dusty air of a clock tower.

Then I did something that could bring me down: I promised to give her my drawings. That meant I would have nothing to refer to when I went to work on the new clock. And yet I was glad to give them to Clare when her eyes filled with tears and she said, "I have never had anything so beautiful."

Next morning early—we were leaving at noon by wagon for the north—I dressed and left before the others were awake. First thing I did was climb to the tower and look at the clock.

After studying it awhile, I realized I had it complete in my memory. The clockwork was in my head forever. Assured, I took one more look around and went down the stairs. Outside a little snow was beginning to fall, so I held the collar of my coat with both hands and set out.

I hadn't gone ten steps before I saw him, skulking in the shadows.

Not knowing what to say, I said nothing, but walked past him. I wanted to glance back to see if he was following, but I didn't, not until getting to the town gate. Then I halted and turned. There he was, hunched and somber, with a lacing of snow in his black hair.

"What are you doing? Are you following me?" When he just blinked, I took courage and added, "Do you think I'll run away? From you? You can't make me run away. And I don't want to run away. I want to work on the clock. I'm not afraid of you at all."

My face burned from my having uttered such outrageous words, yet I felt buoyed, too, by my boldness—and then by him. Because Martin kept behind me, maybe thirty paces behind, as I walked down the snow-covered road to the fork that led me toward the tiny graveyard. Where the wood began, I halted and studied him. He was taller than Hubert had been, but not as sweet-looking and certainly not as handsome.

"Don't follow me in here," I told him.

Martin blinked again, but stayed where he was, at the side of the lane, when I stepped into the dark wood.

There was a winding path among brambles and between

leafless trees. Branches were circled in ropes of ice. Ahead, suddenly, I saw the graves, a dozen of them blanketed by snow with their dark crosses outlined softly in white.

I sat down among the graves, feeling the wet cold seep through my clothes.

"Niklas," I said, and waited.

Clouds jumbled above me, showing themselves through a tangle of black branches. It was so quiet. The air around the tiny graveyard was made softer by the falling snow.

I said, "You hear me, don't you. Now listen carefully, dear Brother. I've come to tell you I must leave. What I mean is, leave this part of the world. Today, Niklas. Now."

The air was quiet, like the graves. The crosses above the snowy mounds had the look of arms outspread in a kind of silent joy. It was not a bad place, it was a good place. Everything here belonged here, in the snowy silence.

"I know you'll always be here," I said. "You and Rabbit and the others. Snug here. All of you secretly. God has put you here to be safe."

As usual I didn't tell Niklas my own secret thoughts, that somehow I would take him with me in my mind. That part of him would leave here and go with me. That he would travel where I traveled, perhaps far, far from Rabbit and the others. That sometimes we would be frightened together and unhappy in a loud world. But such truths he would learn later. At this moment, when he was being told that I was leaving this place, it was important for him to know that in another way he would always be safe.

Finally I got up and retraced my footsteps through the undergrowth. Beyond the wood, sitting in the lane where last I'd seen him, was Martin. He got to his feet when he saw me.

Why was he here? Why had he followed me? But before I could give myself an answer, I started to cry.

Cried so hard, I fell to the ground and lay full-length in the snow. Cried without thinking, without knowing anything but tears salting my face and my chest heaving like a boat. I cried until body and soul felt empty, as light as the snow falling.

When finally I sat up, through a blur of tears I saw Martin sitting patiently nearby, looking at me without a frown but without a smile either—his face still looking like carved stone, telling me how strange I still was to him.

"Don't ask me what I was crying about," I told him, angry that he had seen me do it.

He didn't ask.

"Don't you ever ask questions?" Wiping my face on my coat sleeve, I said, "Why did you follow me out here?" But, of course, I didn't get an answer. Rising, I stared at him.

"You don't talk much, do you."

He looked at me.

"Will you tell me why you came out here?"

"So you'd be safe."

He could have said nothing better to please me, but I frowned. "Is that all?"

He just stood there looking.

Well, he didn't talk much, probably never would. But I liked that. With Niklas I had been used to doing all the talking. And around Martin I'd certainly do most of it too. But I liked the idea that he could talk if needed.

I started to walk down the path, turning to motion at him to come along. He did.

We had walked awhile in silence when suddenly he stopped, rummaged in his pocket, and came out with something. Holding it in his outstretched hand, Martin said, "Here."

It was a piece of metal with a diagonal channel cut from top to bottom. The top had a groove.

"Holds better than nails," Martin said.

The thing looked like the wooden-threaded barrel of a winepress, except it was shorter than my little finger and not as big around.

"Hard to make," Martin observed.

I turned it in my hand. Someone had laboriously cut and shaped its channel with a file.

"Fits pieces of metal together. Called a screw." Those were more words than I had yet heard him say. "Smiths making them up north."

Studying the screw, I could see that the groove might fit into a hole in metal and grip the sides. To get the screw out, you'd have to turn the groove in the top. Turn it the other way. I smiled at Martin.

"Yours," he said.

I knew it was valuable, so I couldn't just say, "Thank you." I said, "This must mean a lot to you."

His face colored.

"There aren't many of these, are there?"

"No. Not yet."

I said, "It will be my most prized possession. I'll treasure it."

He stepped briskly forward without looking at me. Because he was so much taller, I had to lengthen my stride to match his. We set out down the road together, although for some time I halted in a bend of it to look back at the distant wood, which had become a tiny bead of darkness on the white plain.